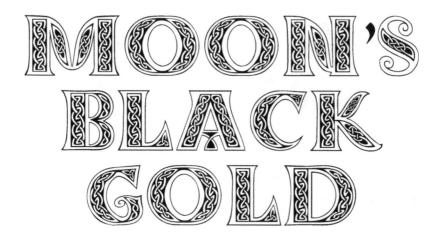

MOON'S BLACK GOLD

R. H. PEAKE

Moon's Black Gold

This book is written to provide information and motivation to readers. Its purpose is not to render any type of psychological, legal, or professional advice of any kind. The content is the sole opinion and expression of the author, and not necessarily that of the publisher.

Printed in the United States of America.

ISBN 978-1-953150-26-4 (Paperback)
ISBN 978-1-953150-27-1 (Digital)

Lettra Press books may be ordered through booksellers or by contacting:

Lettra Press LLC
30 N Gould St. Suite 4753
Sheridan, WY 82801, USA
1 307-200-3414 | info@lettrapress.com
www.lettrapress.com

Moon's Black Gold
by R. H. Peake Lettra Press
book review by Priscilla Estes

"Everett Lunamin had never been one to savor. He had in fact been a gulper of the first rank."

"Black Gold" is coal, the cash crop of southwestern Virginia, and Moon's gold comes from the controversial practice of strip mining, where land is razed for the rich vein of ebony beneath the earth's epidermis. Moon (Everett Adamo Lunamin), fresh from Viet Nam and tired of being "dirt poor," returns to his corner of Virginia, determined to be a rich man. He quickly grabs a piece of the lucrative coal industry to fund a lifestyle he believes will fulfill him. Money does capture respect, security, and the high-school sweetheart of his dreams. But Moon's mountain man spirit is tied to nature, the very flora and fauna strip mining displaces. As financial gains (and a woman) free his mind and soul to concentrate on learning, thinking, and self-examination, Moon's story morphs into an homage to the mountain way of life with all its kith and kin, including Mother Nature raped by strip mining.

Along the way, union strikes, environmental and political tensions, rivalries for coal and women, and even murder keep the stakes high and the storyline packed to bursting. Detailed physical descriptions, the Appalachian dialect, and immersion in the post Viet Nam period in southwestern Virginia keep the story rolling like the mountains in which it is set. "Tan snakes sinuously arranged from top to bottom" choke the mountain ridges. Mountain men, who say "by gonnies" and "hit" instead of "it," explain the origin of "Melungeons" and call each other "honey." Marijuana rivals coal for cash, moonshine is plentiful, and sometimes "legal" is a state of mind. Subtly using the metaphors of mining and nature in an Anthropocene era, Peake uncovers the deep vein of richness within Moon, an Appalachian to his core. The art and culture of strip mining fascinate as much as Moon's journey to a greater self brings joy.

Books By R.H. Peake

From Papaw to Print: A History of Appalachian Literature,
Mapplelodge Publication,1990

Wings Across
Vision Books,1992

Birds of Virginia Cumberlands
Mapplelodge Publication,2001

Soon to be available:

LETTRA PRESS publication

Jaykyll's Joust
Moon's BLACK GOLD
Beauty'S No Biscuit
Love and Death on Safari

ACKNOWLEDGEMENTS

My thanks to Dr. Catherine Mahony for reading the manuscript of this novel and making valuable suggestions, to John Mack Clarke for his helpful suggestions, and to Rhonda C. Peake for proofing the manuscript.

"It is important that we be mindful of the earth, the planet out of which we are born and by which we are nourished, guided, healed—the planet, however, which we have abused to a considerable degree in these past centuries of industrial exploitation."

Thomas Berry
The Dream of Earth

"O powerful love! That, in some respects, makes a beast of man"

William Shakespeare
The Merry Wives of Windsor

HOMECOMING

Before the sun glowing bright yellow descended over the ridge through the haze of ground fog rising after the spring rain, the man had begun to climb the path that led to the top of Pine Mountain.

Tall and thin, dressed in worn denim, he strode with the air of a man with a purpose.

In the gradually lengthening dusky dark, he could not see far in front of him and had to walk carefully, looking down often to avoid the mud holes that were left in the otherwise dusty track. Every now and then he forgot and miss-stepped and a foot fell into water colored dark with coal dust dropped from the haul trucks, wetting his foot through the cracks of his footgear and leaving a grimy dark film.

The discomfort of wet to s could not erase the pleasures of the late evening. He took a s nsuous delight in the towhees and pewees calling quietly, the dew forming on the leaves, the light breezes moving through the treetops, and a gray tree frog giving out its resonant, mournful *yawwwwup* from the darkening recesses of the woods.

After pausing several times to look at the gleaming sunlight descending over the mountain, the tall, dark-haired man turned his lean frame and moved up the dusty road—dryer walking now after the rainwater had begun to sink in—muttering to himself.

"Tired of being dirt poor. Mean to get some money. Nah, I'll not bother too much how I get it. Don't care what Mamaw and Papaw say. I can't eat trees, and I don't want to live on 'possum and groundhog neither."

In fact, though, he did care what his grandparents thought and he worried about what they would say when he told of his plans. They didn't like the destruction he was planning.

The dust here and there made little clouds around his boots and formed a layer on the legs of his jeans and the boot top showing through them. The red ball slowly moved over the trees onto the dirt road winding up the mountain and beyond, casting its glow on the walker moving toward the top of the ridge. Whenever he stopped, he looked around eagerly, not to rest so much as to drink in the scenes around him and to consider homecoming as an intellectual fact—to take in without deep thought the sights, sounds, and smells. Hungrily, he looked ahead to the next ridge. He'd been a long time away. The fact of homecoming was caught in his mind. He thought of the story of the prodigal in the bible his Mamaw had given him.

"There won't be no fatted calf for me, but I've got a stake and I'm gonna make it count. Ain't nothin' nor nobody stoppin' me," he said to himself.

He'd made slow going since leaving the bus at Coeburn. He had stopped so often to drink in the sights and sound. He wanted to get started with his mining project, but he wanted to be ready when he did. There were still many devils running around inside his head.

He had to get his head right before he'd bother with business. Just now he wouldn't have his mind enough on making money. He'd be more comfortable with the old folks for a few days. Mamaw and Papaw had raised him after his pa was killed by a roof fall. His ma had remarried, and Moon hadn't liked his stepfather all that well. He turned in his mind thoughts about the bus ride.

On the bus a fellow from Clintwood had told him of the money people were making stripping coal. A good foot shorter than Moon, he was beginning to gray around the temples, but there was a boyish twinkle in his brown eyes as he looked up at Moon.

"Howdy do, Boy, my name's Fred MacCloud," he said, extending his hand.

"Glad to meet you, Fred, mine's Moo—Everett A. Lunamin. Just call me Moon."

"What's the *A* stand for, if that's not too nosy?"

"Why, no, it's Adamo. That's *Eye-talian* (Lunamin felt comfortable saying it that way now. After all, he was home) for Adam. My great- grandmother was *Eye-talian*.

"Don't say. She come from over to Dante? I've got cousins at Dante."

"Yep, she was a Caruso from Dante."

"Well, Adamo, I guess you and me's cousins. My great-grandma was a Caruso from Dante too. Where do you live?"

"Up in Whiteoak Hollow. I'm Archibald MacC oud's grandson. Big John Lunamin was my pa, but he was killed in the mines before I was born."

"Shoot! I was in the mine with your pa when he was killed by that roof fall. A shame, it was. I was lucky enough to make it out. He was a good man. You don't say that old buzzard Archibald MacCloud raised you?"

"Yep. Won't deny it, Cousin. My Papaw's a MacCloud. So I reckon we're kin more ways than one. Now, tell me what's happened here while I've been in Nam."

"Lord take me, boy, if they ain't makin' money faster'n the folks in Washington can print it. Why, old Ricky Burnett, he didn't have nary a dime ni h three year ago and now he's a millionaire. Bought him a dozer on time for a start."

As he listened to Fred talk about all the newly acquired wealth that was being gathered in the Southwest Virginia mountains, Lunamin told himself that some of that money had to be his. He had to be getting his own million. He could see some problems heading his way, though. His mamaw and papaw liked strippers about as well as they liked copperheads and rattlesnakes. Lunamin excepted, Vietnam veterans weren't real high on their list either. They didn't favor running off to Canada the way cousin Abe had, but they didn't like the war either.

"Fred, do you know anybody who can run dozers who ain't already workin'?"

"Not many. But I'm your man if you want me. I just quit my job last week."

"Why's that?"

"Didn't like the way they worked. No care for the land and overloaded their trucks to litter the highways. You can tell, just by lookin' at the highways, which way the coal tipple sits. The haul side of the highway is black with coal dust. Overloadin.' Common practice, but not mine. Don't cost much more to do stripping right than to do it wrong. In this case it costs less. Don't lose so much coal, and coal at the tipple is money."

"Cousin Fred, you've got you a new job once I get my stake aworkin.'" They shook.

When the bus reached the forks where the Whiteoak Hollow road turned off, Lunamin stopped the bus and climbed off to begin the long walk to his grandparent's home place. At the top of the first ridge he had stopped to take a deep breath. He could see ridge upon ridge opening out to the haze of the horizon.

The ridges close to him looked as if they were being choked, constricted by huge tan snakes sinuously arranged from top to bottom, each separated from the next by a strip of green. Here and there, a strip miner's snaky path around a mountainside left close to the top of a ridge a bit of green sticking up like the feather bonnet of an old cigar- store Indian that Lunamin had seen in a magazine. But something was squeezing the life out of these Indians. The green bonnet seemed an island of green above a brown constrictor trying to squeeze the Indian to the death.

"Used to be lots of Indians here before the white man run 'em out," Moon thought. "I probably got some Indian blood in me even if Papaw says we're Scotch-Irish. Wonder how them old Cherokee or Shawnee'd like their happy huntin' ground now. Old Chief Benjy'd make another raid, I bet. Wouldn't like his huntin' grounds all tore up. Still a happy huntin' ground for that black gold, though, and I'm gonna start huntin' 'fore the good stuff's all gone."

The cooling air nudged him from his reverie. Seeing that the sun was close to disappearing over the ridges, Lunamin began to pick up his pace. Alert, then, like a cat stalking his prey, he moved quietly but quickly down the road.

COUSINS

Shifting his Datsun carefully into a lower gear, George Landsetter slowly eased by the coal truck in the left lane. He didn't like to take chances.

Coal dust fell like dark rain on his maroon car. "Damn, more dirt and scratches."

He speeded up to pass the truck.

"Damn overloading." He sighed with re ief when he pulled ahead of the truck.

Landsetter wished he could do something about that problem.

The waste as well as the filth it created bothered him.

He thought of all the rains that had gone into the making of that dark dust, the oceans of rain that had had to fall on the fern forests while the great trees grew tall and died and fell to decay in the ancient swamps to make this dark mist possible.

A vision of the Pennsylvanian landscape came into his mind, full of fern tree forests but no dinosaurs. Primitive reptiles were just coming into being on the land and sharks were putting in an appearance in the oceans. The Appalachian trough was slowly subsiding and most of the time the land surface was just a little above sea level. As areas had subsided and returned to the sea, they were quickly filled with erosion from the surrounding lands that were being uplifted.

The land in the trough was flat and near sea level. Great swamps extended throughout this landscape, densely covered with vegetation that was continually maturing, dying, and shedding needles or leaves or being broken down by storms. Once down in the swamps, the fallen material thickened into huge bogs of peat preserved from decay by the stagnant swamp water. Then these swamps fell below sea level and were in turn covered by eroded earth.

Age upon age, this process occurred many times, and the layers were compressed again and again. As age wore into age of Pottsville time, the peat was changed into beds of bituminous coal that formed the Pocahontas, the Pardee, and the High Splint.

George had been away from the coalfields a good many years before he had taken the job with the reclamation people eighteen months earlier. He had kept in touch with far Southwest Virginia from reading the mail from his father and mother. Landsetter had grown up in the city as well as here, but even before they moved back to the mountains, he had listened to talk and had been part of the many trips back for family reunions. They had come from these hills where so many of their family still lived, and they had returned in time for George to spend his last years of high school here.

He wasn't exactly a mountaineer, but he wasn't a city boy either. Now, after four years of college, and a couple of years working on a master's degree in geology, he had cast his lot with his mountain relatives. He wasn't entirely comfortable seeing some of his kin getting rich from digging the bones of the Pottsville era, but at least a part of the proceeds were staying in the mountains rather than heading to Pittsburgh, New York, or London.

George didn't begrudge anyone's earning honest money as long as that person had a care for the environment and for what few laws there were governing the gathering of this black rock. He did begrudge those miners who paid no attention to what they were destroying and cut every corner to increase their profits. Both cautious and careful, he hated carelessness and wastefulness.

As Landsetter drove from the town out into the countryside, the dusky dark began to envelop him. After about a quarter of an hour, he turned off the paved road onto dusty dirt and gravel. In the hollows, where the road curved sinuously to follow the streams, dark came earlier than on the ridges.

When he turned a sharp bend, the glare of his car's headlights touched a tall figure walking in the road near the left side. As George approached, the man stepped carefully off the road, stuck out his thumb, and waited for the car to pass him. George pulled to a stop just beyond the man, whose tall form seemed familiar.

The hitchhiker peered inside the open window of the Datsun, but George couldn't make out his face, George recognized a familiar voice when the hitchhiker asked if he could get a ride to Winding Fork.

"Moon? Is that you? How've you been, Old Buddy?" "Is that you, George? What you doin' here?"

"Came back 'bout two years ago. Got my master's degree and a job with the reclamation people. You want a lift to Winding Fork?"

"If it won't put you out, I'd be obliged, cousin. I do believe Mamaw wrote something 'bout you workin' with the reclamation people."

Lunamin squeezed his lanky frame into the Datsun. The two men bore a strong family resemblance. Both were tall, over six feet, although Lunamin was dark-haired and a good three Inches taller than Landsetter, who was blond and bearded. Their mothers were both the daughters of Archibald and Serafina MacCloud. George's mother, Cary, was a couple of years older than Moon's mother, Verna. "Moon, how come you're out here walking."

"Just home from the army—I flew into Roanoke and came on the bus from Roanoke to Abingdon and took the Coeburn bus from Abingdon."

"Why didn't you let somebody know? We could've met you in Roanoke and given you a welcome home party."

"George, I didn't want to see people—didn't want no big party. I had some thinkin' to do, some plannin.'"

The cousins rode along talking about the old days and the folks along Winding Fork. George's parents had temporarily moved back to the mountains many times when work was scarce in Cincinnati. He and Moon had become close friends on his trips back to the homefolks. On George's returns to the mountains, the two boys had gone hunting and fishing together whenever the opportunity arose.

In the city George had been a good student and athlete at his metropolitan high school. At the small high school he attended up Winding Fork, they played football, basketball, and baseball. George had been a welcome addition to the teams his last two years back and a star in the classroom also. After graduation, he had gone on to college at Ohio State University and Virginia Polytechnic Institute and State University while Moon had drifted from one job to another until he ended up drafted into the army and sent to Vietnam.

"I heard lots of boys are getting' rich around here now, cousin." "Coal's going for forty-five dollars a ton now and moving up, so I guess a fellow could get rich."

"You makin' your second million yet, George?" Moon chuckled. George waved the thought away. "I just try to get the land put back, Moon. That won't make an honest man rich. It won't even make him popular."

"Well, now, you should get you some of this money while you can. I aim to. Black gold, cousin, that's what it is. Black gold just waitin' for us to scoop it up and haul it to the bank."

George could look into the future and see Moon bragging about making it big. He feared that Moon might cut corners to achieve success.

"I reckon we'll have a word or two before long, Moon."

"Just don't g t in front of my big dozer when I push dirt for the big bucks, George."

Moon laughed at the picture he had painted. George didn't laugh. Moon had hit a sore spot. Landsetter had already been too close to a few dozers pushing dirt the wrong way. Their talk switched to memories of their high school exploits as the car moved along through the summer evening.

"George, you remember that time we won the state championship in basketball?"

"Sure do. We couldn't have done it if we'd listened to old coach Backforth. He didn't know his rear end from a bushel basket. Why, the only coaching we got that did us any good came from Papaw MacCloud yelling instructions on the sideline. Papaw was a pretty good coach. He saw some of the best—including Glenn Roberts. Why some folks say he was the one invented that one-handed jump shot and Roberts got it from him."

"That last game was a snap, but the one before that, that was tough. You ran in front of that guy who was tryin' to catch me. I just laid the winner up with a second to go."

"We had quite a party after that game."

"We sneaked in some beer and moonshine afterwards."

"I'm surprised you remember." George slowed down. "You were drunk."

"Shit, George, I held my liquor pretty well."

"Sure, you never passed out. But dribbling a basketball down the hall in your shorts at two o'clock in the morning yelling 'Dunk it, dunk it,' wasn't exactly the action of a sober man."

"I didn't wake up many people."

George laughed. "'When he is drunk asleep or in his rage,' as Hamlet says."

"That was just high jinks, Shakespeare. You still like to quote the bard, I reckon. Miss Jarman always went ape when you did that in English class. You had her number, all right." Moon gave George's shoulder a playful slap.

After they had gone another ten miles, George pulled in at a mailbox and drove up a lane to where a white clapboard house sat waiting. When George had stopped the car, Lunamin eased his tall frame slowly from the small car as he gazed up at the house.

"You comin' up to the house, George?"

"No, I just talked to the folks yesterday. You go on up, Moon, you've got some catching up to do. I'll see you in a few days. You still sweet on Susan Stanard? I saw her in town the other day."

"I guess I'll look her up pretty soon. We wrote some while I was in Nam."

"I thought you'd camp out over at the Stanards as soon as you got home. You find another girl over in Vietnam?"

George wondered if Moon were having second thoughts about his campaign to add Susan to his trophy shelf.

"No way, George. I'll be seeing Suzy in a few days. I'll call her tomorrow."

As Landsetter turned the car around and headed away, Lunamin stood a long time looking up at the white clapboard house glowing in the last rays of sunshine before he began trudging up the path to Serafina and Archibald MacCloud sitting on the front porch.

Moon was worried they would not approve of what he planned to do.

THE OLD FOLKS

Climbing up the hill as the dark settled in, Lunamin could see three people sitting on the porch.

"How do Mamaw, Papaw. I'm glad to see you—good to be back." Moon kissed Serafina and hugged Archibald MacCloud. Looking past them he saw a blonde, well-dressed woman who reminded him of his mother. It was his Aunt Cary. He greeted her with a smile as he climbed the steps.

"George picked me up on the road and gave me a lift, Cary." "Mighty glad you made it back, Moon. Did George tell you about the close call he had at Dab Whacker's strip job the other day?" "No. He didn't mention it. I reckon they keep him busy."

"That's certain," Cary grunted. "Those damn strippers don't pay any mind to what's safe or how to treat folks. If you live near one of Whacker's jobs, you need to watch out for rocks coming through the roof and hitting you on the head. We're not safe even in town."

Serafina nodded agreement and Archibald slapped his knee to show his approval. "Some people will do anything to get a little bit of money," the old man said.

Lunamin decided that he'd hold his peace. It didn't seem like the right time to announce his big plans.

"Why didn't you let us know you were coming, Moon," Serafina scolded. "We could have had some other people in to see you, and I could have readied your room."

"Mamaw, I just wanted a quiet homecoming. I didn't want to see anybody much."

19

For the next hour they talked about the war and caught Moon up on the current neighborhood gossip. When Cary left, Moon pleaded a need for rest and asked where he should sleep.

"You wait here awhile with Archie. I'll ready your old room."

Before going to bed, Moon and Archibald talked about old times—hunting and fishing experiences—and planned for a 'coon hunt as soon as the weather was right. It was like old times. Moon wondered if Susan's father would still call him a damned Melungeon

Moon's father, Big John Lunamin, had died young. He had been 4-f despite his size because of flat feet, but he could dig more coal than two average men. He had had his eyes on Verna MacCloud when they were in high school, and he had managed to persuade her that he would be a better husband than his rival, James Jenkins. John Lunamin and Verna publicly announced their intentions of marrying in the spring. Their plans went awry when John and several other miners were killed in a roof-fall at South Fork Mine in February. Fred MacCloud and some others had barely escaped to tell of it.

Everyone in Winding Fork thought of John and Verna as married, so nobody was greatly surprised w en Verna produced a baby boy in September. According to old mountain custom, a relic of the frontier when courthouses were non-existent and preachers came around only occasionally, they were considered married by the community even though they had not obtained a license or "stood up" before a preacher.

Archibald MacCloud came home from his army post to make sure that John Lewis Lunamin was listed as father in the official records so that his grandson would not carry the stigma of bastard through life.

Several years later, after the war, Verna married James Jenkins when he was demobilized from the army. Along with his desire to wed Verna, Jenkins still harbored an intense dislike of his dead rival, whom he had taunted and accused of being a Melungeon.

Moon knew the Melungeons to be a group of mysterious people who at the beginning of the twentieth century lived mainly along the mountain ridges of Southwest Virginia and nearby Tennessee. Calling themselves Portuguese, they kept apart.

"Papaw," Moon asked, "Are folks still knocking Melungeons?"
"There's still some objecions, but it's better now. 'Sides, you're a vet."

Moon remembered being left behind when his mother went to California. When the first settlers of the westward migration in colonial times had come to Southwest Virginia, they wanted the rich bottomland farms they found in the possession of the Melungeons. Before and to some extent after the Civil War, being classified as a person of color in Virginia disqualified a man from owning land, so the newcomers simply labeled the dark-skinned Melungeons people of color and took their land. Categorized as people of color, these Melungeons were dispossessed of basic rights as well as their rich bottomland. Long after the legal restrictions disappeared, a social stigma remained. It was not surprising, therefore, that many persons who had Melungeon blood preferred to call themselves Scotch-Irish.

To call a person a Melungeon was still an insult not to be ignored in the 1940's, so when James Jenkins had once called Big John Lunamin a Melungeon devil to his face, a fight had ensued. Big John had bested Jenkins both in that fist fight and in a later altercation over Verna. and John had bested James in courting Verna also. James Jenkins still carried a grudge years later and didn't want to rear what he termed "Big John's bastard boy." Jenkins wanted to head west—without Verna's baby boy.

Archie had told Moon about the leave-taking. "Don't you worry none Verna. Your ma and me'll raise this little feller," Archibald had comforted her.

"Thanks, Pa, I hate to leave him, but Jim wants to try his luck out west, and he don't want to take Everett. My boy'll have a better life with you all than with a step-pa that don't want him."

Verna had brought her and Jim's two children back to the mountains almost every summer to visit, but other than for those infrequent visits, Moon saw nothing of his mother. She wrote him, but Archibald and Serafina had seemed his real mother and father even though he called them Mamaw and Papaw.

Moon promised himself he'd show folks what the son of a Melungeon could do.

The next morning Lunamin stretched himself as he looked across to Walnut Ridge. The swirling mists hung down in the valleys below the blue-green ridges of Pine Mountain as the sun rose to the loud hum of seventeen-year locusts. He had slept well, the best sleep he'd had for a long time. He heard a squirrel barking on the ridge and thought about the coming fall and squirrel season. He pictured himself moving quietly through the woods to a good squirrel stand, and his mouth watered a little at the thought of having some squirrel meat with biscuits and gravy.

In the distance some hounds were baying. That brought to mind some late night fox and 'coon hunts when he and George gathered around the fire with Papaw and others listening to the dogs and swigging good moonshine. It was difficult to find good stuff nowadays, because the revenuers had put so many blockaders out of business. But Papaw had his contacts.

"It's good to be back home in the mountains," Moon mused as he walked off the back stoop and turned toward the kitchen garden on the left of the house.

Mamaw's garden was always a pretty sight with hollyhocks, marigolds, cosmos, four o'clocks, coxcombs, and zinnias adding color around the edges with the corn and beans rising up behind them. The pea vines were starting to brown on the sticks and twigs holding them off the ground. The Irish potatoes were beginning to die down, but the tomatoes and squash were still blooming, their large unripe green and ripe red fruits hanging down from the tomato vines and a few of the green cabbage plants had split open, grown impatient at waiting unharvested.

A tall, heavyset woman with graying hair was bending along a row of kale, cutting the large, curly green-blue leaves and placing them in a peck basket.

"That sure is a pretty garden patch, Mamaw!" Moon called.

Grunting agreement without looking up, the woman finished gathering the greens before she stood up, smoothed her calico dress and finally looked over at Moon and smiled.

"Well, Ev'rett, you finally out of bed? I don't see how a young'un can sleep so long."

Moon stretched to his full height. "Now, Mamaw, I'm a man grown."

Serafina patted his hand. "You'll always be a young'un to me, I reckon. Think you can eat any of this truck I'm collectin'?"

"Sure do. Been dreamin' 'bout tomatoes, beans, corn, and garden greens with fatback. Don't look like I've got to dream much longer."

She handed him her basket. "Well, make yourself useful and take along some of this to the house for me. Put it up ferninst the sink."

After Moon had finished this chore, he walked out to the front porch. Papaw MacCloud was sitting in the swing looking out over the hills. His lined face was still handsome and his gray eyes gave off a steely glint. His blue shirt showed signs of wetness that indicated the old man had been out working and was just now taking a rest.

"How do, Papaw."

"By gonnies, Ev'rett, did you finally get up? Boy, the day's half gone. I'd think you was a city slicker if you wasn't my young'un's whelp."

"Sleepin' late's a way to forget the army and Nam, Papaw."

"We're glad to have you home from there, Ev'rett. Just don't want you to sleep the rest of your life away. Verna asked about you. She called last week. Said to give you her love when you got in."

"How's the family? Serena and Tom?"

Moon's omission of his stepfather went unremarked.

"Verna says James just got a promotion. He's head of plant security now. Tom's in college. Serena's plannin' to marry."

Moon had had letters from his mother when he was in Vietnam, and Serena had written him a few times. Moon's memories of his mother stemmed largely from her visits back to Winding Fork during summers when she brought Serena and, later, Tom to see her parents and Moon. Verna had always brought presents—clothes and playthings for Moon. Other than these visit, pictures, and gifts on his birthdays and at Christmas, Moon had few other memories of Verna, who had left him with her parents when he was two and she married James Jenkins and moved west to California with him.

Moon had liked the toys. They were store bought. He had lots of other toys that Papaw made for him—wooden trucks and autos, a train with four or five cars and a caboose, stilts to walk on and pretend he was a giant. From old tires Papaw made a swing and another toy in the form of a horse to hang up and ride. Always, when the novelty of the new store-bought toys had worn off, Moon found Papaw's toys more fun. After Verna's visits, Moon felt deserted, but his hurt healed quickly because of the love Archibald and Serafina heaped on him.

His half-sister Serena was just two years younger than Moon, blonde and blue-eyed. As soon as she was able to walk, she tagged along with him everywhere she could when he let her, even though he made fun of her pigtails. Two years younger than Serena, his half-brother Tom followed as quickly as he was able. Brown-haired and chubby, he had trouble keeping up. When he fell behind, he cried until they let him catch up.

When Moon had reached nine years old, he had a band of two loyal followers to play Indian to his chief. Moon showed them where to find salamanders, turning over logs in the woods and rocks in the streams, and how to tie a string to a June bug's leg and follow it as it flew. He showed them his secret hiding places and his climbing trees. He taught them to make leaf whistles, to taste teaberry leaves, and to chew cherry birch bark.

Together they found birds' nests, and his tribe watched as he stole a young crow from its nest and taught it to talk. Moon's pet crow was a center of their attention for several summers before it became a casualty to a nearby farmer's gun turned against all crows because of some black marauders in his corn patch.

Moon's tribe climbed the big rocks up the mountain at the back of Papaw's place—he as chief Bengy and they as his warriors. They killed and scalped settlers by the dozens, undeterred by the troops sent to quell Indian uprisings. As they grew older, however, games changed. By the time that Moon had become a teenager and had killed his first deer, he felt that he was too grown up to play much with *children*. He still was given the responsibility of looking after them, but their relationship had undergone a transformation. Moon made a point of being grown up. He hunted and fished with the men and did a man's work.

"I killed my first deer this past fall," he told them by way of explanation about why he would not play the old games."

"What's that got to do with anything?"

Moon kicked a ball. "Serena, I'm not a kid anymore."

Besides Moon's standoffishness based on his assumption of manliness, his brother and sister had begun to perceive the gulf between California culture and what their father scoffingly termed *hill ways*. Serena thought his new behavior toward them must be part of hill culture.

"Dad says that mountain people are backward. They stick to hill ways instead of keeping up-to-date."

Tom chimed in, "Dad says moving to California was the best thing he ever did."

They didn't use the term *hillbilly*, because Verna drew the line there, Moon knew, telling them to mind their tongues.

Moon responded to his brother and sister with a scorn born of hurt, "What do you know about anything? You're citified." He threw a rock up the ridge. Moon calmed when Verna tried to restore peace.

"There's more to be learned about how to live by spending one day with Ma and Pa at Winding Fork than in a whole year in California," she lectured.

Despite their mother's defense of mountain culture, as Serena and Tom grew older they were less comfortable being followers of an older brother they were beginning to think of as countrified. He was someone their California friends termed a hillbilly, even when he became captain of the football and basketball teams at Winding Fork High School, the hero of all the young men and the heartthrob of many of the young women around Winding Fork. They remained Moon's brother and sister, but they more and more lived in a world disparate from his.

Moon sat down on the porch steps and followed his grandfather's gaze over the mountains blue with haze, ridge giving way to ridge in the distance. He felt himself drift into a sort of drowsy trance. It was good to be back home.

"I'm glad to be back in Windin' Fork. I never did figure out why we had to be in that jungle halfway 'cross the world."

"Hit's a shame, Moon. I'm as patriotic as the next fellow, but Eisenhower was right when he talked about the dangers of a military-industrial complex. Them's fancy words, but it's just another way of sayin' to watch out for big business bastards that'll make money while the workin' man sweats and bleeds. Same old story as us miners have lived."

"Papaw, I aim to get in on the other side."

Archibald MacCloud gave his grandson a long, searching look— like a man trying to decide what kind of bad joke was being told him. Finally he managed a few words.

"Just don't get too far above your raisin' boy."

"Don't intend to sleep too much. Talked to cousin Fred Caruso MacCloud on the way from Coeburn. Me and him's goin' into the minin' business."

"Fred's a good man. He works hard and he's honest. Where's the money comin' from, honey?"

"I've saved some. It don't take much to get into the strippin' business I heard."

Archie shook his head. "You aimin' to be one of them damn strippers? Why, they'd tear up their mamaw's graves to get a little bitty seam of coal."

Moon cracked a knuckle. "There's a right way to do it and a wrong. Fred wants to do it right. So do I, Papaw."

Archibald MacCloud didn't answer Moon for a long time. He gazed at the distant ridges for what seemed to Moon even longer. Finally he cleared his throat and spoke, "George says that he has a time keepin' a lot of these stripminin' bulldozer jockeys from pushin' the hills into the streams. Them fellows are in such a rush to cash in they don't even bother with the timber and don't give a damn about the fish."

"Papaw, I'm ready to rake in some money, but I'll not give George much trouble."

The two men sat together looking over the mountains, listening to the vireos sing monotonously and a broad-winged hawk blowing his high-pitched whistle as he circled above the ridge.

Moon felt sad. He knew he had not pleased his grandparents with his performance in high school. They thought his excellence in sports caused him to neglect his books. Archibald MacCloud had had little formal schooling, but he read voraciously. And he thought about what he read. He always worried that Moon had taken no greater interest in books. Still, Moon felt, he kept abreast of the world. He hoped the folks would come around.

A yellow-billed cuckoo's gulping *kawp, kawp, kawp* interrupted Moon's thoughts. Papaw MacCloud looked down at Moon sitting on the steps below.

"There go s a rain crow. Goin' to rain this afternoon. Well, honey, your mamaw and me was worried while you was away. We're right glad to have you home. If you're dead set to strip, I know somebody with a servagorous seam of met'lurgical coal who's hot to make money. I'll talk to our cousin Isaiah."

Their talk drifted into politics and the war. Archibald MacCloud had been in two World Wars. He had enlisted twice to fight in what he believed to be just causes. He had to pull some strings to get into WWII. He couldn't believe that his country had any business being in Vietnam and blamed the scurrility of Lyndon Johnson and other politicians for getting America into it.

"Even if that man was a Democrat, he done his country a great disservice."

For Archibald, this was a difficult admission, but Moon agreed wholeheartedly, "We have no business bein' there."

Their discussion moved on to the economic situation in the nation. The price of coal had followed the price of oil in the late 1960's. As the oil companies worked to maximize their profits, the high prices of oil increased the desirability of coal-fueled power despite the growing awareness of the pollution and damage to the environment and to human health that coal could cause. Leaders touted the use of nuclear energy, but coal remained the only feasible large-scale substitute for oil. "Nixon's pushin' for that Alaska oil pipeline. He wants to take controls off natural gas. Folks want nuclear energy. You'd think they've forgot about coal."

"Do you reckon any of that stuff will go through, Papaw?" "Well, might be. Some say Nixon favors strip-minin' coal, too.

May be so. May be not. There's lots of people don't want us burnin' high sulfur coal. Bad for the lungs. Kills trees. So they say."

Moon and Archibald agreed that the coal industry would prosper in spite of people's reservations about the environmental problems it caused. The nation would not be able to do without coal, and the price was likely to go up. But despite their prescience, they could not look ahead to see just how much money coal would bring in just a few years. "With coal prices goin' up, I don't see how I can go wrong, 'less there's a drastic change. There's no way coal can be replaced."

"That's right, boy, demand for energy just keeps goin' up. Long as there's coal, somebody's goin' to want it dug."

"There's talk about closin' down power plants that use coal." "Don't worry. The politics of it won't allow that to happen. They may build some of them nuclear plants, but they'll need the coal- burners. No way around it. Besides, there's just as big a *broohawhaw* about nuclear as about coal. You don't need to go after them contracts for the power companies. The best money's in the high-grade coal.

Hit's easier to get that low-grade coal, and lots of those fellows goin' after it don't give a hoot for what they're doin' to the land."

Archie made a fist.

"You have anybody in particular in mind?"

"Well, if you want to call names, Dave Blackmun and Dab Whacker'll do for a start. They get the coal and move it as fast as they can. They tear the hell out of the watersheds and let the run-off ruin the streams. Gettin' hard as hell to find a stream to fish for trout in even with the put-and-take hatchery fish we have to put up with nowadays."

"Papaw. People I ran into overseas would call you an environmentalist."

"Moon, I don't need no earth days and teach-in's and Councils on the Environment to tell me the land's bein' ruined. I see it with these here two eyes."

"Strip mines ain't pretty, that's a fact," Moon said, shifting his seat.

Archie went on, "I can remember my daddy tellin' how passenger pigeons came into these mountains in big flocks. They're long gone. I don't need no Endangered Species Act to tell me that wild animals get the short end of the stick. Trouble is, most people makin' the decisions had rather save a couple of hours flyin' across the Atlantic on an SST or have a big pipe ine to Alaska or somewheres else to bring 'em gas for their fancy cars than worry about havin' animals to look at and hunt." "You're right, Papaw, but worryin' over it won't stop people from wantin' coal and oil. I'm tired of fightin.' I just want to show all the rich bastards that I'm just as good as they are. I'm goin' to show Suzy's folks what real money is. Way things are agoin' I figure I can do it strippin.'

I spent too much time overseas fightin' a stupid war and watchin' men die for something' we never understood."

Lunamin quieted, and he and Archibald MacCloud sat silently for a time looking out over the mountain ridges. Over all, the fighting in Vietnam hung like a bloody pall—made real each night for Moon by bloody scenes on the evening news and in his mind. Lunamin heard all of the political noise around him, but he never doubted that coal would provide his way to wealth and the ability to hold his own with the power brokers of society.

Everett Adamo Lunamin had returned home from the now-despised war in Vietnam to a situation hitherto largely unknown in the coalfields. With a little good luck, Moon thought, enterprising young mountain men could now make their fortunes in this region more noted for its human poverty than its mineral wealth.

Finally Archibald began talking again.

"Hit seems right for some of the local boys to be makin' some money from the riches around us, Moon. I don't deny that. They're just getting' back some of what was stole from us in the 1890's and early 1900's. Land agents were thicker'n ticks on a coon dog buyin' up mineral rights for big wigs back east and in England. Why Isaiah Timmons' pa thought he was makin' a shrewd bargain—sold some of his mineral rights for almost nothing,' pennies an acre." Archie spit a stream of tobacco juice.

"He wasn't the only one got to k, was he?"

"No, those of us that didn't was few. My daddy was one of the lucky ones."

"Papaw, lots of guys I met in Nam can't fit in back here. People some places yell at 'em. Even spit on 'em. We just did what our country asked, and lots got killed or hurt bad. It's not our fault the jackasses in Washington didn't know how to fight a war. I'm better off than most. I plan to blot our my nightmares with a bulldozer and a front-end loader."

"As long as you do it honest, I reckon Serafina and me can live with it."

"I want to get some money all right. I want to show all those bastards who think we're dirt. I want to show all those people who look to Richmond and Philadelphia and New York that I'm some-body who counts. I want to show Susan Stanard and her family what a Melungeon can do. Right now I'm about as pop'lar with Tom Stanard as horse-piss."

"Don't lug a chip on your shoulder, Moon. That's not goin' to help none. I cut trees for Ritter lumber, cut every tree worth a damn from off these hills, and then I worked in the mines. The only way us workin' men got something besides the hind tit of the cow was by joinin' the union."

Archibald MacCloud was a union man to the core. Moon respected Archibald's views, but he thought that union men, for all their bitterness toward the companies that owned the mines, did the bidding of their corporate masters, however they might rail against them. Lunamin wanted to be part of what he saw to be a new breed of mountain men.

"Papaw, I want to be part of something new. I'm g in' to join the Old Dominion Surface Miners. Pal Fador and Gabe Wheeler belong. They made it big in the 50's. They rub shoulders with doc-tors and lawyers and deep mine owners and all the other folks that look down on us in the hollers."

"Serafina and me, boy, we want the best for you. We don't care to object to the mess some strippers are makin,' but you're our boy and we'll stick with you. Just try to do it right. Make sure you don't forget where you come from."

FOLLOWING THE 'COON DOGS

Two days after Moon returned to Winding Fork, a cold front brought cloud cover to hide the sun and moon for a time. It seemed a good time for a 'coon hunt. Papaw invited Moon and George to hunt with him. Moon couldn't help thinking about night patrols he had been on in Vietnam, but he found the sounds and smells of the Appalachian woodlands reassuring. The shadows cast by this moon when it came out from behind the clouds held no terrors for Moon. He could almost imagine himself and George as teenagers following Papaw on the hunt.

"Like old times, ain't it?"

"Sure is, Moon. I think of the old times, too, listening to the hounds. I wonder whether the two of us will be going on many hunts together after you begin the strip-mining business."

"It won't make a difference to me." Moon brushed these thoughts aside, though, because the hunt demanded his complete attention.

The cloud cover wasn't complete, and there were moments when the landscape was illuminated with a brightness that gave everything a ghostly glow. As they listened and followed Archibald's old blue ticks Sap and Sookie up the ridge, the moon appeared only fitfully from behind the clouds. Most the time they had enough light from it so that they didn't have to use their flashlights, but Archie knew the way well enough that he could traverse the terrain without needing to see it well.

They moved up to the head of a stream near the top of a hollow over the first ridge from the house and looked for 'coon sign. As Archie had foretold, there was plenty. The dogs had picked up a scent without much difficulty and begun the chase baying at a run.

The enthusiasm of the dogs was matched by the excitement of the men who followed them. There must have been at least a couple of raccoons, but they split up after about a half-hour's chase. The dogs hesitated at this point. After a bit of sniffing around, the dogs decided on the trail to follow and the group was off again. Moon and George were beginning to be a bit winded, but Archibald MacCloud did not seem to be breathing hard.

"You boys been livin' too high off the hog and sittin' around? I hate to think you young fellers can't keep up with a 'coon."

"You go on, old man. We can keep up." Moon didn't like to admit being out of shape.

The 'coon they were following didn't tree. He went down in a hole instead. Sap and Sookie were standing at the hole barking when the three of them caught up. Archie sized up the situation.

"I reckon we'll have to smoke 'em out. We probably should have waited for a night with a little more cloud cover."

Fanning out, they gathered branches and brush to make a fire. "Now, we don't want too big a fire, boys, just enough to get the critter to come out to get some fresh air. Don't want to kill 'em in there and have to drag him out. Get some green stuff to make some smoke. Smoke it out, not kill it in the hole."

Moon gathered an armload of brush and carried it back to Archie. "I don't know as I want to kill anything tonight, Papaw. I'd just like to see old brother 'coon come out and grin at us."

"Honey, you let me do the shootin' then. I promised Serafina some wild meat, so I got to take me a 'coon back home. You grab this bottle and sit down by the fire and rest.

Moon took the pint of moonshine that Papaw handed him. He and George found a nearby log and sat down. They passed the bottle between them, taking only one swig apiece.

"It's sure like old times, George. You just don't know how good it feels to be back home in a woods where the smells are familiar and you don't have to worry about booby traps, snipers, and friendly fire."

"It's been a long time since we sat around a night fire in the woods, Moon. I reckon I'm glad to have you home even if you're going to be giving me trouble soon. Look at those clouds scudding across the moon. The wind's picking up. The front's moving in fast."

"Be lucky to get this ole 'coon out and cared for before the rain comes. How's it agoin,' Papaw? Any sign of that varmint?"

Archie peered at the amoke. "Just give 'em a little more time. I think he's comin' out."

"Would it were done quickly, the bard might say," George joked.

Moon laughed, took a second swig from Papaw's pint bottle and passed it over to George, who followed suit.

Moon smacked his lips. "I see you still have connections, Papaw. This here's good stuff."

"Got it from old man Timmons," Archibald said as he helped himself to a pull off the bottle. "He don't hold with makin' bad liquor, and he's one blockader knows how to hide his still house. Ain't no revenuer got him yet. Won't neither, unless some Judas gives him up. Won't be me. The good Lord has done give us the corn and the know-how. The government should keep out of it as long as a man don't go commercial. Hit's something Timmons does just for family and good friends."

"Which category do we fall into, Papaw?" George asked. "Both, honey. He's my fifth cousin."

Moon felt the mellowing effects of the liquor as he watched his grandfather. Archibald kept his eye on the hole and his smoky fire next to where the raccoon had gone to ground and the actions of Sap and Sookie sniffing around it. When he saw that they were becoming more agitated, he passed the bottle to Moon and grabbed his shotgun. The discussion ceased as the raccoon began to stagger out of the hole. George and Moon shone their lights on him as he came out, dazed, and stood grinning at them until he rolled over dead as the shot from Archibald's gun did its work. As the old man walked over to pick up his game, George and Moon put out the fire.

"Hit's big. Didn't damage him much, I'm pleased to say. Hit'll make a fine skin to hang on the barn to dry while Serafina serves the meat on the table," Archibald surmised.

On the way back to the house, Moon and George and Archibald talked about past hunts. The years faded away. The manhunts in the jungles of Vietnam became a distant memory for Moon. He was enjoying returning to a way of life that had been taken from him. The death of the raccoon had seemed natural, part of the order of life—a world away from the hunting of men in an Asian jungle.

Breaking a long silence, George turned Moon's thoughts elsewhere. "Have you seen Susan yet?"

"No, I've talked to her on the phone."

"Did you know she's been seeing Rod Mashburn?" "She didn't mention it."

"Word is Rod's supplying her with pot. That Suzy gets it free. Thought you ought to know, cousin."

"Thanks, George. I'll see what Suzy has to say. I don't want a smokin' wife, hash or tobacco. Rod's bad news even if he is a cousin." "Yeah. But he appears to be making a good living dealing in marijuana. Our old teammate and cousin Earl Campbell's working for him. I guess Rod's paying off the sheriff. Probably in pot. I hear the jail's a great place to buy maryjane."

"Suzy never had anything to do with Rod in high school. She thought he was stuck on himself. I've got to hear it from her own lips."

LOVERS' QUARREL

Moon had less than a week to think about what George had said. He and Suzy had made their first date for the Friday after his homecoming. George's news had taken Lunamin a little aback. He wasn't surprised to hear that Susan had dated somebody else. He hadn't expected her to sit at home all the time he was in Vietnam, but he was surprised to hear that one of her choices for an escort had been Rod Mashburn. Susan had given him a cold shoulder when he had approached her in high school because Rod had had a reputation of being a womanizer even then. Moon worried that Rod's access to marijuana might have caused Susan to view him with less hostility, but he felt that Suzy would not have allowed Rod to add her to his list of conquests.

With Moon, Suzy had always been quite adamant about maintaining her virinity for the marriage bed. She wasn't very conservative about many things, but even though she had a penchant for trying all the new fads, she had been very determined to follow her mother's advice about sex. Moon and Suzy had argued about that. In high school they had also argued about pot smoking. She was eager to try it, but Moon opposed any smoking and made no distinction between tobacco and pot. Even though she termed him a stick-in-the- mud, Susan acceded to Moon's wishes. Moon had been out of step with the majority of his classmates, but once he became a star athlete, nobody thought much about his determined abstinence, as they attributed it to his desire to stay in good physical condition for athletics. Suzy's seeing Rod Mashburn and the possibility of her

35

smoking pot troubled his mind as he knocked on the front door of the Stanard home.

A dark-haired, dark-eyed young woman dressed in a red blouse and blue jeans answered his knock. Susan Stanard seemed even prettier than Moon remembered.

"Hello, Moonman." Susan smiled as she moved forward into his arms and lifted her face to be kissed.

"It's good to see you again, Suzy."

"Come in and say hello to Mom and Dad while I finish getting ready."

"Do I have to? You look great."

"You haven't seen them for years. They expect it." "They never liked me."

"You just didn't fit their idea of what husband material for their daughter should be. Athletics, the stock cars—Dad thought your greatest ambition was to become another Richard Petty. I just objected to your being a grease monkey."

"I learned a lot workin' with those stock cars. I'll be able to put it to good use, you'll see."

"Mom and Dad would have b en a lot happier if you had gone to college."

"With what? I didn't have the money."

"You could have taken that sports scholarship they offered you at Emory and Henry."

"Yeah. But it didn't pay all the bills. I'd have had to work and go to school to . I couldn't have stood that for four years. Lack of money—that's what they have against me. I aim to show them, and you, and some others. I'm goin' into the strip-minin' business. There's money to be made there."

Despite his objections, Moon dutifully went to say hello to Mr. and Mrs. Stanard, who were always polite, though, it seemed to him, politely condescending. In their late forties with the beginnings of gray hairs, the Stanards still dressed in slacks, coat sweaters, and saddle oxfords as they had during their college days at Vanderbilt. The subjects of family background and money always crept into their conversations with Lunamin—and always with the implication that they had them and he did not—and did not appear to have any prospects of obtaining the money necessary to expunge his lack of appropriate genealogy and education.

This evening, when the subjects came up, Moon took pleasure in announcing that he had embarked upon a business venture.

"There's money to be made in minin' these days. I've started a new company, Lunar Minin'. I'm plannin' to do some surface minin'. My grandfather helped me find a seam of high-grade metallurgical coal. I expect to start minin' right away, but I want to do things right. We're not goin' to push the timber over the hill. Before we mine, we'll timber, but that should bring in a good bit of money considering the good stand of timber on the tract."

After he had stopped, Moon thought that Tom Stanard looked at him with a more kindly expression. He even gave Moon a genial smile. "I'm glad to hear you're going to try your hand at something that has good prospects. There certainly is plenty of money to be made in mining these days."

Louella Stanard's smiling face indicated to Moon that she too approved of his business plans, even though he detected a note of surprise in her voice when she spoke.

"I hadn't realized you were such an ambitious young man, Mr. Lunamin. I don't seem to recall your having much interest in business."

"Vietnam changed my mind about a lot of things."

To Moon's surprise and satisfaction, Mr. and Mrs. Stanard walked to the door with Susan and him as they left.

"Have a good time, dear," Mrs. Stanard called after them.

If the mere announcement of my intentions produces this effect, Moon thought, a mild success might be sufficient to render me fit husband material. He felt his campaign to achieve acceptance well underway.

Later, after dinner and a movie, they drove to the top of Pound Gap and sat in the moonlight. They kissed eagerly and engaged in heavy petting until they had become thoroughly aroused. Moon pleaded for Susan to let him enter her, but she told him that she was as determined as ever to save her virginity for her wedding night. She guided Moon's hand to her sex and grasped his, just as she had during their high school days and after graduation before he left for Vietnam. Afterwards, they watched the clouds scud across the moon and Lunamin pointed out the circle around it that foretold rain.

"That circle around the moon foretells rain. I wish I could read your father as easily as I can read the weather. I think he approves of my minin' venture. I could see his eyes change when I told him. I told him I planned to do it."

Susan laughed, "I'm sure he was as surprised as I was, but I think you're imagining things if you think you can tell what he's thinking. I can't. I'm certain your announcement didn't hurt. Dad and Mom are family mavericks who acquired a vision of bucolic bliss during their college days at Vanderbilt. They think that living close to nature makes them and their children better people. They call themselves Agrarians."

"What's an Agrarian?"

"I'm not quite sure. It has something to do with living close to nature. As far back as I can rememb r, my uncles and aunts have poked fun at my father and mother's lifestyle. 'Tom,' Uncle Josh would tell my dad, 'You have a good head on you. You could run for the legislature or do something else worthwhile, but you just sit out here and live off your inheritance. You manage pretty well, I admit, but a man of means ought to make his place in society, not spend his time looking at birds and feeding foxes and 'coons.' He'd laugh, of course.'

"Dad would just smile and reply that he was doing as much business as he wanted taking care of his money and that of the people who paid him to take care of theirs. I guess he's made a pretty good living at that, but I don't want to spend my life with foxes and raccoons. I don't want to live with the wild animals. I don't dislike raccoons. I just don't want them as close friends. I want to live like the rest of my family—near a place where there are department stores that carry the correct fashions along a street where there are sidewalks."

Moon realized that Susan had never accepted her parents' view of the way to live and looked forward to escaping from what she termed "the wilderness" to return to what she considered civilization with those whom she considered the normal members of her family. When she and Moon had dated in high school, Susan had made clear to him that she didn't intend to marry anyone who would take her to live in any place more rustic than a town with a population of at least 5,000 people.

"I've spent enough of my life with groundhogs, 'possums, and skunks. I relish the thought of a house with a sidewalk in front, or at least within a few miles," she had said.

Moon had felt obliged to defend life in the hollows and along the ridges, "Not all skunks live in the woods," Moon had retorted, "some of them stink up neighborhoods in towns and some of them even walk around on two legs, wear suits, and run for town council."

Tonight, as they sat quietly in the moonlight, Susan, from habit— without giving her actions conscious thought, Moon suspected— pulled out a cigarette and began to light it.

"You know how I feel about that Suzy."

"Oh, yes. I guess I forgot." She put away her lighter and put the cigarette back in her purse.

"What was that? Tobacco or pot?"

"That's my business. You don't have the right to determine my smoking habits."

"I suppose Rod Mashburn does, then. I hear that's where you get your supply of hash. I hear cousin Rod has quite an agricultural operation."

"What if it is? That's my business."

"If we get married, it'll be my business, too. I don't want a pothead for the mother of my children."

"You're getting way ahead of yourself, Moon. I think it's time for you to take me home."

"Okay. But you can't have me and Rod Mashburn too. And if you decide on me you're decidin' against tobacco and pot."

"You're still a poor boy, Moon. You don't have a chance unless you change that. You've been my favorite for a long, long time, but you'll have to have a healthy bank account before I marry you. I'm looking for a man to take me out of this wilderness. My dad and mother like to feed the chipmunks and squirrels and watch the turkeys strut across the yard, but I want to live in a place where I can walk down a sidewalk a few feet to visit a neighbor or the corner drugstore. And I want a place to be proud of."

"I'm aworkin' on that. You just remember what I said."

AGRICULTURAL ENDEAVORS

I t wasn't long after Moon and Suzy's date that the state police raided one of Rod Mashburn's pot-growing operations. They didn't put Mashburn out of business entirely. By no means, but the news of the arrests, and the sophistication of the operation drew attention from as far away as Roanoke and Knoxville and beyond. Word went around Clintwood and Winding Fork that somebody had tipped off the troopers.

"Rod suspects you tipped off the police," Suzy told Moon. "How do you know?"

"Rod told me he suspects you when I called him to tell him that I won't be needing any more marijuana."

"Let him suspect what he wants."

* * *

The incident attracted the attention of the press far outside of Southwest Virginia as the AP and other press services picked up the story. Reporters swarmed into the county. One of the reporters from the Roanoke *Times* had been a casual acquaintance of George Landsetter at the university in Blacksburg, where they had both been active in the hiking club while George was working toward his master's degree. When Jennifer Coffey came to Big Stone Gap to cover the pot arrests, she looked up George and asked him to help her with the background for her story.

Jennifer seemed prettier than George had remembered. J,. Maybe it was her casual stylishness that impressed him. He remembered a thin, drably dressed young girl. She had certainly filled out since their hiking outings, but she still had the burning desire to be a successful news reporter. That had amused him during their college days, but now he found it difficult to laugh at her. And her blue eyes were as blue as ever, he thought.

George took the newspaper lady into Hardee's for breakfast so that she could meet some of those who thought themselves the local movers and shakers—some real talkers. George could tell what kind of story she had in mind to write. One like the *National Geographic* had done a few years earlier—poor, benighted Appalachians that have dropped out of the mainstream, depending on hand outs to get by, and following the course of least resistance by growing marijuana. They ordered coffee and sat at a booth. George warned her that she must alter some of the misconceptions that she had brought with her.

"Now, Jennifer, if you're looking for local color like shucky beans hanging from the rafters, Hardee's is not the place to go. Hardee's is contemporary—the new Appalachia. Like the new South, it's average American. If all you've read about the coal counties in Southern Appalachia (that's pronouncted Appuh-latch-uh unless you're a northern missionary lady or a mountain person rying to get above his raising) comes from the newspapers or magazines, then you don't really know much about us. We're not all on food stamps."

"George, do you mean there are no poor folks here?"

"Look, I know that you can find things here to fit all the stereotypes, but I can go anywhere in the United States and do that. I could get a good story about the homeless in New York or Washington, D. C., or some other big city. The only homeless here are the winos who choose to be that way, and they're hard to find unless you hunt them out under the railroad overpass in Norton."

"Oh, George—you're going to tell me that this land is full of milk and honey and there's no poverty or injustice. All those tales of bad mining practices and pot growing are just that, fairy tales."

It was plain to see that she lacked real understanding of what he was trying to tell her. George tried a different approach.

"I didn't say that. You can't do a story here in Central Appalachia without talking about coal. And coal's been a dirty business. No matter whether you're talking about the early days or now. In the beginning it was pretty much just hard on people. Now with strip mining it's hard on some people and hard as hell on the land, but it has made some Appalachians rich. What I'm trying to tell you, it's complicated, not the simple poor-folks story you came to write. For some, pot growing seems an easier road to riches than strip mining. Most people around here who grow pot don't do it because they're starving."

"I'm willing to be enlightened if you've got the time."

"That makes you an unusual item around here—an outsider who's open minded about hillbillies. That, by the way, is a term that I can use jokingly but you can't. If you use it, it's a fighting word— sort of like *nigger* used by a white man."

"George, I'm Appalachian. I'm from the mountains of Southwest Virginia myself. I'm from Roanoke."

"That's a laugh. Even a townie would find that funny." "What's a townie?"

"Town Appalachian. Trying hard to forget what their Mamaws and Papaws did to survive up in the hollows. Trying to forget that they made moonshine to survive and smoked corncob pipes. Trying to be carbon copy middle class."

George thought about what else he could tell Jennifer. She might have a passing familiarity with mountains and mountain people in the Blue Ridge or in some place where there's no coal. She had probably watched the Waltons on TV. It came to him that telling her about Moon might be the best way to explain some of what he was trying to get across. After all, his cousin Moon was becoming a sort of Appalachian Horatio Alger, and he and his story were complex enough to let her know that everybody in the mountains isn't a simple soul living the old ways or a pauper in need of food stamps.

"Okay, Jennifer, I'm going to tell you about my cousin Moon. He's not a character out of the comic strip even though that might be what got him his nickname. His full name is Everett Adamo Lunamin."

"Adamo?"

"Moon's great-grandmother was Italian. She came from Dant (that's spelled D-a-n-t-e, like the poet). Moon would have said Eye-talian in the old days. The name shows you that everything here isn't simple. The coal companies brought in lots of people from Italy and Central Europe. So names like Caruso or Brobosky and Malesky are fairly common here. The coal companies had to bring in a lot of Europeans. They needed the manpower. Appalachians didn't make good miners."

"That seems strange."

"They didn't want to go down in the mines—not because of the danger so much, though coal mining has always been dangerous. But the darkness. They didn't want to do the Devil's work. That's one of the ideas they brought with them from the British Isles. Miners dig down toward Hell. They're doing the Devil's work."

"I guess the Devil is still very real in these mountains."

"Yeah, that's truth. If you've read Hamlet, remember the ghost under the stage in the cellarage is in Hell. And that is not far off to describe the conditions in the early mines. It really was Hell down there. Just read about life in the coal camps and about the mine disasters. Dante and other coal camps that the coal companies created weren't heaven on earth either."

"I find it hard to believe it was as bad as you say."

"Basically Dante was a semi-prison until the second generation of miners learned to speak English. Miners often got paid just in scrip, company money that had to be used in company stores where very high prices were changed. That's one reason strip mining (surface mining as the people at ODSUM call it) attracted Moon and others. They could get at the coal without going underground and without being quite so beholden to the large coal companies. They could mine on their own terms and not be taking orders from some mining company with headquarters in Pittsburgh or New York."

"So Moon and other strip miners are just good guys trying to live the American dream?"

"That's right. They want to enter the mainstream. Be middle class—even upper class if they get rich enough. Be their own men, not depending on Pittston or Westmoreland. And Moon's tour in Vietnam didn't make him as conscious of the environment as it did of the need to make money. He didn't like to see the bodies blown to pieces or burned by napalm, but for the most part his mind stayed here in these mountains. They sustained him. I reckon he spent a lot of nights in Nam thinking about the fellows back home hauling in the money with the coal while he was watching his buddies sweating blood and guts in the Indochina jungles. When he came home, he had to find a place here. I had a college degree and got my job without too much trouble—it's not going to produce riches if I stay honest, but it gives security. Moon didn't have a college education, but he saw his way to get ahead and he took it."

"But you and Moon butt heads, I'll bet "

"There's no doubt about that. We go at it real good. But Moon is a lot better than some others. It has b en a wild time with people getting rich fast and then losing it just as fast. Moon is making money and keeping it better than most. He pretty much follows the laws and treats people well while some of his competitors break the laws and trample and cheat people. Funny thing, though, many of them either don't clear as much money as Moon or, if they do, they squander it. It's an old story in the coalfie ds. Boom and bust. Millionaire one day, poor man the next."

"But Moon's not growing marijuana."

"No, coal can be dirty, but coal mining is legal if done right. Moon's too set on becoming legitimate to dirty himself with pot. But the people who're behind those fellows that got caught have the same dream as Moon. Those sinners just don't care as much about where the money comes from or whether or not the saints think well of them.

"Do you know any of these pot growers?" "Might be."

"Would you introduce me?" "I might, but I have a price."

"What's that?"

"You'll have to meet Moon, too." "Is he good-looking?"

"Lots of girls in high school thought so. He's a couple of inches taller than me and dark-haired."

"Sounds interesting. Is he married?" "Not yet, but he's got plans."

"Too bad, but it's a bargain. Now, what about the pot mogul?"

"He's another cousin of mine, Rod Mashburn. He's good-looking too. You'll have to promise to use anything he tells you just as background. It wouldn't be too wise to cross him."

"How does he manage to get away with his operation? From what I know so far, there was a real pot-growing factory in the abandoned mine the state police raided. There were rows and rows of plants growing under ultraviolet lights."

George looked around to see if anybody was listening. "Rod is too smart to get caught with his plants. Anyway, Rod didn't have his whole operation there. The only men they arrested were the hired hands that tended that particular piece of the action. They don't even have any personal contact with Rod. Besides, Rod pays Sheriff Bo Mulberry a handsome amount to protect him. Folks around here tend to look on growing marijuana as a legitimate substitute for moonshining. They're still a little angry that they aren't allowed to legally turn their corn into liquor."

"Then how did this raid happen?"

"I reckon the state police didn't let the sheriff in on this arrest. They'd tried to close down some of Rod's operations before, but somebody always warned Rod or somebody close to him what was coming. By the time the state troopers arrived, all the plants had been moved. This time was different."

"I guess you're right about this story being more complex than I thought."

George felt that he was making some headway in educating Jennifer about the background of her story. Still, he wondered whether she really did understand the desire of Lunamin and others to snatch their share of the region's wealth. An outsider just couldn't fully comprehend the anger of the local people about their being cheated out of their fair share of the wealth that their black gold had created.

"I know you came to do a story on pot growing. That's all right, but you need to meet Moon and hear how he feels about surface mining. He hates pot and pot growing. Maybe you will find it interesting to quiz him about that, too."

SUCCESSFUL DIGGING

By the time Lunamin had put his stake to work in Lunar Mining for a few months, the price of coal had gone up to fifty dollars a ton and was still rising when he and Fred began to see the profits from their first job. Fred had brought along another cousin, Acie Hankins, a first-rate mechanic.

Competition for good mechanics was fierce, but Fred had persuaded Acie that he should take a chance that Moon would hit it big with this rich seam for which Archibald had helped him contract the mining rights. Moon had offered Fred a p rcentage of Lunar Mining, and Fred told Acie that he would give him a fourth of his twenty per cent to him just to keep it all in the family. Another cousin, James Earl Campbell had joined them, too. He had been working for Rod Mashburn, but after the state police raid on Rod's operation, he had decided that he wanted a line of work a little more honest.

Unlike the majority of surface miners, who were in such a hurry to get to the coal that they pushed the timbered slopes over into the hollows, Moon and his partners took a little more time. They timbered before mining the coal.

Fred saw to it that Moon did things the right way, even though it meant waiting for the coal. "Moon, don't fret. We may lose a few dollars by timberin,' but I don't think so. Not the way coal's goin' now. We may even gain. Another week coal could be up to sixty dollars a ton."

Moon lifted a beer and took a swig. "I want to do things the right way. Besides the timber money will come in handy."

The timbering was no problem for them since all of them had already worked felling trees. Many were experienced loggers from their youth, so dealing with timber did not present them with a great obstacle, and their bulldozer could make all the roads they needed to bring in the trucks to haul out the logs. The tract had good oak and some big poplar. They made quite a few dollars timbering besides getting enough firewood to supply all their families for the winter. They even made some money selling firewood.

By the time they had finished working the timber, Moon had contracted to deliver his coal at Norton for 62 dollars a ton, not quite as much as Fred had predicted, but good enough to guarantee a sizable profit. The seam was close to the surface at one point. Uncovering it was relatively easy. So Moon bought a front-end loader on time, and they started loading whatever trucks they could wrangle into working their job. Moon had to pay wages and meet his loan payments, so he needed the coal to move as fast as possible. He took any trucker he could get. A thirty-ton truck or a sixty-ton truck—whatever would haul Lunar Mining's coal. He found enough vehicles to move the coal to the tipples fast and in a steady stream.

At the end of the first week, Moon made an early start to the mine. He wasn't in a hurry. He just wanted to enjoy the ride in the Ford pick-up he had bought used. The sun was just rising over the ridges to the east of Pine Mountain as he pulled out of Archibald's drive. He drank in the beauty of the ridges stretching out before him as he congratulated himself on his good luck. Lunar Mining's cash flow that first week of mining had been more than enough to pay the truckers, pay on Lunar Mining's loans, and have a tremendous profit left over. The first week's profit had astounded him. As he rounded a curve, a gray fox stole across the road ahead of him. Moon laughed as he watched the animal disappear. "I feel like the fox who raided the henhouse and got away Scot free," he thought.

When Moon reached the trailer that they were using for an office at the mine site, everyone was waiting for him. "Boys, we've had a good week. It'll be a pleasure to go to the bank this afternoon to get the payroll. But right now, we need to get to work and get that coal rolling to the tipple another day."

Crowding around Moon at the end of the day, Acie and Fred were happy to see the first week's bottom line as everyone waited for their pay.

"By Satan's forked tail, we done cleared forty-two dollars a ton on this here coal!" Acie chortled.

"And done it right," added Fred. "There's no coal along the highways from our trucks. We didn't overload. A body can make money without wreckin' everything in sight."

Moon practically glowed good feeling as he handed out the paychecks.

"You men have worked hard; you've earned a bonus. We have to keep it up, keep the coal movin.'"

If they could keep the coal moving to tipple, Lunamin thought, he might soon be a wealthy man. Coal was showing no signs of going down in price any time soon. Now was the time to dig what was rapidly truly becoming what he and his fellow strippers were calling it and what Merle Travis had sung ab ut—Black Gold. A few months of digging this gold and he would be a millionaire. If coal prices held here for just a couple of years, Moon and his partners would be rich beyond anything they had imagined.

The men thanked him as they took the checks that he handed them. After the others had left, the cousins stayed and talked for a time. Acie sat in a glow, having drunk half a bottle of 'shine. The curly black hair that spread around his ears framed his balding head. His midriff betrayed a tendency to spread forward above his belt, the result of having eaten a little too much meat and potatoes too often. His coveralls were spattered with grease.

"I sure do favor bein' a partner in this here Lunar Minin.' I think I could enjoy being rich. I'd strut my stuff."

In the corner sitting on a chair tilted against the wall was another happy miner. His shock of orange-red hair tended to flop down untidily over his pale green eyes. Moon had been waiting to give Earl his paycheck.

"Moon, honey, just give me my paycheck and let me go. I got things to do with that money. I want to see how it feels to spend some honest money," Earl Campbell joked. "I'm ahowlin' at the Flamingo tonight."

"Don't forget to duck," Fred advised.

Earl put on a hurt look, and then doubled up with laughter. "Hell, Fred, I know how to take care of myself. A young'un's entitled to some fun after workin' like an idgit all week. I'm a young wolf ready to howl at them lovely females."

As he handed Earl his paycheck, Moon growled, "You've worked hard. You've done a good job. There's a big bonus here, cousin. Just make sure to get back to work Monday. I took a chance on you. Don't blow it by goin' back to that pot pushin.'"

"Okay, okay. I'll do my work. You just let me be. I didn't swear to become a choir boy just because I took this job."

When the other cousins had left, Moon and Fred discussed their good fortune. Fred was jubilant. "Moon, I reckon we've done real good so far, and we done it right. That gives me a good feelin,' almost better'n the money."

Moon grinned, turning his eyes to the sky.

"Now, honey, get that smirk off your face. I don't mind the money at all."

"If we can keep sendin' coal to tipple, there'll be more. From rags to riches, Fred, that's us, praise the Lord."

"Sure is. I thank God every day. Make way for us millionaires."
"Say, do you reckon Earl is clear of Rod Mashburn's operation? I don't want any trouble with Rod, but I don't want Earl messin' around with Rod's business either. You know he was a messenger boy for Rod, and he hauled and sold a little—and smoked a little on the side."

"Earl tells me he's through with all that. I think he's tellin' the truth, at least as he sees it. He's a good worker, Moon. Hit's hard to find fellows who'll work as hard. He's a little bit crazy, but he don't mean no harm. Just be ready for the practical jokes. He'll probably hook Acie into some of them, too."

"Yeah. And he's family. Reckon we'll just have to take the chance and put up with the hot feet and the unhooked battery cables. I think it's a price we can afford. We'll soon see."

IN THE DITCH

George looked over the yawning abyss with a careful eye while Lunamin stood beside him and smugly watched the humming machines across the huge cavernous pit, satisfied that the huge amounts of earth his machinery had moved meant money in the bank. That seam of four-foot metallurgical coal under the Lee formation was guaranteed to make him a wealthy man with coal going for 80 dollars a ton and still rising. With few regrets for the forest he had displaced, he reveled in the piles of gray rock his D-12's were pushing aside. They had moved a great deal of material since that first week that Lunar Mining began digging coal.

Huge rounded boulders and jagged shafts of rock rested where a road had once run up to Isai h Timmons' home place. They rested in the roadway like a mixture of starved giants and obese and rotund interlopers throwing a picket line across the roadway. They possessed a kind of beauty. Boulders of gray sandstone (some showing a bright pink underb lly and others showing veins of rust-red) offered signs of the iron ore that had prompted eager men to try to create an industrial complex at Big Stone Gap during the first big Southwest Virginia coal boom in the 1890's. They were trying to create what they finally did produce at Birmingham, Alabama— George and Moon knew— the steel center of the South. It had turned out that the veins of iron in Southwest Virginia were too small for commercial purposes, and the first boom went bust. New times were at hand. Lunamin was determined to take advantage of them. He would succeed. This job was only the first step to riches.

"Listen to my dozers hum, George. You'd have a hard time findin' a richer sound out in these hills, honey."

In this term of address, George recognized the old mountain way of expressing good fellowship. The relish with which Moon expressed his satisfaction was not lost on Landsetter. He felt a little conflict of interest as he made his answer.

"Well, maybe they sound better to you than to me, Moon. You've blocked that road. Why don't you get one of your machines out there and fix that blocked road so old man Timmons can get out of his hollow?"

"Now George, you're talkin' money. I've got to move this coal fast. I have a contract to meet and I've got bank payments to make. Lordy, honey, I'll get old Timmons' road cleared out when I have time."

"You want me to fine you, Moon?"

"George, you know you can't do nothin' to me worth shucks. Bear with me, old buddy. Tell you what, I'll work on the road myself when a dozer's free."

George nodded agreement and climbed into his tan government pickup. Soon he was heading off up the road to the next strip job. It was hard to argue with Moon. He had been dirt poor all his life. Moving mountains of dirt to dig his way to riches seemed only fitting to him and many others in thes mountains. It was as if the heavens had opened up and showered gold upon a people who had been trapped and cheated and euchred and shoved aside by what the world outside liked to call progress.

It was as if the mountaineer's fierce God had suddenly turned benign and rained a deluge of gold upon those who would put forth the sweat to dig for it. The older folks couldn't approve seeing the valley pastures (poor and overgrazed though many of them were) lifted up to the hills and the hills, full of nut trees and squirrels, brought down into the valleys. Young men like Moon had fewer regrets. They were developing a new sense of self-sufficiency from this leveling of their native hills.

To them, the older frontier spirit of subsistence living didn't seem as satisfying as this newer way of the machine. They were in control now. It was with more than the cupidity of self-interest that they fought attempts to regulate their mining. They had become the apostles of progress bringing the modern world to their land, enabling themselves and their neighbors to hold their heads up among any people from the outside.

After all, George thought, compared to some of the strippers, Moon was a model citizen. He timbered before mining, and he didn't wait years with rusting machinery sitting on a job before he did reclamation work. No, if all strip miners were like Moon, he'd have an easier job.

A loud *Zang* interrupted George's thoughts.

Without giving much conscious thought to the matter, he put his head down low and headed his truck for the ditch. The next shot hit his right front tire. George felt he was lucky to be off the road before this. Lunging out the other side of the cab, he yelled up the mountain slope, "Timmons, what the hell are you shooting at me for?"

Across the pasture and up in the trees, an old, gravelly voice answered, "Jest remindin' you of your duty. I got to have me a road. Only ways I can get out now is goat like, clamberin' over them boulders Moon piled on my land. Remember, I hit what I aim at."

George looked up to the spot from which the voice had emanated. He saw a thin, stooped man in blue coveralls holding a rifle. He looked tired and forlorn, George thought.

"I just talked to Moon, Isaiah. He's going to fix your road soon as he has a dozer free. Now let me get this truck back up on the road and change my tire."

"All right, George. You stop by after my road's fixed and I'll give you some truck from my garden to make up for that tire. I don't want to be ornery, but I got my rights. These damn strippers want to tear up the whole world it seems. They don't own me. Moon don't have the right to block my road even if he is kin."

After George changed his tire and headed to the next strip job on his schedule, he had time to consider the deep divisions that surface mining was bringing to these mountains. Surface mining had produced a more complex social structure than had previously existed. When deep mining was the only industrial force in the society, things were simpler. You were management or you were a worker. There wasn't much in between except for those who held to the old ways of subsistence farming.

What merchant class there was in the old days aligned itself with the mine owners and their managers, who tended to look to the outside world for their ideas of what a society should be. If you wished to enter the industrial world and stand outside the old frontier barter culture of the mountains, you were either a union man or anti-union. People often felt obliged to choose sides.

How to answer the question of the mining ballad—"Which side are you on?"—was a pressing matter. You became either "a union man/ or a thug for J. H. Blair." There had b en no room in between. Now, surface mining was offering those w o had been oppressed in their own land an opportunity to enter the money economy without completely giving up their mountain heritage.

The older folk like Timmons and Archibald MacCloud didn't see the destruction of their fields and woods and water in the same light as the younger men who sought to bulldoze their way into the larger American society of the twentieth century. There was bound to be conflict between those holding to the old ways and those who saw themselves as the new breed of mountain men.

Fred MacCloud and Moon stood between the two groups, a foot in each camp. They wanted to be part of the new economy, but they didn't want to destroy all the old life to achieve his end. Fred exerted considerable influence on Moon, and for this reason as well as because Moon wanted to be able to face Archibald MacCloud without hanging his head in shame, the operations of Lunar Mining created far less destruction than those of men like Dave Blackmun and Dab Whacker.

Their only goal was amassing money as quickly as possible by whatever methods seemed quickest.

"Yes," George told himself, "if Moon were the worst I had to face, my job wouldn't be too hard."

WASHING IN THE BLOOD

In addition to being careful about his stewardship of the natural world, Fred MacCloud was a god-fearing man. He wasn't pushy about his religion. He just kept inviting Moon to come to Sunday service. Having used his best powers of persuasion on Lunamin without success, he had concluded that Moon could profit so much from a little divine guidance that he decided to resort to a little bribery. Fred resolved to appeal to Moon in a way that would be hard to resist. Fred promised him a really good home-cooked Sunday meal.

"Just attend a Sunday service, Partner. Jauncie will bake you an apple pie."

Finally, after weeks of Fred's pleas, Moon decided to attend services at the Holy Lamb Tabernacle. He thought maybe he'd hear something to ease his guilt about adopting a line of work that displeased Mamaw and Papaw. Fred had told him that Lamb o' God Flannary had good words to say about surface mining. Besides, Jauncie MacCloud baked good pies.

The service at the Holy Lamb Tabernacle began with the singing of a hymn. Fred lined it out for the congregation. Fred intoned the line, and the congregation sang it,

> Some have fathers gone to glory Won't you tell
> me if you know?

Fred lined on,

> Will our fathers know their children When to
> heaven they shall go?

After the first hymn, Fred continued with

> I am a poor wayfaring pilgrim
> A-traveling through this world below.

And

> Oh, my brother, take this warning:
>   Don't let old Satan hold your hand.

After these hymns, it was time for the preaching. Old Jeems Wright got up and gave a prayer for the preacher, the preaching, and the reception of it by the congregation.

Then Lamb o' God Flannary got up and marched to the pulpit. Tall and heavyset, the preacher walked to the pulpit with a determined gait. In the pulpit, he prayed silently for a minute and then spoke.

"I come to prepare you for the Lamb o' God! Sinners, hearken to the call. You've a choice to make. Will you be washed in the blood o' the Lamb or will you burn in Hell's fire? Do not call your brother fool because he gives his worldly goods to the Lord. Whoever calls the giving man a fool shall burn in the fires of Hell according to Matthew 5:22."

Already feeling a bit warm, Lunamin looked around him to see how the other people were handling this pronouncement. Then he turned to listen to the preaching again. Flannary was being caught up in the spirit.

"Brethren and sistren, there's those among us that live with no thought of what's to come. The fires of Hell burn with a powerful flame. Pain, indescribable, unending, everlasting, tormenting pain—that's what the sinners feel. Can't you see them writhing as the pain eats at their innards? The torments of those poor people in Vietnam are just a hint of what Hell's fires are like. Napalm for the wicked, that's what old Satan serves up. Aaah! Look at those flames, see the sinners writhing in pain, screaming, see their flesh coming off in layers as they burn. Look at them! They chose. They can't choose a second time.

They had the chance to choose. They chose these torments of Hell, not the Lamb o' God. They can't be washed in the blood."

Moon could see some of the ladies sitting in front of him squirming. The gray-haired Jones sisters seemed especially moved. Ella Jones put her head on her sister's shoulder and cried. Moon couldn't help wincing a little himself, because the mention of Nam and napalm brought back to him some scenes that had been as much of a hell as he could imagine.

"I can't believe that Satan can do much worse than that," he mused.

To clear his mind of those scenes he jerked his attention back to the sermon. Flannary was really getting warmed up now.

"Brethren and sistren, have you been washed in the blood of the Lamb? Have you been up that Hill of Cavalry? Aaaah now, there be sinfulness in this world. Hit'll grab you when you least suspect it. You've got to be strong and climb that hill. Don't stay on the wide valley track. Aaaah, if you climb that hill just once, then the dirt of this old world can't touch you …aaah brethren and sistren, we're all sinners like old Adam and Eve. Eve bit that apple for all her children. Now, there's folks around who says there's no Hell. Don't listen to false prophets. There are hell fires and they burn the wicked with a powerful, searing flame. I can see the sinners writhing in those white-hot flames. They're screaming for mercy."

There were groans from the congregation. These gave encouragement to Lamb o' God.

"We can't help it. We're bad. We're mean. Sinners, listen to me. We are bad and mean, but we have hope because of Jesus. If you'll just believe, friends, sweet Jesus will save you. Wash your dirty linen in the blood of the Lamb. That blood can clean any dirt. Brethren and sistren, that blood can clean any dirt! It's God's heavenly, holy soap, God's super suds. It's got all the super ingredients anybody can ever need. There's no dirt can stain the hard heart once that super holy soap gets used. Just up and say, 'Lord, I don't care to use those holy soap suds!' All you've got to do is say, 'Give me that soap and wash me clean, Lord!' Tell him, 'I don't care a bit, Lord, to wash my filthy soul.'"

Lunamin wasn't sure that he wanted to wash *all* the dirt off. He was just beginning to hit pay dirt in a big way and it looked just fine to him. He wanted to enjoy it for a while. He guessed he was one of the sinners. He found it difficult to continue to follow the preaching. His mind kept slipping back to those coal seams. They were rich. He'd had to cut a few corners (not many, Fred saw to that) to get the coal out, but then, as the preacher said, we're all sinners.

"What's the use of trying to fight it too hard," Moon thought. "Besides, sinners make more money." He almost laughed aloud and glanced around him to make sure he hadn't made any noise.

The faces around him seemed still intent on what Flannary was saying. Moon's attention returned to the sermon when he heard the preacher use the word *mining*. The man of God was working even harder now. He'd taken off his coat and he seemed to have grown taller. "Brethren and sistren, I feel the spirit moving me something powerful. The spirit is lifting me up on the wings of that great speckled bird. The spirit is atelling me that God ain't against strip mining, friends. He wants his children to be fed, and if it takes getting that coal out of the ground with monster machines, then the spirit moves us to use those big machines for all they're worth.

Moon could hardly believe his ears, but he liked what he thought he was hearing.

"Make'em hum, brothers, but look out for the poor and the needy when the black stuff turns to gold. Don't forget the hungry sparrows that flock around our valleys and our mountainsides. Don't forget folks that wait at the church door in the name of sweet Jesus, the risen Christ. Do unto others good things and the Lord will do good things for you."

Moon was glad that God was on his side after all, but he still wanted further confirmation. So, after the sermon, he made a point of spending some time with Lamb o' God Flannary as the preacher greeted and shook hands with departing members of the congregation.

"Let me get this straight, Preacher. You say that God don't object to strip minin' and strip miners?"

"That's right, Mr. Lunamin. The Lord never begrudged a man's honest labor."

"I'm glad to hear that, 'cause some of my family's dead set against my surface minin'. They say tearin' up the mountains is sinful."

"Moon, the Lord put that coal there for a purpose. Man's lot is to toil for his bread. So I guess toiling to take the coal out of the ground is the Lord's will as long as you do it honestly, put the land back right, and don't forget the needy."

The message was getting through clearly to Moon now. It was all right with God if he tore up the hills to get at that coal as long as he put the land back, but the Lord wanted his cut of the loot. When the collection plate came around the next Sunday, Moon put in a hundred- dollar bill for all to see.

"That ought to make the Lord happy," he thought, satisfied that he was establishing his credentials as a go -fearing Christian. He still worried that Papaw's God couldn't be bought off so easily. "Papaw wouldn't agree with Lamb o' Go . Strippers' big machines are the Devil's toys the way Papaw and Mamaw see them."

Moon felt certain that Archibald MacCloud's stern Calvinistic God expected a great deal more of strip miners than Lamb o' God Flannary's. Still, Flannary was considered an upright, sincere man of God. He believed in the power of the Holy Spirit, and he proclaimed his belief no matter who was listening.

"If Lamb o' God thinks surface mining is honest labor and not sinful, I reckon it's all right." This conclusion did a great deal to soothe Moon's conscience and quiet the echo of Papaw's condemnation of strip miners, but a nagging doubt remained.

TRASH

The meeting was held in the offices of the local power company. A group of people calling themselves Concerned Citizens for Sane Energy (CONCISE) had invited some speakers to talk about ways to clean up the area roadways. One speaker had come all the way from Germany to talk about German methods of recycling. Despite the worthwhile aims of the group, somehow rumors had spread around the county that plans were afoot to develop legislation to abolish strip- mining forever. These rumors had reached some of the more belligerent members of the surface mining association. ODSUM members had been discussing these rumors well before their monthly meeting.

ODSUM's monthly gathering met the same evening a block away from where CONCISE presented its program. The miners' gathering hummed with discussions of how best to deal with this threat to the American free enterprise system. They had heard the rumors that the CONCISE people were communists organizing against surface mining. Some ODSUM members counseled violence. Chief among these, Dab Whacker and Dave Blackmun snarled at those who shied away from hasty action.

Both Whacker and Blackmun had physical strength. Blackmun was a tall, broad-shouldered mountaineer who had played an outstanding defensive tackle for his high school football team. His dark hair and face presented a contrast to Whacker, his ardent supporter. A little younger, Whacker was shorter, fair-haired, and quite muscular. He generally spit a stream of the tobacco he chewed before offering his opinions. Both pushed their workers hard and both gambled so recklessly with the money they made that their antics created talk all through the area.

Moon was the most outspoken among those who opposed doing anything unlawful or violent, so the two vented their spleen on him.

"You're mealy-mouthed. All you want to do is talk," Dave groused at Moon and others that opposed them. As the meeting went on, the talk became louder and more heated. Dave called Moon a chicken- livered coward.

Dab seconded his buddy, "Nobody has the right to tell us how to run our minin.' We need to do something about that bunch of Commies opposing us."

B. G. Hooper, Moon, and others—skeptical that there was any imminent threat—cautioned no action at all until they knew what actually was happening.

"We could hurt our cause by precipitous action," Hooper advised. Educated in Pennsylvania, Hooper dressed nattily and had impressed ODSUM'S search committee with his articulate and sophisticated defense of surface mining when they had interviewed him for the position of Executive Director of their or anization. He commanded attention when he counseled caution. "There's no doubt we have to worry about people who seek to harm our liveli- hood, but we don't know that this meeting has anything to do with those efforts," Hooper concluded.

Hooper's words had a calming effect. Even Blackmun and Whacker became less belligerent, Moon observed.

"Let's send a force to reconnoiter. If it's no good they're plannin,' then we can decide how to handle them," Blalock Mullins suggested.

"Let's send Lunamin and Dave Blackmun to find out what these folks are up to," Dab Whacker chimed. Whacker's proposal was much more reasonable than anything he had heretofore said. Perhaps a sense of relief caused the group to receive his plan with enthusiastic applause. The surface miners left their meeting confident that Moon and Dave would find out the truth of the matter, although the chosen two didn't relish their mission and were less sure of success.

The leaves on the Norway Maples that spread over the court-house lawn had turned bright yellow in the October sun, and Moon couldn't help noticing their beauty as he and Dave passed the Courthouse and walked across the street to the suspect meeting. Moon also spied George Landsetter and another man entering the power company's building.

Lunamin was not the only person enjoying the autumn color. George and Harry Painter, the organizer of this clean-up meeting, had noticed the beauty of the maples and the late October sky. Before going inside, they looked around them and breathed deeply the brisk air of Indian summer. They didn't really want to go inside and hear about trash, but they were bound to do their civic duty. The county needed to clean up, no doubt about that.

Inside, they found seats at the back of the room and sat down to hear trash talk. Looking around, George saw that there was a good cross-section of the community. The audience included Susan Stanard's parents. He wondered how they felt ab ut their daughter's dating a surface miner. At any rate, he was glad that they were here to support cleaning up the county.

The speaker was giving a slide presentation showing what German cities had for many years b en doing about waste disposal. In modern incineration plants, trash disappeared, burned, and came out as recycled metals or recycled organic material that was spread on the city parks and, for a reasonable price, lawns and gardens, bringing life out of refuse and generating heat to run the city at the same time.

As the audience marveled at the efficiency of German trash man-agement, voices drifted in from the hall. They grew louder. George moved to the door hurriedly because he thought he recognized Dave Blackmun's and Moon's voices.

"By God," Dave Blackmun was loudly asserting as George approached, "I'll turn this county into a desert if that's what it takes to get the coal out. Black rock is gold, buddy, and I'm gonna get my share of that golden hoard before any of you environmental bastards has a chance to stop me."

With a nodding head, Moon seconded everything that Blackmun was saying to the stranger they had cornered against a soft drink machine. Every now and then he interjected a "Give 'em hell, Dave."

By the time George reached them, the cornered man was looking a bit scared. "What are you doing here, Moon? Isn't trash disposal a little out of your line?" George asked.

"What do you mean, trash disposal?"

"Come on in and see. We're looking at how Germans handle trash disposal in their cities. That's what we're doing, talking trash while the sun shines. We want to clean up all the trash lining the roads around here."

"Nah, now, we heard there were fellows goin' around tryin' to write and pass a law to outlaw all surface minin.' Honest, George, isn't this meeting in opposition to strip mining?"

George laughed. "Sorry to disappoint you and Dave, but ODSUM isn't as high on the civic agenda as trash. Got to take care of trashy folks first, Moon. Then we'll go after the forces of destruction and environmental evil."

A voice from behind George supported him. "That's right, Moon. We're trying to clean up the environment. We want to get the litter off the highways. This meeting has nothing to do with mining of any kind."

George laughed again as Moon looked over his shoulder and saw Tom Stanard. Moon grinned sheepishly, mumbled an apology, and turned to leave with Dave following meekly behind.

Still laughing, George called after them, "You don't have to leave, you know, we need all the help we can find to get rid of the trash."

Though all had ended without incident, Moon was embarrassed by this episode, and it made him a bit more cautious in accepting the attitudes of the other members of ODSUM. He resolved not to jump to conclusions or hot-blooded action in the future on the say-so of the likes of Dave Blackmun and Dab Whacker.

Relieved at the peaceful ending of their expedition, Lunamin could not help worrying a little about the impression he must have made on Tom Stanard. He hoped that he had not ruined his chances of convincing Susan's father that he was a worthy match for Susan.

STRIP MINE SYMPOSIUM

The fears of ODSUM possessed some foundation in reality. A group was working to pass effective legislation governing the reclamation of surface mines. LEAPS (Let Our Environment Alone, Please, Strip Miners!) members were calling attention statewide to the abuses to the land occurring in Southwest Virginia in the name of jobs and getting coal to market.

ODSUM members expressed outrage at the notion that any group of *do-gooders* would stand in the way of their machines. Bumper stickers appeared on numerous vehicles proclaiming 'We Dig Coal.'

B. G. Hooper wrote letters to the editors of the local papers accusing Heidi Leaves and her followers of un-American activities. He convinced a majority of the ODSUM members that LEAPS was simply a hotbed of radicals, part of a Communist conspiracy against American free enterprise. When they heard about the symposium on surface mining that LEAPS planned to sponsor at the local community college, the more hotheaded members of ODSUM desired some action. The group as a whole, Moon included, did not wish any violent confrontation, and B. G. Hooper counseled against it in spite of his misgivings.

"That's just the sort of thing they want. They can milk that sort of thing for lots of press coverage. Don't think you can win that way. Besides, some of us have been asked to participate. We need to go and present our case, whether or not we get a fair hearing. In addition to the Southern Mining Council, Heidi Leaves has enlisted the Southern Council of Christian Churches. We can't fight God with violence."

Moon remembered the episode with the people who wanted to clean up the county's trashy roads. He and a majority of the members agreed with B. G., but Dave Blackmun, Dab Whacker, and a few other members disagreed with this moderate position. Outvoted at the meeting, they decided among themselves that Hooper's way would do for public consumption, but they needed more strenuous action to throw the fear of god into the socialist, commie sympathizers that LEAPS was bringing in to tell them how to run their mines.

Despite his views, Hooper agreed to appear on the program of the symposium. "If we don't go and give our side of the story, nobody will hear it. We have to participate," he told association members. Moon and others offered to help Hooper present the case for surface mining. A diverse group of people convened in the college auditorium.

The symposium had many speakers offering different perspectives on the effects of surface mining and the need for effective legislation to govern it. Hooper and several members of ODSUM gave presentations emphasizing the economic benefits that the group's operations were bringing to the area.

"This region has been depressed for many years," Hooper told the gathering. "Pictures of poverty-stricken Appalachians have graced the pages of many national magazines and widely-distributed books. The region does have great mineral wealth, but this has not always benefited the people who live here. Surface mining has enabled many local people to better themselves and their neighbors through the good old American way: free enterprise."

Many of the other speakers agreed with Hooper that surface mining had brought benefits to the region, but they were less sanguine than Hooper and other ODSUM representatives about the other effects of the practice.

Local lawyer and author Harry Caudill spoke next. Tall and thin, Caudill's few wisps of hair were graying. He adjusted his glasses and read from his book *Night Comes to the Cumberlands* sections that detailed the devastation that had been wrought in neighboring Kentucky counties where surface mining had proceeded unchecked under what was known as the broad-form deed. It allowed owners of the mineral rights to do whatever might be needed to the surface of the land in order to recover the minerals.

Then he added a few comments that suggested the passion with which he viewed the subject. "Why, they take people's houses and push them over the hill. It's no wonder that some of our folks have confronted strip miners' bulldozers with rifles. You people here in Virginia don't have to deal with anything as bad as we have in Kentucky. Parts of Eastern Kentucky look like a lunar landscape. Things are better here, but I'll bet you have some lunar settings here in Southwest Virginia, too."

Moon felt obliged to speak in defense of his operations. "I'd be happy to show you a minin' operation that's done with regard for the environment, Mr. Caudill."

A woman's voice answered him. "Perhaps you could give us all a tour some day soon, Mr. Lunamin." As she sp ke, a small, red-haired young woman approached Caudill to take her turn at the podium. Dressed in a blouse with a tee short over it and a khaki skirt, Heidi Leaves gave little indication of her energetic ways other than the motto on her tee-shirt: We Dig Deeper than Coal.

Heidi spoke for the majority of participants when she attacked the callous mining practices that were raising up high walls fifty or more feet high a few feet from neighbors' houses, breaking their walls apart with blasting, and causing their water supply to disappear.

"Have you been without water? Ask the people who line up at that spring in Norton how hard it is to haul all their drinking water thirty miles. It's mighty nice of old man Jessup to let them get water there, but many of them have to drive weary miles to get that water. We don't want to stop surface miners from earning a decent livelihood. We just want them to do it in a more responsible way."

During the question-and-answer period, B. G. Hooper responded. "ODSUM members are responsible members of the community. They provide jobs, give money to local churches and charities, and they have established locally owned businesses. Just look at the locally owned banks in this region. As for high walls, I think we could argue that they have aesthetic value. Look at all the people from all over the world who travel to see the stark landscapes of the Grand Canyon, Zion National Park, and the Badlands of Wyoming. I think strip mining could encourage the local tourist industry."

That comment provoked considerable laughter. Even Moon found it comical.

Listening to B. G. Hooper's concluding remarks, Moon looked over at George. His cousin could hardly keep a straight face. He was smiling as he rose to make his presentation.

He tried to use his best English. "After reviewing the current state of the Virginia laws, I've come to some conclusions about what would be appropriate changes in the law. I'm not in favor of putting that land back to the approximate original contour in all cases. I can even see some benefits coming from high walls, although I don't myself find them as aesthetically pleasing as Mr. Hooper does."

The loud laughter caused him to pause.

"The best thing that can be said about high walls is that they provide nesting sites for rough-winged swallows in the cavities in the sides of the high walls and phoebes in the tree roots overhanging their edges. But a lot of deer chased by dogs fall over these high bluffs and break their necks. I'm a deer hunter. I don't like to see deer die in such a senseless way.

"As I see the problem, it is considerably more complex than Mr. Hooper or Ms. Leaves have suggested. The main problem is the erosion that comes from land that has been surface-mined but not reclaimed. It fouls the streams as badly as any run-off from deep mines. And surface mining often uncovers soil that, if left untreated, will not grow anything for twenty or thirty years. All that time the erosion continues. That's the main reason we need better reclamation laws."

Moon could see that George had the attention of his audience now. He found that he didn't disagree with what his cousin said, especially about high walls killing deer. After all, he was a hunter too. "Better reclamation is economically feasible," George continued. "Reclamation work at Fishpond Lake near Jenkins, Kentucky, was done without legal compulsion simply because the mine owner thought that he had a duty to leave the land in no worse shape than he found it. Proper reclamation doesn't present problems for operators who prepare for it before and while they are taking out the coal. There is no need for huge high walls or fouled streams. In my opinion, they don't add beauty to the landscape."

The audience laughed and clapped. They were not inclined to subscribe to Hooper's notion that strip miners added to the natural beauty of the region by their mining. Even Moon found that difficult to accept. The majority thought that legislation on the national level would be necessary to control surface mining practices.

Undaunted, Hooper spoke yet again, in rebuttal. "We should be careful not to create more inefficient government bureaucracies. Mr. Landsetter has admitted that excellent reclamation has taken place without laws requiring it: actions done freely by free men. We should avoid aiding and abetting creeping socialism. American free enterprise is the cornerstone of our system. America needs capitalism, not socialism. These miners simply want their part of the American dream."

Hooper convinced some of his audience of the good intentions of the members of ODSUM. Their conversion was short-lived, however. Even those who accepted Hooper's version of surface mining were outraged when they left the meeting and walked to their vehicles. They found that their tires had been slashed, and some were emblazoned in white paint with the words *Commie.* Since the tires of Hooper and other surface mining advocates had been spared, the victims drew a logical conclusion: proponents of surface mining, probably members of ODSUM, had attacked them.

"These guys play rough, Heidi," one of the out-of-town guests observed.

in check."

"Is this the sort of thing you put up with all the time?"

"Usually it's not this bad. Phone calls at two and three o'clock in the morning with nothing to be heard but heavy breathing. That's the usual *modus operandi.* Ask George. He gets calls, too."

George was just walking up to them and overheard. "Not as many as you, Heidi. I'll admit that heavy breathing at two o'clock in the morning can ruin a night's sleep."

Walking to their untouched vehicles, Moon and B. G. Hooper cursed the knife-wielders. At the symposium, they had tried their best to present ODSUM's members as caring, law-abiding pillars of the community. This violence negated everything they had tried to accomplish. Moon had heard talk. He had a fairly good idea of who was responsible.

"This mess is the work of Dave Blackmun and Dab Whacker.

They're 'bout as smart as a retarded 'possum," this is their work.

"Well, if they keep up with this violence, they'll practically guarantee that there'll be some kind of reclamation law passed on the state level, and probably on the national level, too. The media are always looking for something sensational to print, and the public outcry for legislation follows," B. G. said.

"B. G., maybe there ought to be laws to rein in the likes of Dave and Dab. Those people made some good points. I don't think Lunar Minin' will have any trouble with the laws. We already do most of what's bein' prop sed. Fact is, a few laws might level the playin' field for those of us tryin' to do things right," Moon said.

"I'd be careful about expressing those ideas at an ODSUM meeting, Moon."

"Those two jackasses will ruin things for all of us if they're not reined in. Besides, Papaw always taught me to respect the land. I've got to do something."

HEIDI LEAVES

George waited with Heidi Leaves until all of the people with slashed tires had had their cars towed and Heidi had arranged a place for them to stay while their automobiles were fitted with new tires. George marveled at the speed and efficiency with which Heidi worked.

"A whirlwind in a petite, pretty package," George thought, admiring her.

When the last beleaguered guest had b en cared for, the two of them sat down on the bumper of George's truck and congratulated themselves on the success of the symposium.

"Any doubts about the success of the symposium disappeared when people saw those slashed tires, George."

"I'm surprised they left my vehicle alone—reckon they didn't want to rile me too much, Heidi. What about yours? I don't see it anywhere."

"I bummed a ride here. So they didn't have a chance."

"You should take up fortune telling. You sure it wasn't somebody on your payroll?" George laughed and Heidi joined in.

"No. But I might have paid somebody to do it if I'd thought of it. "I don't think it was my cousin Moon's handiwork. His grandfather and grandmother wouldn't approve of anything like this, and he wouldn't want to shame them. I don't think he would be a party to this."

"I hope you're right. He seems to be level-headed." "He's trying to do things right."

"I wish all of ODSUM's members did." "Do you need a lift home?"

"Sure do. You offering?" "Yep. Hop in."

On the way to Heidi's, George told her about some of the attempts that had been made to intimidate him or buy him off. "A fellow could get rich in this job if he had a mind to."

"How close are you to your first million?"

"Not very. I reckon I have a few too many scruples to become rich fast."

"Well, I think you're a great guy even if you're just a poorly paid public servant."

"Thanks, I'm doing necessary if under-appreciated work."

When they reached Heidi's, she turned to George and smiled up at him. He couldn't help thinking how attractive she looked.

"Come on in George. I'll fix us some dinner." "Are you sure it's no trouble?"

"I'd appreciate the company. You can he p."

In her small kitchen, Heidi put Geor e to work with salad fixings while she threw some spaghetti no dles in a pot of boiling water and heated up some sauce from a jar. Then she took an apple pie from her freezer and heated an oven.

After the table was s t, Heidi poured each of them a glass of red wine. Once the two were seated at the table, she proposed a toast. Lifting her glass, she waited for George to lift his. "Let's drink to the success of the symposium and its support by slashers unknown."

"And to the efforts of LEAPS," George added.

When the apple pie was eaten and the dishes neatly arranged in the dishwasher, Heidi poured each of them another glass of wine and ushered George to her great room and the sofa there. He sat where he was directed and Heidi sat down close beside him.

"That was a great meal for such short notice, Heidi. And this wine certainly hits the spot."

"Thanks. It's good to have someone to share it and the day's success with. Are you comfortable?"

"Sure, how about you?"

"Well, I'd be more comfortable if I could snuggle a little closer." That said, Heidi moved closer to George and put one hand on his thigh. "Now, that's better, don't you think?"

George was a bit taken aback by Heidi's brashness, but he was also very much aware of her touch an d a faint odor of roses that emanated from her. He was hardly aware of putting his arm around her.

"I'm not sure what to think. You certainly have pretty hazel eyes," he observed. "They set off your hair."

"Why don't you imagine me as a reclamation job. The first thing to do would be to have me stripped."

"But I'm not a strip miner."

"I could strip for you. Then you could go to work reclaiming."

Raising herself, Heidi pressed her lips against George's and kissed him with great energy while running her fingers through his hair and down his neck.

"Now, didn't you enjoy that?"

George had to admit that he had enjoyed it. In response, after a slight hesitation, he repaid her kiss with another and ran his fingers through her hair.

Heidi had unbuttoned her blouse and unhooked her bra. She took George's hand and placed it under her bra. Feeling the warmth of her breast against his palm, he began to wonder if they were moving faster than was wise.

"Heidi, I think we ought to slow down." "Why? Don't you find me attractive?"

"Very. That's the point. I'm not sure how well I can resist that attraction."

"Why resist?"

"Maybe we're moving too fast."

"You're a good-looking fellow,. I admire your character, too. I can tell you want me. That's quite obvious."

"Okay. I think you're beautiful. I long for your touch. I'd like to go to bed with your right now."

"Well, why don't you let me decide just how far we take this? How do you know I want to bed you tonight?"

"I'm confused."

"Poor George, why don't you just kiss me again?"

Later, as George drove back to his townhouse, he wondered if he could have handled the situation better. Heidi certainly was a desirable woman, and she definitely seemed to desire him. He believed that his cousin Moon, had he been confronted with the same situation, would have proceeded differently. George shook his head as if in an effort to clear his mind and sighed.

He didn't sleep well that night. His insomnia stemmed only in small part from his worry that Moon had been involved in the tire-slashing incident. He was also wondering whether he should pursue a relationship with Heidi.

THE CODE

Despite B. G. Hooper's warning, Moon decided not to remain silent at the next meeting of ODSUM. The coal symposium had started Moon thinking about the ethics as well as the economics of surface mining operations. Fred's tutelage had convinced Lunamin that the two were not antagonistic to each other. The more he thought about mining practices, the more he saw that men like Blackmun were not only giving surface miners a bad name, they were poor businessmen. Their methods were not just obnoxious to the people they hurt. These practices were also economically inefficient and often counter-productive.

"Fred's right. It's just as cheap to do minin' right if you plan ahead," Moon had told George the next time they talked after the symposium.

"I'm glad to hear you say so, Moon," George had congratulated him. "You're already doing most of what you should. Planning ahead actually allows you to mine more economically while lessening your impact on the environment."

Moon's bottom line provided plenty of evidence to support their conclusions. After all, he cleared a greater percentage of profits than Dave Blackmun and Dab Whacker. Lunamin wasn't prepared to accept all the criticisms leveled at their industry at the symposium, but he could see that ethical mining practices had not hurt Lunar Mining's bottom line.

They made money timbering before mining, and they found more people willing to agree to their mining because they had heard that Lunar Mining looked out for the interests of the landowner.

Besides, people who were treated well were less likely to damage mining equipment. Lunar Mining had to deal with far less damage from vandalism than Dave Blackmun and his ilk. Those uncaring miners often lost mining time dealing with such things as sugar in the gas tanks of their bulldozers and front-end loaders or other kinds of vandalism.

Though not ordinarily a very reflective person, Moon turned these ideas over in his mind and discussed them with Fred.

"Dave Blackmun and his crew undid all the goodwill B. G. and I created at that symposium. Those folks decided all the bad things they'd heard were true when they saw their slashed tires."

"Moon, honey, besides being wrong, it don't help none to hurt the folks you want to like you. Dave Blackmun's not right smart. He'd be better off practicin' the golden rule than actin' like a two-year old idgit."

"I've been thinkin' 'bout it since the symposium. We make more money doin' things the right way than Dave and his kind do cuttin' corners."

"Moon that's music to this old coot's ears. You are finally seein' the light. Dave Blackmun and Dab Whacker are mean. They're also poor businessmen. They'd do better treatin' people in a Christian manner. Those two don't have sense enough to bell a buzzard."

Moon determined then that it was his place to speak out at the next surface miners' meeting. When new business was called, he rose and said that he had an idea to propose.

"We need to do something to counteract the bad publicity we received as a result of the tire-slashin' at the surface mine symposium. I've been doin' some serious thinkin' and talkin' to people in our business. We need to have our own code, call it a code of conduct, a set of rules settin' out the right way for us surface miners to act. No need to wait for the legislature to pass laws that may be unnecessary and bad for us. We'll beat 'em to the punch. Set up our own rules."

Dave Blackman, Dab Whacker, and a few others glowered at the mention of tire slashing.

"You been talkin' to that red-headed Commie bitch Heidi Leaves, Moon? She the one who told you to dump this on us?"

"I haven't seen Heidi since the symposium, Dave. I bet she'd call my proposal a cynical, self-servin' attempt to avoid harsh laws."

"I call it a chicken shit way to give in to our enemies!" Dab Whacker yelled.

"Let's keep this meeting civil," B. G. Hooper interposed. "I think we ought to hear Moon out. So far what he's proposing sounds sensible to me."

"Fred MacCloud has always told me," Lunamin continued when quiet returned, "'Moon, it don't cost no more to do it right than wrong.' I've decided he's right. As a matter of fact, it may cost less. It came to me during that symposium. Some of thezz things people were askin' for seemed silly—like puttin' the land back to its original contour. We need some flat land in these mountains. But a lot of what they said was right. If they passed their laws today, Lunar Minin' wouldn't notice the difference in our bottom line. We already do most of what they want and we sure ain't losin' money. If ODSUM adopted a code of conduct, it wouldn't hurt our bottom lines. It might even make them look better."

Moon had caught the interest of the majority of those at the meeting, but Dave and Dab and a few others remained unconvinced. "I don't want nobody (and that includes you, Lunamin) tellin' me how to run Red Dog Minin.' I'm an American and proud of it. I want my rights. I want the liberty my ancestors fought for and won."

"Damn right, Dave," Dab Whacker added, "we ain't shrinkin' violets like Moon. We don't give a f… what people think about the way we get our coal out."

cvvgghhhgh"No, you don't, Dab. You're such a jackass you'll just keep blowin' everybody's houses apart until they pass laws to stop you. I don't want to take away your rights as an American, Dave. I have just spent a part of my life in Vietnam defendin' those rights. But I want to do my part to keep America beautiful."

"Who you callin' a jackass, good buddy?"

"You, Dab, and Dave and anybody else who throws in with their way of thinkin'.'"

Dab had been making his way to the podium where Moon was standing. When he reached the podium, he hurled a huge fist at Moon, who ducked and hit Dab squarely in his mid-section. Whacker doubled up in pain, gasping for breath. "I'll get you, you Melungeon bastard," Dab growled when he caught his breath and started toward Lunamin again.

Moon gave Whacker another jab. "I don't want to fight you, Dab. But I ain't goin' to be your punchin' bag no matter how filthy your tongue gets," Moon said as he backed off out of Whacker's reach.

Seeing that things might easily get out of hand, B. G. Hooper rushed to the podium and rapped his gavel for attention. "Let's have a committee to discuss Moon's proposal. I'm appointing Dave, Moon, Blalock Mullins, Dave Wrangle, and Hugh Beverley. Meeting adjourned."

When Moon told him about his proposal and its reception, George laughed.

"Did you expect a shout of acclamation?"

"I expected a negative reaction from Dave Blackmun, Dab Whacker, and some others, the ones who slashed the tires." Moon was genuinely surprised that he and Whacker had come to blows.

"Did you think they would embrace reason with a bear hug instead of offering a fist?"

"No, but I didn't think they'd try to start a fight there at the meetin.' I believe most of the members of ODSUM went along with what I said. They're most of them good men. I think we'll get a code of conduct.

"I hope you're right. If you do, will all the ODSUM members abide by the rules?"

"Most will. Some won't. You know Dave and Dab will keep blastin' away no matter what. Anyway, it's an effort to do the right things."

"I agree that it was a start. You have a long way to go to convince Blackmun and Whacker and their bunch. I'm glad to have you for a cousin and not Dave Blackmun or Dab Whacker. I'd be hard pressed to admit kinship to those two in spite of mountain traditions of sticking by one's kin."

Moon had no intention of accepting defeat at the hands of Blackmun and Whacker.

"You'll see cousin, I'll get that code yet."

DENVER

During the following weeks, the coal business boomed, and Lunar Mining rode the upward economic forces. Acie and Earl began to press Moon to take some time off and go with them to Los Vegas. He could leave Fred in charge. They'd talked to other miners who had gone out there for a good time gambling and womanizing.

Lunamin was tempted to do some celebrating because he had managed to persuade the surface miners' association committee appointed by B. G. Hooper to agree to draw up a code of conduct to present to the membership. Lunamin was skeptical about going with Acie and Earl, because he knew of their hard drinking, gambling, womanizing, and love of playing practical jokes. He just didn't trust the two of them, especially since Earl loved to play practical jokes and Acie usually went along with them. Besides, he was sure to be their victim, especially if he drank enough to lose some of his self-control.

But they kept telling him of the fun they could have, and he began to weaken despite his misgivings. He didn't want anything to spoil his plans.

"I'm goin' to marry Susan Stanard. I don't want any stories about wild escapades gettin' back to her before I convince her to marry me. I haven't convinced her or her parents yet."

"You should have some fun, Moon. If you're plannin' to get hitched, that's all the more reason to go and have some fun before you give up your freedom," Earl argued.

Then Lunamin had a thought. George was cautious to a fault and levelheaded enough for two men, He would go with Earl and

Acie, but he'd take George along to make certain nothing really bad happened. But George was not easily persuaded, especially when he found out who else was going along. He too was aware of the penchant these cousins had for practical joking. George had a sense of humor, Lunamin believed, but Landsetter claimed that he had outgrown the sort of low-brow, pie-in-the-face jokes Earl and Acie liked to play.

"I worry," he told Moon, "I'm a mine inspector. People might think there was a conflict of interest. If I'm caught partying with some of the surface miners I'm supposed to inspect, it will cause trouble. They won't see me as a disciple of Aldo Leopold anymore."

"Who's this Leopold fellow?"

"Just a man that told us how we should treat the environment."

Still, George and Moon went back a long way. Lunamin kept pleading. "You know I haven't had much time to have any fun since comin' back from Nam. And you don't seem to be makin' much of a splash in your spare time."

George finally agreed, reluctantly, to go along. He told Moon he was going to make sure that the group didn't get into any real trouble. "I reckon I have to go along to look out for you. You're too impulsive a fellow, especially when you've been drinking."

The flight from the coalfields to Los Vegas passed slowly. Moon and Earl and Acie enjoyed the drinks in first class and played poker, oblivious of the other passengers and the rough weather over Kansas. George slept between cocktails. While he sipped drinks, he and Moon discussed their differences.

"George, I just want to get my share."

"I don't blame you for that, Moon, and you generally do your jobs the right way. But there's strippers like Dave Blackmun who don't give a damn how much damage they do just as long as it gives them a few more dollars, and the truth be known, it wouldn't cost that much more to do it right. You're proof of that. You've done better than Blackmun. "Sure have," Moon chuckled. "Don't tell, George, but Dave's not right smart. He just doesn't want to be bothered with tryin' to do it right."

"Then why do you throw in with him?"

"Got to, I reckon. Got to stick together against all of you do-gooders—you and all those environmentalists like Heidi Leaves. You'll do us in if we don't fight."

"Folks who run with dirty dogs get fleas."

"Yeah, but they live a sight longer. I'm still workin' on that code, and I've made some progress. The committee Hooper appointed agreed to draw up a sample code to present to the membership."

"That's positive. I know you're trying to do the right thing, but you better think about what I'm saying, cousin. Men like Blackmun will get you into trouble. They won't stop at talk and they don't care where they drive their dozers."

During the layover in Denver, they ambled to the bar in a lounge and continued preparing themselves for the excitement to come. Earl and Acie sat at a table while George and Moon took seats in front of the bar. Soon Acie and Earl were laughing. It was obvious to George that they were planning some skullduggery when they invited a pretty girl in a gray business suit over at their table for a drink. George slipped off his bar stool and took up a chair at Acie and Earl's table.

"Honey, we need your help to settle a bet," Acie told the rather voluptuous young redhead with pouty lips who went by the name of Shirley.

"Why do you need me?"

"Well, you see, we've got a bet on about whether or not you can get our cousin Moon over there (he's that tall, dark-haired, good-lookin' fellow at the bar) to buy you a couple of drinks. I say you can; Earl here says you can't. We'll pay you thirty dollars to help us."

"Is that all I have to do?"

"Sure is. Two drinks settle our bet in my favor and you'll have earned thirty dollars. If you can't get more than one drink, or none at all, Earl wins, but you still will have earned thirty dollars."

"Seems like an easy way to earn some money, and maybe some drinks. I'll do it."

The three of them watched and listened as the girl walked over to the bar and attempted to appropriate the stool that George had vacated. As she did so, however, she seemed to slip and fall over upon Moon.

"Oh, excuse me, I'm sorry I'm so clumsy."

Moon exuded chivalry. "It was probably my fault. I was taking up a lot of space. Are you okay?"

"Yes, I think so."

"My name's Everett Lunamin. My friends call me Moon. Let me buy you a drink."

"Well, thanks. My name is Shirley. I'll have a gin and tonic."

As Moon and Shirley sipped their drinks, they struck up a lively conversation. George, Acie, and Earl watched with great interest and attempted to make out what was being said."

"Earl, old buddy, I'm halfway to winnin' that bet." "Don't crow too soon, old rooster."

The three voyeurs did not have long to wait before Moon and Shirley began indulging in a second round of drinks.

"All right, now, Earl, hand over that fifty dollars you just lost."

Earl did not hide his chagrin as he reluctantly handed Acie the fifty-dollar bill. "You win, but remember, you have to pay Shirley her thirty dollars."

Acie did so with a grin w en Shirley came over to collect her money. He tried to get her to stay, but she declined, saying she had to catch her plane to Little Rock. "I'd love to go back there and spend some time with Moon. It was fun. I feel a little guilty taking your money."

George wasn't surprised when Earl began to challenge all comers to deny the beauty of his amazing tattoo of the girl riding a fish, but Moon's belligerence toward the fellow sitting next to him at the bar did surprise George. He guessed that Moon felt a little unhappy about losing Shirley's companionship.

Moon had liked the looks of his neighbor on the next stool and had struck up a conversation. He was surprised to find that under the cowboy's tanned face and worn jeans there beat a heart tuned to the land ethic of Aldo Leopold.

"Is there good money in ranchin'?" Moon asked.

"That depends on the quality of the range, on the weather, and on the price of beef and how much damage you're willing to do to your range," the rancher answered.

"Push the beef and damn the range, I say." Moon was smiling, but the joke didn't go over well.

"The trouble with some folks is that they don't like trees and grass and birds. The good Lord put them all here for a purpose, and we're supposed to take care of them. We all need clean air and water. And we all need to hear the birds sing."

"Good buddy, you talk like one of them environmentalists causin' us coal miners all the trouble back home."

"Yeah, I guess I do like grass and trees and animals." "Hell, can you eat grass?"

"No, but my cows really like it. They sure as hell can't eat coal."

Moon had had some more drinks by now. Added to what he had had on the plane, these made him more belligerent. He had listened patiently to George's complaints on the plane and had held his temper. But he didn't feel a need to humor this cowboy.

"Good buddy, you hand out a lot of shit, cow shit!"

"You're coal shit! I've seen pictures of those god-awful holes you guys make. You're trying to turn forests into deserts."

"Go to hell, you son of a bitch!" Moon grunted as he swung at the cowboy, who ducked.

As the bar erupted, George sought cover. From his safe position, he watched Moon flatten the cowboy. But the cowboy had friends, and Moon was soon alongside him on the floor. Earl rushed to help Moon. He added a couple of men to the growing pile of bodies on the floor. Then a couple of the cowboy's friends punched Earl at the same time, and Acie rushed in to even the odds. Bodies were piling on the floor next to George, who was finding his hiding place becoming crowded, so finally he stood up. There was only one more cowhand standing. Seeing no alternative, George did his part and tackled the lone adversary, knocking him down on the pile and falling on top of him.

"Friend," he said to the man under him, "let's call this a draw." George was happy to hear muttered agreement. "Let's get these jackasses out of here," he added.

George felt lucky to pay the bartender for the damages and get Acie, Earl, and Moon on the plane for Las Vegas without further trouble. An uneasy feeling about what might happen in sin city had crept over George. If the main bout was to be anything like the pre-liminary, they might be heading for trouble.

"Moon, promise me no more fights this trip."

"Now, George, that didn't amount to much. I'll pay you back for the bar bill."

"Thanks. But you know I shouldn't be going to Vegas with you. It's what's called conflict of interest. I don't want it to end up in the newspapers. I can see it now. Our pictures spread over the front page of the *Coalfield Endeavor* and the caption reading "Mine Inspector Carouses in Vegas with Strip Miner.""

"Cousin, you worry too much."

Moon put back his s at and went to sleep, leaving George awake to worry. The rest of the flight was uneventful, and George occupied himself reading a copy of Rachel Carson's *The Sea Around Us.* It did not completely turn his mind from his worries about what might happen in Vegas.

VEGAS

The lights of Vegas were bright enough to dazzle the eyes of good old boys from the Southwest Virginia coalfields. Moon had booked them into a suite at the Sands. When they walked through the door, they stood for a moment, dazzled. For a few minutes, they walked around to take in the rooms.

Looking out the window, George had to admit that Moon was going first class. "This is quite a view. Look at those bright lights."

"By gonnies, Moon, this young wolf is achin' to howl again."

George's fears weren't eased any by Earl's announcement, unoriginal as it was. "Earl, don't you do anything but howl. Just don't do that where it'll cause trouble," George snapped.

"Hell, George, all you do is worry. If I get into trouble, I'll tell everybody I never knew you. I sure don't want to admit I'm cousin to such a chicken shit environmentalist."

Moon interposed with good humor. "Now, cousins, don't ruin our trip. Let's have us some fun. I'll bankroll you five hundred dollars apiece. How's that? You can gamble it away or do whatever else you want with it. Let's meet back at the room at eight o'clock, then go eat."

Wandering through the casino, George watched Earl's attempts to pick up women with amusement. For a while he watched the play at the blackjack tables, then he sauntered over to the slot machines and began to play. After he had played a few minutes with no success, Earl happened by and tried his luck. Even though the third slot machine that he tried paid off with a rattling horde of coins, Earl found slot machines too tame for his liking.

"Lucky at slot machines, unlucky at love, Earl," George laughed at Earl as the coins tumbled out.

"How would you know about either?" Campbell muttered. Earl did not seem to appreciate either his luck or George's laughter. He gathered up his winnings and stalked off looking for female companionship.

"Don't forget to come back to the room on time, Earl," George called after the departing figure. He continued patiently playing the slot machines but could never achieve anything like the great success that Earl had had with so little effort. He barely managed to come close to breaking even.

Discouraged with the machines, George moved to the black-jack tables. As he made his way to play blackjack, he spied Acie and Earl with a good-looking woman in tow. She appeared to be rather gaudily dressed. George suspected that Earl had found a use for some of his winnings at the slot machine. At the blackjack tables, George had a little better luck than he had had at the slot machines, so he ended the evening a little ahead of the house.

Later, sitting at the bar having a gin and tonic, George struck up a conversation with a man sitting next to him.

"You look like a cowb y. You from around here?"

"No, I'm a banker on holiday. I just thought I ought to dress for the west."

"Having any luck at the tables?"

"No, but I haven't lost much, about eighty dollars. I always put myself on a budget when I come here. So much for gambling, so much for booze, and so much for women."

"You're not married, then."

"Yes, but what's that got to do with having fun in Vegas? If I brought my wife, she'd want to spend all of our time sight-seeing."

"I wouldn't know. Not married. What kind of sight-seeing would you recommend for me and my friends?"

"Well, when you get tired of looking around here in Vegas, there's plenty of beautiful scenery. And you can always go up the road to the

Mustang Ranch. There're some good-looking women up there. And the food and liquor are great. They treat you like a king. They don't come cheap, but they know how to make a fellow feel appreciated."

"Thanks for the tip. I've got some friends who might be safer there than here."

LUCKY MARTIAL

Lucky Martial had entered into Earl's scheme willingly enough but not without considerable incentives being offered her. The five hundred dollars that Earl and Acie promised her had insured her eagerness to help with their practical joke, although she had been reluctant to go along with them without financial incentive.

"You just get him hungerin' and in bed. Let him make out like a bandit if he'll promise to marry you."

"But I'm already married."

"Yeah, but he don't know that," Earl pointed out, "that's the joke." "If I married him, I'd be a bigamist."

"Nah. Nothin' gonna be real, but Moon won't know it's fake."

Acie pulled out five one hundred dollar bills and waved them in front of Lucky, one after the other. "Five big ones, Lucky. We'll give you one now and the others when you get him to the altar. Besides, Moon's tall, dark, and handsome. You'll enjoy your work. I know girls would do it for free or pay for the chance. We checked on you. We payin' you 'cause we're told you have some actin' ability."

Lucky hesitated, then agreed, "Okay. I'll tell my husband something. I'll try to get Moon to propose. But four days is all you get. If things are still hanging after that, you have to give me the rest of the money no matter where matters stand. I'm supposed to deal on Tuesday, and my husband will be suspicious if I don't show up for that." The compact was struck. Acie took lucky up to the suite and introduced her to Moon. Earl didn't go. That way Moon would be less suspicious. After the introduction, they sat down to talk and Acie suggested that they order drinks—rum and cola for Lucky, bourbon for Moon and him. A couple of drinks and an hour later, it was obvious to Acie that Moon and Lucky were enjoying each other's company. Acie was glad to see Lucky was drinking at a much slower rate than Moon. Acie believed her intent on remaining clear-headed enough to carry out her bargain with Earl and him.

They had paid Lucky the one hundred in advance but determined to have her deliver her performance before paying the rest. Her body language told him, though, that she thought Everett Lunamin was handsome. It would be easy money for her. It wouldn't be too difficult for her to make love to Moon, Acie figured. He could tell that Moon had developed more than a conversational interest in this woman, so he sneaked out to find Earl.

"Hit's goin' like a 'possum up a persimmon tree, old buddy. Moon's almost hooked already."

Left alone, Lucky and Moon continued drinking. Lucky switched to bourbon and coke at Moon's suggestion. She was becoming more voluptuous by the moment in Moon's eyes. He had been too wrapped up in making Lunar Mining a going concern to be spending much time thinking about women, even Suzy. Now, bedazzled by Lucky's blue eyes and blonde hair atop her well-endowed figure, he had completely forgotten about Susan.

"Lucky, where do you come from?"

"I grew up in a little town near here, Everett." "The bright lights of Vegas beckoned, eh?"

"I guess so. It was pretty dull in that town—not even a movie theater—just a couple of gas stations, a general store, a post office, and a school. My dad was the postmaster."

"Whatta you do here in Vegas?" "Just deal blackjack."

"I reckon a pretty girl like you gets lots of attention. I'll bet the men flock to your table."

"No, not so many."

"I'll bet they line up to lose."

Moon took Lucky by the arm and led her out on the balcony. As they gazed at the bright lights of the city, Moon put his arm around Lucky, who snuggled against him.

"The lights of the city have always entranced me," she told him. "Yep, they're pretty, about as pretty as your blue eyes. I'll bet the losers keep comin' back to your table just to see you."

"I do have a lot of repeat players," Lucky admitted.

As she said this, Lucky leaned closer to Moon, shivering a little. "The desert cools off fast when the sun goes down," she explained. Instead of answering, Moon pulled her closer and kissed her.

After a long, lingering kiss, Lucky suggested that they go back inside to get warm. "My jacket's inside," she pointed out.

Back inside, Moon fixed them more drinks. As he handed Lucky hers, he said, "This should help warm you up. I have some other ideas about how to keep you warm, Lucky."

"What are those?"

"For starters, I'll rub your feet and legs. Let me help you take off your shoes and stockings." He ran his hands over her legs in between sips of bourbon.

"These are the prettiest legs I've seen in a long time," he observed with the air of a connoisseur.

"You speak like an expert. I'm glad you like them. I exercise to stay in shape."

Moon had now become warm from his exertions and the drinks.

His hands began venturing further up her legs to her thighs. "Everett, I'm getting really warm. You should stop now." "Let's go to my bedroom."

"I can't do that. We just met." "But we're good friends already."

Moon picked Lucky up and carried here to his bedroom, placed her upon his bed, and began unbuttoning her dress.

"Everett, I'm saving myself for the man I marry. I can't go to bed with you."

"What if I promise to marry you?"

"That would be different."

"Okay, we'll get married. How about day after tomorrow?" "Everett, how sweet. But can I believe you? This is too sudden."

Under ordinary circumstances, Lunamin was a reasonably cautious man when sober but a bit impetuous when drinking. Tonight he had challenged his capacity even more greatly than he had in Denver. What caution he now possessed had been numbed by his desire for Lucky and the bourbon he had drunk.

"You don't believe I mean it?"

"Maybe you're just saying that you'll marry me now and then you'll forget later."

"Do bears live in the woods? Here, I'll write it out for you."

Moon grabbed a pencil and paper from the stand beside the bed and wrote, "I, Everett Adamo Lunamin promise to marry Miss Lucky Martial." Despite his great capacity, Moon was beginning to feel the effects of the liquor a little. He had had some difficulty writing the note, but with great effort he had manag d to complete it. He signed it E. A. Lunamin.

He handed the paper to Lucky, "There. You can take that to the bank and the preacher."

"Are you sure about this?" Lucky asked, handing the paper back. After Moon reread his note and handed it to Lucky again for her approval, he began helping her out of her dress and slip, but Lucky stopped him. His efforts weren't to her satisfaction. She insisted on undressing him first.

"You're practically tearing my clothes off of me, Everett. You need to slow down. It's more romantic that way. Let me show you how."

When she had Moon completely undressed, she finally allowed him to remove her bra and panties but then slowed him down and would not let him enter her.

"Moon, are you certain you want to get married?"

"Sure, if that's what you want, Lucky. You've got my promissory note. I need you."

Moon's motor abilities were becoming somewhat more impaired, as the liquor had begun to tell on his coordination. He had difficulty in his efforts to bed Lucky, but she subtly maneuvered herself to help him. George met Acie and Earl at the door to the suite as they all arrived back at the room a little after eight. They looked around for Moon, but he was not anywhere to be seen. The door to his bedroom was closed, and they could hear voices and occasional laughter coming from inside.

Earl had no trouble sizing up the situation, "Sounds like Moon has hisself some fun aworkin.' Looks like food's not the highest thing on his list right now. He's livin' on love." Earl laughed and Acie joined in.

"Yeah," Acie said, "I'll bet he's havin' a ball with a pretty gal." George eyed them suspiciously, "Do you know something' I don't, cousins?"

Acie and Earl looked at each other, then grinned at George.

"Don't go worryin' about it, George. Moon'll be all right," Acie assured him.

George accepted Acie's assurance, looked around for the TV controls, and turned on a football game. He and Earl settled in to watch while Acie drank a beer and ate some chips. They waited for a half hour or so before Moon stuck his head out of the bedroom door.

"Say. Are you boys hungry? Why don't you go out to eat?"

"Well, what about you, Moon? Don't you want supper?"

"Don't worry about me, George. I'll just order from room service. You boys go on and get you a dinner at a good restaurant with a floor show."

"I'll bet we could see a better show right here."

"You'd probably lose that bet, Earl, but you won't be here to find out."

Acie and Earl laughed loudly, salaamed to Moon, and grinned widely as they ushered George out of the room.

Out in the hall, George questioned them, "I repeat, do you two know something I should know?"

"George, don't worry. We just found a pretty little thing for Moon to occupy some time with."

George was skeptical because he knew how Earl loved practical jokes. And he could always persuade Acie to help him.

"Was that 'pretty little thing' the woman in the short red dress I saw you two with an hour or so ago?"

"Reckon so. Pretty, ain't she?"

"Yeah. She's good looking. What else do you know about her?"

"She works here."

"I'll bet she does." "Honest. She deals cards."

"What kind of deal did you arrange for Moon?"

"Don't you worry none, cousin. We'll just have a little laugh. It'll turn out all right," Acie promised him.

Laughing, they ushered George downstairs, out the front door, and to a taxi that took them to a restaurant. They spent the rest of the evening eating, watching the floorshow, and reassuring George that nothing bad would happen to Moon.

Next morning Moon didn't fully remember what had happened the night before. He awoke with his arms around Lucky, who turned toward him and kissed him, thinking this job quite rewarding. She had enjoyed Moon's company. He didn't seem to suffer any ill effects from the liquor he had consumed, but he did appear a little dazed when he saw the note that he had written the night before. Peering out the window, Moon commented on how blue the sky looked.

Enthralled by the snow-covered mountains, Lunamin called Lucky to see.

"I live in the Virginia mountains. I'm attached to them. They're different from the Rockies. Not so high—but beautiful."

"I just love looking at the mountains," Lucky told him. "I love driving up into them and looking at the plants and animals."

"You like the out of doors, too? What's the countryside around Vegas like?"

"I'd rather show you than tell you. Let's take a drive to look at the scenery."

Moon was easily persuaded. "All right, let's go take a look around right now."

Lucky laughed at his eagerness. "You'll have to wait awhile. I've got to go home and change. I'll meet you back here in an hour and a half."

"Let's have breakfast in the room first." Moon called in their order and then pulled Lucky to him. They did not hear the breakfast arrive, but George knocked on their door to announce it.

"Breakfast for Mr. Lunamin is here."

"Just leave it at the door. I'll get it, George."

Breakfast eaten, they showered together. Then Lucky dressed and left to change. When she returned in blouse, shorts, and tennis shoes, Moon met her in the lobby. Once out of Vegas, Moon headed the rental car toward the blue mountains to the west. The desert showed various hues of blue, pink, and red contrasting with the gray tones of the tumbleweeds and creosote bushes. The distant peaks shone in the sunlight, still snow-capped even in mid-July. Drinking in the desert's beauties and those of Lucky, Moon decided he was really enjoying this miners' holiday.

Alongside the road they saw large hawks perched on the telephone poles. By the time they climbed into the foothills, it was late morning and the thermals had begun to rise along the ridges. Above them, they saw an eagle soaring. They watched as it circled higher and higher.

"Stop, Everett, look at the deer." Lucky pointed to a slope on the right.

Moon saw an antlered buck and two doe about fifty yards from them.

"That rack would make a nice trophy."

"I like them better the way they are. They're beautiful."

"Where I come from we think about game animals as meat for the table."

"Do you have deer where you're from in Virginia?"

"Yeah. Whitetails. When they run they raise their tails like white flags. These deer are mule deer. They're bigger'n white-tails but not as pretty."

While Moon and Lucky were viewing natural beauties, Earl and Acie were putting together the final part of their plan. They found the Little Sagebrush Chapel, whose owner, Carlos Atkinson, was quite willing for two hundred dollars to provide fake papers and to rent his establishment on short notice for an afternoon wedding.

"You can have the place for three hours, no more. Just give me twelve hours notice."

"That'll be just fine," Acie assured him.

Then they located two out-of-work actors: Jack Walton, who claimed to be experienced playing ministerial roles, and James Donathan, who had played police roles. Walton and Donathan would be glad to perform for fifty dollars apiece. So Acie and Earl were ready whenever Lucky succeeded in completing her part of the game.

"Earl, we done come in under budg t. After allowin' for Lucky's fee, we've still got two hundred of the thousand dollars Moon staked us." "Yeah, we can still play a little blackjack or hit the slot machines.

I hit it big on them. And George still has most of his. We can hit him up for a little."

When Moon and Lucky returned, they found Acie watching TV. Lucky gave him the agreed upon signal while Moon ordered food and drinks for the two of them in his room, a steak medium rare for him and a dish of fettuccine Alfredo for her. Lucky went in to shower.

"Acie, find a justice of the peace or a minister to marry Lucky and me. Make it fast, Acie. I want to do this tomorrow. Lucky wants to get married right away."

"Don't worry, old buddy. I'll find Earl and we'll get to it pronto.

Tomorrow evening, okay? We'll go out now and settle the details. "Fine. I'll tell Lucky."

Lucky seemed elated by the news. She asked Moon to pour them more drinks while she finished her shower. She came out dressed in Moon's bathrobe. As they ate dinner, Moon turned on the radio to an easy-listening music station Lucky had found. Lucky was enjoying the meal and the music, Moon thought, but she ate her fettuccine and drank slowly. Moon attacked his steak ravenously, so he finished eating well ahead of her and poured himself another drink.

Sitting on the couch, he slipped off his shoes and propped his feet on the coffee table. He watched her breasts appear and disappear under the folds of his bathrobe she was wearing and gazed at her long, well- proportioned legs and thighs protruding from under the table.

"You have a great figure."

"I'm glad you think so. I jog and do aerobic dancing to stay in shape."

When she finished her food and drink, she suggested that they dance to the music. "Montavanni puts me in the mood for dancing. Let's dance, Everett. Some slow dancing," she told him as she rose and came over and pulled him up to her.

Moon wrapped his arms around Lucky and drew her close to him. As they swayed to the music, Mo n began to run his hands over

Lucky underneath the bathrobe. She responded by opening his shirt and running her hands over his chest."

"Everett, I can feel your excitement." "That name for it's new to me."

For another quarter of an hour they continued dancing. Then Lucky told Moon that it was time for him to shower.

"I've had my shower, Everett, but I'll put my shower cap back on and shower with you."

Lucky led Moon to the shower stall and finished undressing him. When they had adjusted the water, she took gel soap from the dispenser and began to apply it over Moon's body.

"How does that feel, Everett?" "Great. Don't stop."

Lucky covered every inch of Moon's body with soap, lingering around his loins, and then took a washcloth and rubbed him vigorously. By the time they had dried one another, Moon was more than eager to have Lucky again.

Late the next morning, after more lovemaking and breakfast, Lucky told Moon that she had to buy a white dress for their wedding. Moon found out from Acie where they were to be married, and told Lucky. She arranged to meet Moon and his entourage at Little Sagebrush Chapel at four in the afternoon. It was agreed that Acie would be Moon's best man and that Earl would give the bride away. George was to be entrusted with the task of finding a gold wedding band to give to Acie at the appropriate time. Moon felt sure that everything was developing according to his wishes.

Moon's decision to include George in the wedding plans forced Acie and Earl to include George in their scheme. They now had to bring George up to date about what was happening because of his being charged with buying the ring. When George had been let in on the joke and coaxed a little, he agreed not to spoil their fun.

"George, nobody's goin' to get hurt. Let's just have a little fun. Moon will be so happy to find out he's not married when he's sobered up that he'll get as big a kick out of it as we do," Acie soothed.

"Okay, okay, I'll keep quiet. But I'm not taking any credit nor any blame."

The ceremony at the Sagebrush Chapel proceeded as scheduled with no problems. The new y self-ordained Jack Walton was waiting for the couple at the door of the Chapel with dark suit and clerical collar. Moon and his escorts arrived promptly at four, and Acie introduced George and Moon to the supposed Reverend Jack Walton.

"I'm pleased to meet you, Mr. Lunamin." "Likewise, Reverend."

As the introductions were concluding, a red sports car pulled up to the Chapel, and Lucky, tastefully adorned in a white dress that reached almost to her ankles, climbed out.

"There's the beautiful bride. All of you come in the Chapel and we'll have the ceremony," Walton instructed.

Walton led them into the Chapel and led Lucky and Moon through their vows. At the end of the brief ceremony, Moon kissed the bride as instructed. Then Acie ushered them into an adjoining room where he and Earl had prepared a reception with a wedding cake and fruit punch spiked with gin. Without much additional ceremony, the bride received toasts and cut the wedding cake. Soon everyone was drinking and eating and wishing the bride and groom much happiness.

Moon did not notice that Acie and Earl exchanged glances every now and then and doubled up with laughter. As the party moved into full swing, the sound of a police siren grew louder and louder as it approached the Chapel. A few moments later, they heard a car pull up in front of the Chapel. Not long afterwards, a man in a policeman's uniform appeared at the door.

"I'm Officer James Donathan," the policeman announced. "I have a warrant for the arrest of Lucky Martial, sworn out by her husband, Herbert Martial. The charge is bigamy." James Donathan handcuffed Lucky and led her away as Acie and Earl held Moon to keep him from stopping their exit.

"What's goin' on here, Lucky?" Moon demanded.

"I'm sorry, Everett. You're a great guy. We had fun, didn't we?" Lucky asked as she took off her new wedding band and gave it back to George.

"Fun? Was that all it was?"

"You'll get over it. Ask your friends."

Until Donathan and Lucky drove off, George had to help Earl hold Moon to keep him from following so that Acie could pay off the actors.

"What'd she mean, ask my friends?"

"Don't look at me, Moon. This is one time George definitely didn't do it."

Acie and Earl couldn't contain their laughter.

"So you two know about this? It's what all you did?" "Moon, you got took," Earl chortled.

"No two ways about it, pardner. We pulled a rusty on you. We done it," admitted Acie.

"Done what?"

"Hired Lucky and those men to fool you. They're out-of-work actors. Lucky's hitched, but we paid her enough for a great performance. I think she enjoyed the job. She had you took in."

In spite of himself, George laughed too as the expression on Moon's face changed from bafflement to outrage to sheepishness in rapid succession.

"Dammit. Were you in on this, George?"

"Not before today. I thought it might as well play out. It was a pretty good practical joke—a cut above what Earl usually dreams up."

"You boys worked hard on this, I reckon," Moon admitted.

"We sure did. We've been hard at work—haven't even had time to play at the tables. We've spent a lot of the money you staked us," Earl pointed out. He spoke with the tone of a man who had sacrificed greatly for a friend.

Acie put his hand on Moon's shoulder. "No hard feelin's, Moon?" "No, I reckon I should've suspected you two were up to something.

I've been spendin' too much time with the coal business. I need a woman. My need and my drinkin' made me a sucker for your scheme."

The four of them spent the remainder of the day and much of the night and the next few days and nights playing various games of chance and watching the floor shows in the casinos. Moon made it a point to stay away from the blackjack tables, but George tried his luck at the game several times, once at Lucky's table. He and Acie and Earl had decent luck and went home with money in their pockets. Moon actually came out ahead several hundred dollars.

"Lucky in love, and lucky at the gambling tables," George joked. Acie and Earl laughed, but Moon merely grunted.

As they flew back to the coalfields a few days later, Moon had time to consider soberly the recent tumultuous events in his life. Lucky's last words stuck in his mind. She really had enjoyed his company, and he definitely had enjoyed hers. It really had been fun. And he was fortunate to have escaped from his foolish actions. He should have known his drinking limits better. The more he considered his time with Lucky, the more he thought that he did need a woman in his life. What about Susan?

He felt more than a little guilty that he had forgotten all about Susan when Lucky's evident charms had dazzled him. He couldn't help feeling anguish about his lack of self-control. He had dated Susan in high school, and she had written him all the time he was in the army. They had been dating again since his return from Vietnam, but he had not had much time to think about anything other than getting Lunar Mining off to a successful start. The need to pay the bills had dominated his thinking. Besides, without the money that a successful mining operation would bring, he had no chance of getting Susan to marry him.

Now that Lunar Mining had become profitable, he had time to think about other things. It was obvious to him that Susan and her family had been one of the reasons (probably the major reason) that he had become a surface miner. He had wanted to show them that he could be a successful businessman. Although he had forgotten his long- time goal for a time, blinded by his infatuation with Lucky, he now saw clearly that he needed to marry Susan right away. He loved her, he thought. He was certain he was comfortable with her. He definitely desired her. She would be the final jewel to complete the crown of his success, and his bank a count should soon be large enough to satisfy her parents that he was the right kind of husband material. Of course it probably meant leaving Winding Fork or anywhere else near the country that he loved, but he knew Susan wouldn't be happy in what she termed "the wilderness."

No doubt noticing how unusually quiet Moon had become, George interrupted Lunamin's attempts to sort out his feelings and chart his course of action.

"Moon, if you don't mind my saying so, I think this last escapade of yours should stir up some doubts in your mind about wanting to marry Susan Stanard. Do you think you would have fallen for Lucky the way you did if you really were in love with Susan?"

"George, that was the liquor and the help of my friends."

"Have you considered that love might not be what attracts you to Susan? There's no law that says you have to marry your high school sweetheart. I know it's not my business, but we've been buddies a long time."

"George, you're right. It's not your business. You've been readin' too many poets or readin' romance stories. I'm goin' to marry Susan if she'll have me. We'll be fine."

"Not necessarily. I'm of the opinion that Shakespeare's Iago had it right for you when he said love is a lust of the blood and a permission of the will. I think all you need is some more good sex. You got that from Lucky, I believe."

"Yeah, that was good sex, Shakespeare. I thought it was more than that. I reckon it was the liquor workin.' But I'm bound and determined to put that affair with Lucky behind me. I'm g in' to marry Susan as soon as I can get her to agree. It's what I've b en workin' for."

"Well, old buddy, I wish you well. Just keep in mind that Susan's not the kind of girl that goes 'coon and 'possum hunting. I hope marrying her turns out to be what makes you happy."

ANOTHER TRIP

After what Lunamin now considered his narrow escape from Lucky Martial, Moon did not wait but a couple of weeks before he pressed Susan to marry him as soon as possible. His bank accounts had increased prodigiously, and he had prospects of even more. Persuading Susan proved an easier task than Moon had supposed. Once he agreed to build her a mansion in Abingdon—to take her out of what she termed "the wilderness"—Susan had no further objections. She wanted her mother and father to approve, but when Moon had revealed his financial status to her father, their objections for the most part vanished. They still thought Moon uneducated and a bit rough, but they had to admit that he was an honest man who was a rising figure in the community. "Daughter, if you want to marry him, we won't object," Tom Stanard told her.

"But I want you to have a splendid church wedding, Susan. I'll help you with it."

Susan was delighted with her mother's offer. She was very much in favor of having a grand wedding where she could show off her triumph to her friends. Everett, after all, was becoming one of the richest men in Southwest Virginia.

He was handsome. He had always been first on her list of eligible marital partners as far as desire was concerned. Throughout their dating, it had taken all of her will power to deny him the sex he wanted. The trouble had been that he had no money. Now he was rich. And she had exacted a promise from him to build her the grand house of her dreams in Abingdon. She would finally escape the wilderness.

A month after Moon's return from Vegas, the wedding announcement appeared in the newspaper. Susan Stanard was to marry

E. A. Lunamin. Not long afterwards, George Landsetter received an invitation announcing the wedding of Susan Elvira Stanard to Everett Adamo Lunamin at the First Methodist Church of Clintwood on the fifth of October. George took in all of the wedding preliminaries, because Moon called him soon after the invitation arrived and asked him to be his best man. George agreed, but couldn't resist razzing Moon a little.

"Are you sure you're ready for marriage this soon after Lucky?" "You know the bourbon had a lot to do with that, George." "Yeah, but you sure forgot about Susan."

"I dropped the ball, all right, but Acie, Earl, and you gave me some help."

"Don't lump me with them. I just went along with them the last day. I knew that you had plans for marrying Susan. But do you really love her?"

"Sure, George, after all, it's what I've been aiming to do for a long time."

Moon admitted to hims lf that wanting to marry Susan had been one of the things that had prompted his entry into the mining business, but he probably would have done that anyway. He had thought about marrying her a great deal while in Vietnam. How much of his goal was owing to love and how much of it stemmed from a desire to have what was being denied him he had never bothered greatly to determine. He had not reflected at length upon what prompted him toward the goal. The attainment of the goal demanded his full attention— especially now after what appeared to him to be his narrow escape from entanglement with Lucky Martial.

Lunamin was not in the habit of reflecting a great deal before action. Had he been, he might have considered that his goals and Susan's might not be the same or even roughly congruent. On one thing they definitely agreed. His making money in surface mining stood high on both their lists.

Moon was never certain whether the size of the house on what jocular folk termed the miner's Riviera in Abingdon was his idea or Susan's. He had wanted to make a statement to the world about succeeding in a big way, but he hadn't heard about the Riviera before Susan told him that she wanted to live in Abingdon to be near her high school friends that already lived there. She told him she was determined to show her relatives that she was no crazy Agrarian like her parents. The laughter aimed at her parents' way of life by her aunts, uncles, and cousins was still ringing in her ears.

Despite their commitment to rustic living, Susan's family had not especially approved of Moon when Susan had dated him in high school. His family, his seeming lack of interest in anything beyond high school sports, and his unvarnished mountain dialect all had affected their attitude toward him. In subtle ways they had indicated to him that he wasn't right for their beautiful daughter. That still rankled in Moon's mind. With Susan, her parents had been more explicit.

"Does the boy ever talk about going to college—on a sports scholarship, perhaps—or going into a business of some kind?"

"No, Daddy. Moon says that he hasn't got time to worry about the future. He's too busy living now."

"That so. He doesn't seem like a fellow you'd want to plan a future with, then."

"I don't have to marry him, Daddy. Tell him, Mom. I'm going to college this fall—at Sweetbriar."

"That's right, Tom, she has just been admitted for next year.

There's no need to worry about Mr. Lunamin's prospects just now."

During their time in high school, Susan had been too caught up in the joys of being an outstanding cheerleader who dated the captain of the football and basketball teams to worry about what kind of a husband she would need. Unlike some of the other girls at Winding Fork, Susan was planning for college. She would attend Sweetbriar with some of her cousins and date young men from Washington & Lee and the University of Virginia.

Mrs. Stanard had hoped that college life would wipe all thoughts of Everett Lunamin from her daughter's mind. Surely, she thought, Lunamin would not stand comparison to well-bred young men from the University or the other colleges near Sweetbriar. To her mother's great regret, however, Susan did not find any young college man to replace Moon in her imagination. She graduated from Sweetbriar without finding a prince charming, Moon would have his chance to take her away from "the wilderness," she had written him in Vietnam, if only he could amass some wealth.

So a large part of Moon's urge to become wealthy had been stimulated by his desire to overcome the attitudes of Susan and her family. The mansion in Abingdon might not have been what he would have built without Susan's direction, but it seemed to him to be a satisfactory statement of his success, even though he was never certain that it or the place where it was located created exactly the flourish he would have wished to make his statement.

Lunamin did not object to building a large, imposing colonial home. He had definitely wanted to make a compelling, visible statement, and this mansion would do. His main objection was to building it in Abingdon, where his statement to some extent spoke to deaf ears and accosted blind eyes while the audience that he especially wished to reach lived over the mountains. He would have preferred to place it in the town limits of Clintwood, Pound, or some other Southwest Virginia community in the coalfields where people would fully comprehend his message.

Moon had not fully realized until now that Susan's desire to leave what she termed the wilderness was an urge akin to the Israelites' desire to reach the Promised Land after forty years of desert wanderings. The location Susan chose in what was jokingly termed the Abingdon Riviera was the closest to the coalfields that she would accept. Moon decided that was close enough, that the placement of his statement wasn't worth great argument even though it meant some long drives to work for him.

"At least," Moon ruefully told Fred and Acie, "I don't have to commute from Roanoke."

"A woman's supposed to go where her man says," Fred observed. "Give a woman an inch...," Acie added.

"You fellers want me to make Susan walk a few steps behind me when we go to trade of a Saturday? Most people stopped that before Papaw and Mamaw MacCloud were hitched."

When the house was completed, Moon had to admit that it said what he intended. Set on a ten-acre lot at the end of a long, tree-lined drive that made a circle in front of the house, the large two-story brick house looked as though it had been transported from Colonial Williamsburg. Inside, the illusion of colonial elegance continued with the large foyer, hallway and winding staircase to the second floor.

Large rooms on either side of the entrance reflected Susan's desire to reproduce a colonial past.

The main living area belied the colonial atmosphere of the front rooms. It extended along the hallway to the rear of the house, where there were a family recreation room, den, master bedroom, modern kitchen, and a spacious utility room. There were upstairs bedrooms for children and overnight guests. The front rooms were reserved for social functions such as bridge parties, cocktail parties, and other social activities that Susan already had planned in her mind.

"Everett, it's just what I imagined it would be," Susan told him when he brought her to see the completed house.

"You'll have to give it the finishin' touches. I just followed your instructions."

The wooded areas on either side of the drive were Moon's idea. He thinned some trees but left hickories, beeches, and oaks (all the nut- bearing trees) as well as whatever hemlocks were on the site. For the under story he left dogwoods, native azaleas, and rhododendrons. The only lawn he permitted was part of an acre immediately surrounding the house. Even there he left a few large hardwoods to shade the house in the summer.

The Lunamin-Stanard wedding occupied the ladies of Winding Fork and Clintwood for several months. The preparations, rehearsals, and the actual event provided ample material for the Winding Fork column in the *Coalfield Endeavor*. The Clintwood society column was not to be outdone. It always managed some inside scoops about dresses or other equally important matters.

Susan's mother spared no effort to create a major social event. She worried that Moon's family would not hold up the groom's end of the social obligations surrounding her social drama. She conveyed her fears to Susan forcefully. In turn, Susan badgered Moon about the rehearsal dinner.

"Moon, honey, your family have to give a rehearsal dinner. Mother will be furious if there isn't a spectacular rehearsal dinner. Will you speak to your grandparents about it?"

Hiding his concern, Lunamin soothed her, "Okay, don't worry. I'll take care of it."

It wasn't the cost of the dinner that worried Moon. Mamaw and Papaw presented a problem. They took a dim view of all the fuss being made over this wedding. It took all Moon's powers of persuasion to get them to agree to host the rehearsal meal. Finally, after Moon had pleaded for days and enlisted George to help him convince Archibald and Serafina, his grandmother gave in.

"Archibald, we need to do this for the boy. It won't cost us nothing but the time and dressin' up."

Moon knew that when Mamaw used that tone, he had won. "Just send all the bills to me, Papaw."

The dinner went off without incident, Susan's mother was delighted, and Moon was relieved. The write-up in the paper was glowing. He followed Susan's mother's orders for all the subsequent events.

Moon's best man, George, saw to it that Moon had an excellent bachelor party before the wedding. George booked a large private room at the Flamingo Lounge. Besides a real strip-tease act by a voluptuous blonde, Moon was treated to a striptease act and a skit in drag performed by Earl and others, who recreated Moon's interlude with Lucky.

Moon took the joke in good humor, but he swore all those assembled to secrecy. "I sure don't want Susan to find out about Lucky before the weddin.'"

The wedding (guests and the newspaper accounts said, and everyone else later admitted) was Mrs. Stanard's triumph. Music from *Lohengrin* and *Carousel* lent an air of culture to the wedding ceremony, but Moon hardly heard the music. He felt very tired when the vows were completed and he was told to kiss the bride.

After all the preliminaries, the wedding and the reception following were something of an anticlimax for Moon, who found considerable solace in the punch bowl at the reception.

Keeping a watchful eye on his charge, George reminded him of his problems in Vegas resulting from too much drink, "That other bowl is safe, Moon. Why don't you confine yourself to that for the rest of the time."

Moon dutifully limited his intake. "Thanks for lookin' out for me, George. I wouldn't want to botch this event with too much liquor. That spiked punch *is* pretty strong."

For their honeymoon, Susan had decided that they should go somewhere that would be fashionable and elegant. The historical interest that had prompted the design of their house also informed Susan's decision on where they were to honeymoon—Williamsburg. Having braved the rice throwers outside the church, they drove off in their highly decorated vehicle, Moon's Ford Mustang with windows chalked and tin cans tied to the rear. The car had a festive look.

Knowing the likelihood that Acie and Earl and others would do something like this, Moon had prepared by parking a getaway car several blocks from the church. He and Susan got into their festive chariot and drove the few blocks to where he had left a new Mercedes. Laughing, Moon transferred all their gear to the new car.

"How do you like this Mercedes?" "It's beautiful. When did you get it?"

"A few days ago. It's your weddin' present."

For their first night, Susan had picked a room at the Martha Washington Inn in Abingdon to avoid the long drive to Williamsburg until the next day. Built in the last century, this imposing building had enough history attached to it to satisfy Susan. The tall columns standing over a wide porch led into wide doors that opened to a spacious foyer. Their room was furnished with reproductions of Georgian furniture, including a four-poster bed whose posts tapered to a pineapple design. Two wing chairs covered in blue velvet complemented the bed. Along the edge of the ceiling the off-white walls had a blue edging of wallpaper decorated with gold *fleur-de-lis*. The only nod to contemporary America was a large TV set on the low table across from the bed.

"I love this room, Moon," Susan exclaimed as he carried in their luggage.

"You sure you didn't have a life during colonial times?"

Susan laughed, "You know I majored in American history at Sweetbriar."

"You must have made all *A*'s."

Moon flipped on the TV and turned on the news while Susan showered. As Moon took his turn in the shower, she watched a version of Tennessee Williams' *A Cat on a Hot Tin Roof*. She continued watching after Moon joined her and put his arm around her. "Why don't we turn of the TV now?"

"Let me finish watching this show first."

Moon did not express his irritation directly. He found the newspaper that he had picked up at the front desk and began to read. Before long, he drifted off to sleep. His conscious mind next registered Susan's voice.

"Wake up, Everett."

Moon could detect a note of anger. "Is the movie over?"

"Yes. You went to sleep. Fine thing. I thought you couldn't wait to get me to bed."

"I reckon it's been a long day. You know how much I've wanted you."

Moon pulled Susan to him. Kissing her deeply, he undertook a physical defense against her accusation of inattention by running his hands under her nightgown and massaging her breasts as he had on their dates. Tonight Susan was more responsive than he had imagined she would be. Before the dawn arrived, her demands had taken Moon to the limits of his stamina. He was glad that George had persuaded him to limit his intake of alcoholic punch.

The drive to the Williamsburg Lodge the next day was a long one—eight hours even though they went well over the fifty-five mile an hour speed limit. Susan demanded to drive the last leg of the trip. Moon told her to watch out for state troopers and began reading the newspaper he had begun the night before. Heedless of his warning,

Susan became occupied with the scenery and did not s e the police-man who pulled out from behind the trees near Zion's Crossroads. When the flashing light of his patrol car finally caught her atten-tion, she pulled over and stopped. The young officer was very polite, almost apologetic.

"Ma'am, do you realize you were speeding?"

"I guess I was watching the scenery and forgot to look at the speedometer, Officer."

"You were going almost seventy in a forty-five zone."

Susan smiled at him. "I didn't realize, officer. I'm so sorry. The car is new. It was my wedding present. We just got married yester-day, and my husband gave me this car. I'll keep my mind on my driving from now on."

No doubt influenced by Susan's manifest charms, Moon thought, the policeman let her off with a stern reprimand.

"I reckon I'll have to watch the speedometer the rest of the way." "You'll do no such thing. I'll be careful."

It was with a sense of relief as well as anticipation that they drove into the parking lot of the Williamsburg Lodge and went to their room. They showered and had dinner in the dining room before retiring for the night. Together alone again, Moon picked Susan up and dropped her on their king sized bed and kissed her. Laughing, Susan unbuttoned his shirt, pulled it off, and then undid his belt.

"I'll let you finish," she said as she began undressing. "Wait," Moon told her, "I'll do that."

They engaged in another active night of lovemaking before dropping off to a deep sleep from which they did not wake until late the next morning.

Their honeymoon was a busy one. Moon would have been will-ing to spend all of their time in their room, but Susan had other plans. After breakfast at the Lodge, that day they took in Colonial Williamsburg, the Governor's Mansion and the Raleigh Tavern in the colonial section of town, where they ate delicacies that had suited the palates of early Virginia gentlemen and their ladies. The next day they visited several of the James River Plantations. Ensuing days they toured Berkeley, Carter's Grove, Evelynton, Sherwood Forest Shirley—all these began to run together in Moon's mind.

"Susan, how do you remember which one is which?"

She laughed. "It's easy, Moonman. You just remember something special. Which one has the cannonball in the out building, which one claims the first Thanksgiving feast, which one belonged to the man who helped fire the first shot at Ft. Sumter to start the Civil War. Really, honey, you should have a little more interest in history."

At the week's end, he couldn't remember which plantation had the original Thanksgiving and which one was the home of President John Tyler. He did remember that the Tyler home, whichever one it was, held the record for the longest frame house in nineteenth-century America. He was proud of remembering that.

Moon wished now and then that Susan had a little less interest in history.

Not that Susan scanted bedtime activity. Moon was amazed at the amount of energy she showed. He could hardly believe that this was the woman who had denied him full sexual satisfaction for so many years. She could look at houses and grounds all day and demand a full night of lovemaking. She appeared to need very little sleep. Moon was somewhat puzzled until he became aware of the aroma that began to permeate their bathroom. Though not very familiar with marijuana, he finally placed the odor. When he asked Susan whether she was smoking pot, she became very defensive.

"What makes you think so?" "The smell in the bathroom."

"What if I am? Do you have any complaints about its effect? I haven't slighted you any, have I? If anything, you've not provided all the sex I wanted."

"No, that's not the point. You've satisfied me thoroughly. I just don't want a wife that smokes—tobacco or pot. You knew that before we got married. Besides, if you become pregnant, it could hurt the baby. You don't want that and neither do I?"

"Aren't you rushing things? I'm sure I couldn't be pregnant yet."

Nevertheless, Susan reluctantly gave in to Moon's demand that she quit. The odor disappeared from their bathroom.

THREESOME

everal months later, Susan missed her period and suspected she was pregnant. A month later, she missed again, and her visit to her doctor confirmed her pregnancy. She wished that Moon was with her more to share the pregnancy, but he was busy at Lunar Mining's operations. Some days at the mines were so long that Moon spent the night with his grandparents rather than making the two-hour commute to Abingdon, so Susan sometimes went for days without seeing him.

"I miss you, Moon," I want you to share this pregnancy, and I also miss having you in bed with me every night. I'm pregnant, but that doesn't mean I can't make love."

"Honey, I miss you, too, but it's a long drive back here from the mines. At midnight, sometimes I'm just too tired to drive home. I'll try to get Fred to handle more, okay."

"All right, but I'm going to need some help when the baby comes." "Let's hire somebody to help you, Suzy."

They soon hired a woman to help Susan with the housework, but neither the company of Elvira Popper nor her many social engagements satisfied Susan. Elvira's sharp, hawk-like features fitted her efficient housekeeping but did not do justice to her ability in the kitchen. She cooked gourmet meals for Susan's entertainments and served them with silent efficiency, but her taciturnity prevented her being an affable companion for Susan.

Susan telephoned her mother every day, and the course of her pregnancy made the newspaper social column in Clintwood. Her high school friends who had moved to the Abingdon Riviera provided her with companionship. They had put forward her name for their clubs and introduced her to the shops and eating places that their social set frequented. She played a great deal of bridge and attended numerous tea parties, but she remained dissatisfied.

On weekends Moon and Susan attended the First Methodist Church. Although Moon did not feel comfortable with the formality of the service, he went to please Susan and to keep up appearances. After all, Fred reminded him that he needed to go to some church and get right with the Lord. Dinner at the Inn usually followed the church service. Sometimes Susan's parents joined them. Infrequently, they drove to Clintwood to spend the afternoon there with Susan's parents, but Susan was always reluctant to visit the wilderness, even to see her parents.

On some of these occasions, but even more rarely, Moon persuaded Susan to visit his grandparents. Archibald and Serafina tried hard to make Moon's wife welcome, but to her they remained a part of that wilderness she had spent so much effort escaping. Susan was jealous that Moon's time was occupied with Lunar Mining, but she was not willing to make long drives to Winding Fork so that they could have more time together.

With minor deviations, this routine continued during Susan's pregnancy and for some time afterward. Moon had talked matters over with Fred, and they had decided that Moon could spend less time at the mines. Fred could handle day-to-day operations whenever necessary.

The pregnancy proceeded without difficulty. Susan was careful to eat properly and follow her doctor's orders. Luckily, Moon was home the night when her water broke, and he took her to the hospital. He made arrangements to be absent from the mines for a few days after that so that he could visit Susan and then bring her and the baby home. Now that they were a threesome, the happy family spent a great deal of time showing off Andrew Stanard Lunamin to their world. Moon and Susan spent more time together and visited Winding Fork more often so that Andrew's grandparents and great-grandparents could see him. Freed from the pregnancy, Susan pursued an even more active social life than before in order to occupy her time while Moon was away. Like the majority of her friends, Susan did not breast feed her child. It was not fashionable. It might cramp her social life. Their housekeeper Elvira Popper now doubled as a baby sitter. Elvira showed no displeasure with the arrangement; in fact, she doted on Andrew.

At the bridge table one afternoon, Susan complained to her friends about what she considered Moon's neglect of her. She expressed her opinion that the honeymoon was supposed to last at least six months or a year or two years.

"He spends all of his time at the mine—even on weekends sometimes."

Laughing, her bridge partners exchanged knowing glances. They were all women whose husbands had business interests and other affairs that often kept them away from home. Many of them were the wives of surface mining company owners or executives. They found her complaint familiar but treated it with amusement, though with sympathy.

"Some of us think of it as benign neglect," Jenny Warbuck advised. "You mean you enjoy being alone?"

"I mean you can learn to enjoy neglect. You don't have to be alone. You can find interesting ways to fill the time."

"I've tried. Bridge, service clubs, church work—I do all the right things."

After the others had left Jenny Warbuck helped Susan and Elvira clean up. Later, she and Susan sat and talked. Propping her feet up on a footstool, Susan pulled out a cigarette pack and offered it to Jenny.

"Susan, if your loneliness arises just from lack of male companionship, that's a problem easily solved."

Lighting up a cigarette herself, Susan gave Jenny a puzzled stare. "What do you mean?"

"It's not hard to find a man who'll pay attention to a good-looking woman like you."

"You mean I should have an affair?"

"It certainly fills the time, honey. And there's plenty of men— lonely or not—who're hungry for sex."

Jenny was a tall, well-proportioned woman. She had been a model. She wasn't bad looking. Susan couldn't believe that she would have trouble keeping a husband interested.

"Oh, I know some good-looking men who like sex, but I don't think I can do that."

"Worried about being faithful? Haven't you heard about the business trips these surface mining moguls take? I say don't get mad, get even."

"Don't you think that's a little cynical, Jenny? So far, Moon hasn't taken any trips away from those damn mines." Susan remembered Everett had told her Hugh Beverley and Dave Blackmun had asked him to attend some meetings (coal symposia, they called them) but Moon had not been willing to leave Lunar Mining's operations even for those meetings.

"Then you're lucky. It's just a matter of time, though. They all go. Believe me, Susan. I know." "But they're on business."

"Mainly monkey business. The business part is for the IRS."

Susan and Moon often argued about her smoking and her perception that he was neglecting her. She could not accept Moon's response that she should try to do some of the things that he liked. She thought of their most recent conversation on this topic.

"Why do I have to go out in the woods with you?"

"I thought you wanted to spend some time with me. I'm spendin' my time at the mines tryin' to make the money to provide the lifestyle that you crave. I think you could do some things with me when I have some time off."

"Yes, with you, not with the chipmunks and snakes."

"If you really wanted to be with me, you'd take a walk or two in the woods."

"That cuts two ways, Moon. Why not spend some time doing the things that I want to do?"

Though almost obsessed with achieving the success of Lunar Mining, Moon missed his time in the outdoors hunting, fishing, and just listening and looking. His attempts to entice Susan to share his love of being in the woods and on the water met with little success. The only time that Moon could get her to share the natural world with him at all was on picnics with her family to the Breaks Interstate Park or Flannigan Reservoir. He could do some fishing with Tom, and Susan would even accompany them on hikes if her mother went along.

If Moon suggested anything in the out-of-doors just for the two of them and Andrew, Susan always had an excuse or some other activity planned. So Moon began to spend more time at Mamaw and Papaw's at Winding Fork rather than making the drive back to Abingdon, especially after Andrew was old enough to stay with Mamaw and Papaw.

When Andy reached three, Susan often had Moon take the boy to Winding Fork to stay with Archibald and Serafina. At Winding Fork, Moon frequently encountered George, who was a regular visitor. On one of these occasions, Moon told his cousin of his frustrated attempts to lure Susan into outdoor activities.

George restrained himself from telling Moon "I told you so," but he couldn't be too sympathetic. "Moon, you ought to have suspected Suzy isn't an outdoor girl. Didn't she always talk about escaping what she termed the wilderness?"

"Sure, George, but visitin' the woods or a lake ain't livin' in the wilderness. She lives in the damndest mansion in town. She belongs to all the clubs, and she travels to Roanoke to shop every other day it seems."

"Maybe when Andy is older, she'll go with you more."

"I reckon you may be right. I hope so. I ain't spendin' all my life goin' to tea parties."

LUNAR FLASH

The first time that Earl proposed putting a car in the local races, Moon refused. He remembered how negative Susan and her family had been about the time he had spent with stock car racing before he was drafted and sent to Vietnam. Earl brought up the idea of putting a car on the track over and over again. Finally, Fred gave him some support.

"Moon, Jauncie talked to her first cousin about it. He's a really sharp tax lawyer. He said that it could be a tax write-off. If we do it the right way, we can list it as a business advertisement or a public relations expense."

"Yeah, Moon, I've got the perfect name," Earl chimed in, 'Lunar Flash.' We can use our company logo. You've done stock. We have guys workin' who'd be more than happy to work on the pit crew. I'll bet you'd like to get into the pit again yourself."

"Well, I reckon I would, but I don't think Suzy would like it." "Shucks, Moon, are you pussy-whipped already? Susan sure is a looker, but a real man don't let his woman tell him what to do."

Moon lost his temper. "You shut your mouth, Earl. What do you know about women?"

"Now fellows, let's not fight about it," Fred interrupted. Trying to calm the two belligerents, he spoke about the tax advantages that would make it relatively inexpensive to put a company car in some races.

"Besides the taxes, it might help encourage the young men to stick with the company, Moon. With coal boomin' the way it is, we might have trouble keepin' some of 'em."

Moon really did like the idea of being part of a racing team again. After all, he could mix fun with business. And maybe Susan would enjoy watching the races once she went to one. He could get George to come along and keep Suzy company during the race.

"Maybe Susan wouldn't give me too much hell if I presented it that way."

So Lunar Mining emblazoned its existence on the side of the Lunar Flash. Below the name and lightning bolt, the Lunar logo of the man in the moon demanded attention, and under it was the motto, "We mine with a mother's touch." The Lunar Flash, with Earl at the wheel, made its debut a month later at the Lonesome Pine Raceway in Coeburn. Moon had spent a considerable time persuading Susan to attend the inaugural race of the Lunar Flash. He told her that he wanted her to be present for a ceremony before the race. She was to untie a huge ribbon on the Lunar Flash while photographers took pictures for publicity.

"You'll have your pretty face in all the newspapers and on TV," Moon told her, "Think of the impression that will make on all of your bridge ladies. Besides, George is comin' along to keep you company during the race. I'll take you both to dinner at the Martha Washington before we drive over to the race."

Susan became convinced that this race might be worth attending. She did like the idea of appearing in all the papers and on TV. And if George was going to be her escort during the race, she could enjoy talking to him even if she didn't like the racing.

"All right, Moon, I'll go to this race and do my bit for Lunar Mining. I don't want to sit home."

So Susan helped launch the racing career of the Lunar Flash and its driver, Earl Campbell. The Bristol *Herald*, the Kingsport *Times-News*, the *Coalfield Endeavor* as well as many smaller local papers and the region's TV sets all sported pictures of the Lunar Flash, Earl in his driving gear, and Susan untying a huge pink bow on the Lunar Flash while Moon, Fred, Acie, and the rest of the crew stood by smiling.

It was the talk of Susan's social circle for weeks. She basked in the attention.

During the race, however, Susan had been less than appreciative of the Lunar Flash and the other vehicles whizzing about the oval track. She occupied herself with making caustic remarks about the event to George, who was enjoying the spectacle a bit more than Susan, but he readily admitted that stock car racing interested him less than baseball, football, and tennis.

"George," Susan observed, "these cars just keep whizzing around and around. You'd think the drivers would get carsick. And what do all these people come to see? Surely not the race."

"I think the big attraction is seeing the wrecks, Susan," George admitted, "but a good many of them have favorites they're rooting for." "Moon says that the company can write off the expenses. He claims Fred MacCloud's cousin-in-law (he's a tax expert) says they can write off the expenses as publicity and public relations."

"Well, Susan, I don't see why a coal company needs publicity, but I'm certain they can use some better public relations."

"I wish Moon could make money some other way."

"You wouldn't want him to throw in with cousin Rod growing pot, would you? Rod seems to have plenty of free time."

"No, George, don't be silly. But Moon spends so much time with Lunar Mining. He doesn't sp nd much time with me."

"Suzy, he got into mining because he wanted to make enough money to get you to marry him. Don't you think it's a little late to be objecting to how he makes the money you demand?"

"I know, George. I wouldn't want to do without the money. I like the lifestyle it brings."

Just then a three-car pile-up diverted their attention. The yellow flag came out and many cars used the opportunity to go to the pits to gas up and change tires. Earl's pit crew performed well and put him back out in record time, pushing him to the front of the race. He couldn't keep first place but finished third, a finish Fred and Moon considered a great success. Earl himself felt his third-place finish a testimony to his driving skill. He was particularly pleased with the time he had to spend signing his autograph for a number of pretty young girls.

After George had delivered Susan to Moon, he drove home wondering how long Moon and Suzy's marriage would last.

BARBERSHOP BLUES

Passing through Coeburn one Friday afternoon on his way back to Abingdon, Moon stopped at the shopping center to pick up some batteries for his tape player and to get a haircut at Jack Sinclair's. A long, narrow room with four barber's chairs on the left and on the right a number of padded chairs for those waiting for a haircut met Lunamin's eyes as he peered in. Not all of the chairs for those waiting were full—about as good as he could expect just before the weekend. He decided to go in even though one of those waiting for a haircut was Rod Mashburn.

Jack Sinclair's eyes met Moon's and he smiled hello. "You haven't been in for awhile."

"I've been busy at the mine."

"Uh-huh. Counting all that money," Jack laughed.

Sinclair had inquisitive gray eyes that seemed to pierce a person's protective defenses. As usual, Jack was engaged in conversation with those in the chairs in front of him as well as with the subject of his tonsorial attentions seated in his raised chair. Jokes and political comments filled the air.

Moon always marveled at how Jack could keep up continuous conversation and cut hair so expertly at the same time. He never seemed to make an unnecessary motion. Moon wished he could mine coal with as little wasted effort as Jack used in cutting hair. It was worth waiting a little for the expert rather than trusting himself to one of the other barbers.

As Moon eased himself into an empty chair to wait, Sinclair greeted him with a question, "How's the mining business, Moon."

"Not bad, Jack, not bad … the coal's movin' and the price is right."

"Uh-huh. I'm almost tempted to start coal mining myself." A voice from down the line of chairs interjected itself.

"There's easier ways to make money, Jack. Besides, we wouldn't want to lose a good barber. You're a skilled artist. Coal mining's dirty business. Just ask Moon."

Moon turned to look at Rod Mashburn. Except for his long red hair reaching down within inches of his shoulders and his well-tailored suit and matching tie, Rod could have been mistaken for Moon's brother. Perhaps that was part of what irked Lunamin so about his cousin. He thought of some of the easier ways Rod was acquiring wealth and congratulated himself that he was getting dirty with real dirt that everybody could see and not fouling hims lf with illegal dirty operations like those Mashburn engaged in.

"At least this coal dirt will wash off. We may get dog dirty minin' coal, but that dirt washes off easy, Rod " he responded.

Rod made a face and grinned, "That so, Moon? You should see the soap I use."

Changing the subject, Moon turned to Jack. "How's the paintin' goin'? You painted any more waterfalls?"

"No, been doing portraits. Getting pretty good. You should let me do your portrait sometime. Give it to Susan for her birthday or Christmas."

"No time for that, Jack."

"Who says she'd want to hang that up in her Abingdon mansion anyway? It might not fit in with her decoration scheme," Rod interjected, grinning broadly when Moon glared at him and clinched his fists as the others in his audience laughed. Moon's reaction suggested that violence might erupt.

"You shouldn't take Rod seriously, Moon. You know how he loves a joke," Jack tried to smooth things over with humor. "I hadn't realized that Rod was such an expert on artistic matters."

"Sure, cousin Rod's an art expert. And he's always been a comedian. A regular Bob Hope. A real clown. All he needs is a funny nose."

When his turn came, Moon eased himself into Jack's chair, grateful that Rod had left as soon as his hair was cut. He and Jack were just about the only ones left in the shop. Moon was glad. He didn't want any more conversation about Susan—especially from Rod.

"How long do you think coal prices will stay high?"

"Don't rightly know, Jack. I hope it's a little longer. Lunar Minin's doin' okay, but we sure could stand a little more success. We ain't spoiled yet. The coal business ain't that good, but I sure won't complain. I'd give it a couple of years more anyway."

"Uh-huh. That cousin of yours seems to be making money, Moon."

"Rod, you mean. Reckon he is. Don't pay to inquire too closely into how he does it, though."

"Uh-huh. Rumor has it he's got a big farming operation. Has some of it underground still, under lights. High grade stuff, they say."

"Don't doubt it, but I'd rather get my dirt diggin' coal."

"Uh-huh. Rumor also has it the high sheriff's getting his cut." "I'd say you hear pretty good rumors. It's almost enough to tempt a fellow to get into politics to cramp Rod's style." "Thinking about a political career, Moon?"

"Not me. Some people's been pushin' me a little is all. I don't have time for it."

"You'd have my vote." "Thanks, Jack."

On the drive back to Abingdon, Lunamin thought about the prospect of seeking a political post. He might be able to do some good. He might stop a little of the drug trade, maybe enough to put a crimp in Rod's business, but he didn't like to think about what he would have to do to be elected. Besides, it might be dangerous to cross Rod in a way to affect his livelihood.

GLADYS

For several years Moon was faithful to Susan despite having temptation thrown in his path. His faithfulness could not be entirely attributed to his moral character. He was too busy making a success of Lunar Mining to allow his attention to stray elsewhere very much. He paid little attention even to his son, who was too small to throw ball or hunt or do any of the other things that Moon conceived of doing with a son. Having moved them to Abingdon to escape the wilderness and be with her high school chums, Susan had developed a sense of Moon's neglect of her in short order, a sense of victimization encouraged by her friends, who used these feelings to justify their own extramarital flings.

Some time after Lunar Mining had become a multi-million dollar company, Hugh Beverley called Moon on a day when Lunamin was particularly upset about Susan's lack of interest in accompanying him on an outdoor excursion to Hanging Rock.

"Moon, you should allow yourself a little time for fun." "Hugh, I've got to make money while the price of coal is high."

"You know Fred can take care of things for a few days without blinking an eye."

After considerable persuasion and an explanation of the tax deductibility of the trip, Lunamin agreed to attend his first coal-mining symposium on the Gulf Coast—in Mobile, Alabama.

Some weeks later, George Landsetter's surprise must have shown on his face. What he saw when he climbed aboard Delta Flight 104 from Mobile to Atlanta took him aback. It seemed to him that half the money men in the coal fields were on board, all accompanied by strikingly beautiful women.

A grin spread across George's face as he surveyed the scene. The many familiar faces whose eyes met his looked a bit uneasily past him at first, but they relaxed when George began to talk to Moon. He saw John Oxnard, Hugh Beverley, Dave Wrangle, Blalock Mullins, Dave Blackmun, Dab Whacker—why, this seemed to be a special coal operators' flight.

"Do bears live in the woods," thought George, "I have a hold on you fellows now."

"Hello, Moon, I'm surprised to find you here. I thought you fellows always flew on chartered planes. Who's your pretty friend?"

Moon squirmed a little uncomfortably but collected himself to introduce his companion.

"Our charter had engine trouble. Gladys, this is my cousin George Landsetter from Southwest Virginia. George, this is Gladys Stayskill."

"It's a pleasure to meet you, George." "Likewise, Gladys."

"What are you doin' in Mobile, George?"

"I've been at a reclamation meeting, Moon, figuring out ways to make surface miners' lives difficult " George joked.

"Lots of luck, cousin, you people sure know how to pick a place to hold a convention."

"Sure we do. But what about you and all these others? What kind of convention have you been having?"

"We've been to a coal symposium, cousin, trying to find ways to combat all the horrible things you guys foist upon us, but I reckon you could also say we've been hidin' from the troubles of modern life by takin' a dip or two in the waters of the Gulf."

"That sounds like mighty pleasant work, Moon. Have you been helping my cousin Moon with the convention, Gladys?"

The woman beside Moon was beautiful, neither blonde nor redhead. Her brown hair had touches (they looked natural) of both auburn and a lighter color. Her eyes were hazel, tending toward blue. Her conservative gray jacket set her figure off well. George could tell she was well enough endowed above the waist, and two shapely legs appeared beneath the gray travel skirt of her suit.

"Yes, George, I think you could say that I've lent a helping hand. Why, just last night, Everett said that I was helping him greatly improve his management style."

"Well, I'm glad Moon can find such good help. Glad to have met you, Miss Stayskill."

Tired from non-stop meetings, conversations over beer, and a lack of sleep, George found his seat in the back of the plane and sat down, feeling a bit left out. It seemed to him he was the only man there without a beautiful woman beside him.

It took Moon a little time to recover his composure after George's appearance, but Gladys immersed herself in a magazine article about Pre-Columbian civilization so that Moon wouldn't feel the need to make conversation. She was intelligent as well as beautiful, Moon thought. He remembered how surprised he had been when he had found that she not only had a college degree,. She had a master's degree as well. Brains to go with all that beauty.

She wasn't the sort of woman that Moon was familiar with and not what he had been expecting when Hugh Beverley suggested that Moon should join the coal miners' group on their Gulf excursions— coal mining symposia, Hugh termed them, quite tax deductible.

Reluctantly, grudgingly, Moon had agreed to join the group.

"I don't know whether or not I can arrange to leave my operation right now."

"Don't give me that lame excuse, Moon. Acie and Fred can handle anything that comes up and you know it."

That first time Hugh made the necessary telephone calls. Moon's life was about to undergo a great transformation.

Lunamin Mining Company had been borne on the wave of rising coal prices to riches beyond Lunamin's most expansive imaginings when he returned from Vietnam. Moon felt that he had to take two baths a day just to keep from being one of the filthy rich. Joining the surface coal operators' group, The Old Dominion Surface Miners, and marrying Susan had all been Lunamin's steps toward a new life style.

Soon he had also found himself a father, and then he had bought a place in Florida at Susan's demand. "After all," she told him, "All my social set (wives of other surface miners) now have winter homes there," she argued. She had to have a Mercedes to keep in Florida, one that was red rather than cream-colored like her Virginia Mercedes.

Moon never had cared much for Florida as a steady diet, even though he did like to fish on the warm winter days. All his acquaintances had fishing yachts. His miner friends were already jaded with their new lifestyle and were looking for other excitements to match their newly fatted pocketbooks. Lunamin did not buy a boat and would not buy Susan a second mansion in Florida. Her complaints did not move him. She had to content herself with a rather large four-b droom townhouse.

"I don't like Florida," Moon offered as an explanation.

"That's not the point. Almost all of our friends have large homes here. Why must I be embarrassed?"

"If havin' a large townhouse for a few weeks' use a year embarrasses you, then you need to think more about where you come from—where I come from."

"You still haven't washed off the mountain dirt."

"No, I sure ain't. Don't intend ever to wash that clean."

Other kinds of ostentation Lunamin rejected also. He had made his statement to society. He had let them know he was somebody. He didn't have anything left to prove to Susan, her family, and his friends. His self-assurance had grown with success. It had increased both his willingness to confront Susan's materialism and whetted his desire for new experiences and new challenges.

Still, he was fairly cautious about what challenges to accept. He did not heed many invitations to squander his money, even though he did make some fairly aggressive investments in stocks and bonds. He invested in new technologies, but Moon avoided the big poker games held at the Inn in Wise. He heard about them from Acie, who sat in for some of the big betters when they wanted to leave the table but not the game. It was hard for Moon to believe what Acie told him.

"Fifty thousand on one hand? Dab Whacker must've lost what little sense he had."

"Lots of bourbon, cigar smoke, and big stakes—that's what all them boys like."

"Sure would hate to lose fifty thousand on one hand."

"Shit! That ain't nothing, Moon. T'other week I saw ninety thousand change hands on one deal—now that's real money."

"Too rich for my blood. I've got too many things to buy. It ain't easy supportin' Susan's lifestyle—a mansion here, a vacation home in Florida, a Mercedes here, a Mercedes there—they add up. Sometimes it feels like she spends money as fast as I can bank it. Can't afford any poker losses, Acie."

"Now that coal's goin' ninety dollars a ton, cousin, we can afford lots of things, but you're talkin' sense. I'd as soon eat rotten eggs as lose that much money on a poker hand."

When they stayed in Florida, Moon went fishing in the Gulf whenever opportunity offered in the guise of a friend seeking company on a fishing expedition, and Moon had offers several times a week, but he did not want to sp nd all of his time fishing. Bridge playing filled a great deal of his time. He had learned to play bridge at Susan's insistence so that she could have a partner for afternoon and nightly bridge games. With a little practice and some tutoring, Moon had become a passably proficient bidder. At the play of the hand, Moon quickly became more than passable. He became expert—so good that his partners were always ready to forgive him for any mediocre bidding as long as he ended up playing the hand.

Lunamin's bridge prowess pleased Susan. She encouraged him to play more frequently.

"I wish you would play bridge with me more often, Everett. You're a good partner."

"Thanks, Susan. I'm glad to please you, but bridge playin' all day can't replace being in the out-of-doors for me. Flying back and forth to Florida keeps me up-to-date with Lunar Mining, but it doesn't allow for much time in the woods. Besides that, all that time in the air gets old."

Fishing and bridge playing did not sufficiently occupy his time. Restless, he traveled around Florida from the Keys to the Panhandle when he wasn't flying back to Southwest Virginia to oversee the mining operations. He spent a great deal of his time thinking about spring in Southwest Virginia. Moon missed the seasons. Palm trees and palmettos didn't change color.

He remembered the mountains around Winding Fork coming alive in the spring. First, the yellow witch hazel blooms, then the white sarvis, the violet redbud, the white dogwoods, and the golden and orange flame azaleas in quick succession—finally mountain laurel and rhododendron.

Spring in the mountains also meant spring gobbler hunting for Moon. He recalled leaving for the woo s before first light and sitting under the trees behind a natural blind. Listening to robins, and titmice, chickadees, and cardinals beginning to sing and occasionally hearing a grouse drum in the distance as he attempted to lure in a gobbler with his slate hen call. Moon could do a fair hen call without the aid of a slate call, but his slate call tired less easily than he did.

Moon was always happy to leave Florida's warm winters for the cold springs of the Virginia mountains. After Lunar Mining had become a going concern, though, Moon had a good deal of time that he could use if he wanted some recreation. So his protests to Hugh Beverley about having to work were not accurate.

For diversions other than large-stake poker games and other similar displays of new money such as multiple Mercedes, ODSUM members relied primarily upon Hugh Beverley, their favored lawyer, who had invested heavily in their coal operations, to be their guide to new delights. Among those that Beverley devised were trips to the Gulf Coast on chartered planes in order to participate in what were termed coal symposia, purportedly designed to keep the miners abreast of the latest research and practices in surface mining.

Once the entire crew of jovial pleasure seekers had boarded their chartered plane, the flight took a rather circuitous route to the Gulf by way of New York City, where they would meet the stunningly beautiful women whom Hugh Beverley had enlisted from the names that had been provided by his New York acquaintances. After becoming appropriately companioned, the group took off again for Mobile or some other Gulf destination. During the flight, over food and drinks (caviar and champagne for those who desired them—or bourbon and barbecue as Moon and some others preferred) the pairs rapidly got to know each other.

Only the mornings of these conferences were devoted to lectures and workshops, however. After their working lunch, the participants had the rest of the day and the evenings for whatever activities they wished to pursue. It was on one of these trips that Moon had met Gladys Stayskill, a five-foot six, reddish-blonde brunette from Bismarck, North Dakota. She didn't tell Moon much about herself in the beginning.

"There's not really much to tell," Gladys had asserted. "I was abused by a father too prone to drink and a mother who looked the other way. Education offered me a way out—first at the local community college and then at the state university. I went to New York to work on my master's degree, but my need for funds and one of my classmates led me into extra-curricular activities. And here I am."

At first Lunamin was lost in admiration of her body. "You're my Marilyn Monroe, Gladys."

"I don't want to be that. I'm glad you find my body attractive, but I have a mind as well. I want to know what a surface miner does." Lunamin didn't require much encouragement. It wasn't long before Gladys had received a crash course in surface mining, even though she had never seen a D-12 or a D-18 bulldozer or a front-end loader and really didn't know the great virtue of a six-foot seam of high-grade metallurgical coal. It didn't take her much figuring, though, to estimate that eleven hundred tons of coal a day at fifty to ninety dollars a ton added up to quite a bit of money.

"You must be a wealthy man, Everett Lunamin."

"I'm on my way to becomin' one, I hope."

The days and nights that Moon spent with Gladys on the Gulf Coast forced upon him a different perspective on life. Though he could not yet describe what he was learning, Lunamin became aware that this woman who had entranced him had a strong ethical sense combined with an active aesthetic view.

Whatever she did, Gladys liked to do in style, Moon noted, and he had the money to give her the style she wanted. Good foods, good wines—Moon had to work hard to cultivate a taste for wine, because his palate had been trained on corn liquor homebrew, the moonshine made from it, and bourbon. Fine wines and strolls in the moonlight in formal dress were new to him. He didn't particularly like dressing up in a dinner jacket, but he did like Gladys and the life that went with the dinner jacket.

He did express some doubts. "Gladys, I'm not sure that I want to give up bourbon."

"You don't have to do that, Moon, but a little wine with dinner won't exclude bourbon before or after dinners. Though I think you might try a whiskey sour every now and then rather than always drinking bourbon on the rocks."

Before he had met Gladys, Lunamin had not considered that he needed to dress up quite as much as some of his colleagues on these Gulf Coast excursions. She changed his mind about the necessity of formal dress. Once their wedding was done, Susan had never been able to turn Moon to her way of thinking and get him into formal wear, but Gladys made her case in such a way that he agreed without much protest to formal dress when she requested it.

"Everett, money brings with it a social responsibility. The Germans say, 'Kleiden machen leute.' Clothes make the man. They don't, but a great many people think that they do. The sensible way to handle that perception is to make a statement for the benefit of those misguided souls. It doesn't mean that you've given up your principles. You've just adopted some camouflage. You know, when you go out to hunt you wear camouflage. I don't like hunting, but the analogy's a good one, because in social gatherings you're engaged in a kind of hunting."

"Gladys, you shouldn't condemn hunting. It's not all bad. I can see your point, though."

Moon had to admit that what she said made good sense. Overcome by the force of her persuasion and her beauty, he soon cut a dashing figure in a white dinner jacket.

Because Gladys quickly decided that Moon was a likable fellow, both literally and figuratively head and shoulders above the majority of her clients despite his being both socially and intellectually naïve, she concluded that it was her responsibility and would also be her pleasure to show Moon how to live well but wisely. She did not take every dollar she could squeeze from Lunamin, but she did encourage him to spend appropriately.

"It's not always how much you spend Everett. Sometimes you can obtain high quality for less money than you might pay for lower quality. Using money well requires study."

"I'm not sure I understand what you mean."

"You understand cars. You have a Mercedes, you say. Why did you buy it rather than another make? The name connoted quality to you. Were they worth the money?"

"I reckon. I bought them to please Susan. I don't drive them. I prefer my Camry.

"Why?"

"It handles better, it's more trouble free, and it costs less." "There, you've proved my point. I'd say the money spent for the Camry gives far better value than that which you spent for a Mercedes. But I wouldn't have you buy a small compact rather than a Mercedes or a Camry just to save money."

Gladys became determined to show him how to use his money. She insisted that he learn to spend his money to get the best service, the best that life had to offer. It had not occurred to Moon before that spending several hundred dollars on a meal was part of the good life, but he gradually became accustomed to the pleasures of wines gently savored instead of white liquor gulped down to put fire in his belly. Gladys insisted on savoring her meals and her men, and Lunamin became determined to meet her standards.

Everett Lunamin had never been one to savor. He had in fact been a gulper of the first rank. With Gladys instructing him, Moon gradually began to understand and believe what Gladys was trying patiently to show him—that life should be squeezed as hard and as long as one can squeeze the juice from the grape, not gulped nor stinted but savored zestfully.

Gladys was greatly pleased by the aptness of her pupil. She liked being the teacher of this tough, hungry man from the hills. Whenever her friends teased her about having a hillbilly lover, Gladys laughed.

"Girls, there is a diamond in the rough as well as black gold in the hills that Moon comes from. I've staked my claim. I'm mining."

In bed, Gladys also introduced Moon to a tivities that he had not considered highly desirable before—even some that he had not known to exist. His sensory apparatus underwent a major assault during his first weekend with Gladys, who gradually taught him that pleasure delayed is pleasure enhanced. When they first went to bed together, Gladys insisted on undressing him before he undressed her, and she took her time in the process, running her hands through his hair and over every part of his body as she did. Only then did she let him undress her.

After they were completely disrobed, she led him to their shower and had him take a shower with her. Their shower completed, they dried each other. Then Gladys dropped down on the soft carpet in front of Moon and gave him a kiss unlike any he had known before and, as his passion grew, led him to their bed. As they lay together on the bed, she would not let him enter her immediately but instructed him to kiss her breasts, her belly, and her back. Then she again took him in her mouth. Only when she sensed that he was nearing a climax did she allow him to enter her, and even then she required him to remain quiet until his passion had subsided a little.

Finally, she allowed him to move to a climax such as he had never experienced.

"Gladys, I didn't know sex could be like this."

"Just remember, Everett, life needs to be slowly savored."

The next few days and nights taught Moon that he had not been living life fully and that amassing wealth was not so enjoyable as spending it could be."

"Moon, baby," she said to him on the trip back to New York, "a man of your position needs some culture."

By this time, Lunamin had developed more than a casual lust for Gladys. He had begun to question ideas he had always accepted without question. He wondered why he felt such a strong passion for this woman. She termed herself a student and a professional escort, but almost every man he counted a friend would call her a whore. In fact, that term often came up in his conversations with the other men who traveled to New York to meet girls from the high-priced escort service that Hugh Beverley used. Moon didn't use the word and didn't allow anyone else to use it when Gladys was the topic of discussion.

Gladys awed Moon. He thought of her as a princess. He began to wonder whether his relationship with Susan was any less a monetary transaction than his payments to Gladys. Without the money he had made and continued to earn, he would never have been allowed into the Stanard family. Thoughts of this kind were unsettling to Lunamin, who had never been one to question his own system of values. His desire for Gladys was prompting Moon to examine his life and scrutinize his preconceptions about women and life in a way he had never done before.

Lunamin simply could not think of Gladys as a common call girl. She was not in any way ordinary, and she seemed far less mercenary than Susan and her friends. Gladys' opinion was becoming more important to him than the opinions of his friends and the preconceptions that he had acquired growing up in the mountains. He wanted to please her. If she thought that he needed culture, then he thought that it would be worthwhile to acquire some.

"Your credentials impress me, Gladys. You lead me to the culture, honey, and I'll sop it up."

Gladys took Moon at his word. She had more than a passing interest in this handsome Midas from the hills. She took on the role of Pygmalion. Though he was already flesh and blood, Moon became her ivory statue into which she hoped to breathe new life. She reminded him of what he had said as she handed him a reading list \which owed a great deal to Adler's great books library but was pruned and tailored to emphasize books that would appeal to an active man.

"Everett, read the books on this list. These writers have thought deeply about the meaning of human experience. That's why their words are called great books. I've added a few contemporary novels and books about good dining and other social skills that will b useful to you.

You don't need to read them all at once. Just take your time and we can discuss them when you want."

Moon could see she was serious. "All right, Gladys. I'll try. I've never been a great student, but I'll try."

Later, when Lunamin had time to consider the change in his life, he thought it strange that he should have learned so much about life from a girl with an escort service, but then Gladys was not just anybody's girl, as she firmly told him.

"I try to get top value for my money, but I give top value for what I earn. I guess you could say that I think that anything worth doing is worth doing well. I'll bet the originator of that old adage would be a bit surprised to find me applying it to my situation, but I do believe that I perform a valuable service. You may not realize it, but I don't necessarily spend the night or go to bed with my clients. In fact, you're special. And you know, Everett Lunamin, that I don't come cheap, even for those whose company I really enjoy."

Moon had to admit that $1000 a day wasn't cheap, but whenever he recalled his moments with Gladys, especially the moments of lovemaking, he knew that he would have to have her company at any price. She had tutored him in eroticism and life. She had opened possibilities of pleasure and living that he had not imagined to exist.

Like many other men, Moon had looked upon sex as a stab in the dark. It seemed an activity that provided a moment's release from self, accompanied by intense pleasure followed by a deep sense of loss and guilt, feelings he did not like to admit to himself and certainly did not voice to his friends.

Back in high school, with a girl named Karen, he had made his first venture into sex, pretending to be experienced but relying on what he had observed in the barnyard and what he had heard men and other boys joking about. The wisdom that he had accumulated from these sources was sufficient to insure that he had provided mechanical protection against disease and pregnancy and to accomplish the deed of defloration but not to provide him with much control or either Karen or him with much pleasure.

"Is that all there is to it?" Karen had asked afterwards.

"Why sure, Karen, what more could there be?" he had assured her, even though he had been wondering much the same thing.

"If that's true, I think I'd just as soon stick to kissin' and pettin' from now on," Karen had mused. "I can't see there's any more pleasure in goin' all the way. And I might get pregnant."

Moon had not entirely agreed with her conclusion but had preserved his ego by maintaining an air of expertise, "You can't get pregnant. I took care of that. I used something."

Nothing much had happened with the prostitutes in Vietnam to change Mo n's self-centered perspective on sex, although these experiences had made him realize how little he had known previously about the ways of obtaining sexual pleasure. Lucky Martial had advanced Moon's knowledge of sexual pleasure a great deal more, but even after years of marriage to Susan he had remained a comparative novice on the subject of what gives women pleasure. When he and Susan had begun to date again after his return from Vietnam, Lunamin was more knowledgeable about what pleasures he might expect from their sexual activities, but even after his affair in Vegas he was only somewhat better prepared for providing Susan with pleasure than he had been with Karen.

Looking back on his married life, Lunamin recognized that this might have been part of the problem with his and Susan's married life. Despite her adamant determination to remain a virgin until marriage, Susan had a very healthy libido. Marriage had opened the door to great sexual pleasure for her, but she remained unsatisfied with the quantity and quality of the sexual adventures that Moon provided her.

By the time he had come to realize this, however, he felt it might already be too late to do their marriage much good. He now understood the lack of depth in his feelings for Susan. As a result of his affair with Gladys, Moon had finally discovered that his had been a marriage formed more out of imagined passion and social considerations rather than a marriage founded on love.

Unused as he was to examining his life, Everett Adamo Lunamin found these thoughts very disturbing.

Reflecting on his marriage now, he considered that it had been and still was as much of a monetary transaction as his relationship with Gladys. The major difference between the two relationships was that society had sanctioned his business transaction with Susan and not his tryst with Gladys. He and Susan had already grown apart—Moon hanging on to Susan out of habit and his belief that she confirmed his rise in social status, a desire not to shock the folks, a need to adhere to biblical injunctions against divorce, and a sense of obligation to holding the marriage together for their son, Andrew.

Unhappy at what she perceived as Moon's neglect of her and his inability to satisfy her desires completely, Susan had found what she wanted outside of their marriage, Moon suspected. But she stayed with him on account of the same social considerations that had directed Moon and because she wanted the lifestyle that he provided her. His new perspective allowed Moon to conclude that Susan was at heart as much or more of a prostitute than Gladys or Lucky Martial. Only society sanctioned Susan's prostitution.

After Andrew's birth, Susan had gone back to her tobacco and marijuana habits, he felt sure. Although she took great pains to conceal her relapse from Moon, she slipped on rare occasions. He was almost certain she was smoking again. Almost all of the time she was careful not to give in to these habits in their home—certainly never when Moon was home. But occasionally he would find a cigarette butt in an ashtray. When he asked Susan about it, she always claimed that one of her bridge circle had left it. "You can't expect my bridge circle to quit smoking just because you insist that I do," she would tell Moon.

In her efforts to conceal her activities, though, she was not entirely successful. Odors linger in clothes, and Moon sometimes thought he detected the taste of tobacco when they kissed. Her behavior also sometimes aroused Moon's suspicions, but Lunamin could never find concrete evidence to support his belief that Susan was hiding things from him. He felt certain she was smoking pot and seeing other men,

but he had no proof. In rare moments, he thought that his guilty conscience was causing his suspicions. Besides, he had too much to do at Lunar Mining to try to keep track of Susan's every move. And he wasn't ready to hire a private detective to find out for him.

In fact, he concluded, it was b tter for him if Susan stayed occupied and didn't look too closely into *his* movements.

ALL POLITICS IS LOCAL

At a monthly meeting of ODSUM in the early summer, Dab Whacker asked for a couple of members who would be willing to run for the town council of Clintwood.

"I need some help. People are tryin' to close my operation in Clintwood."

"We have heard that you've been using too much explosive material in your blasting," B. G. Hooper admonished. "People on the Clintwood Town Council have been complaining to me. That's not the way to improve our public relations."

"Well, maybe so, but I'm a member of this here group, and I need some support."

Whacker was mining within the town limits, and his methods had prompted a great outcry from those living near his mining operation. The excessively large blasting charges used by Whacker were causing special concern. Cracked ceilings, cracked foundations, and roofs full of holes made by falling rocks had excited intense ire on the part of affected citizens, who were lobbying council members to pass an ordinance banning surface mining within the town limits.

For once, Moon was happy to be living in Abingdon. Obviously he could not be drafted to run for the Clintwood council. He could be called upon for financial support, and he might be expected to campaign for ODSUM's candidates, especially with his kin living in Clintwood, but he himself would not be placed in the public eye.

"I expect your help," Dab said in concluding his appeal. "No tellin' when you'uns will need my help."

Whacker paused and then for emphasis spit tobacco juice in the can that he held for that purpose. While he occupied himself with this chore, B. G. Hooper took the opportunity to encourage all of the members of the association to involve themselves in politics. Hooper agreed that they needed to come to the aid of Whacker even though they might object to some of the methods he had been using.

"We need to have some of our people on the Clintwood Town Council and all of the other town councils in our area. Fairly popular men are needed," B. G. noted. "Especially at the local level, you need people who are well-thought of by those who know them best."

After a lengthy discussion, the group agreed that Dave Wrangle and Blalock Mullins would run for the Clintwood council. The discussion did not end there, however. B. G. Hoop r argued that they needed to think in larger terms, to look ahead to the next election of delegates for the Virginia legislature.

"Not that I think it unwise to attempt to elect town council members favorable to our cause. Not at all," B. G. argued. "We simply can not stop at that level. We need to put up some candidates for the state legislature to help pass favorable legislation and to head off legislation designed to control surface mining.

"We need delegates and senators in Richmond to look after our interests. Take this push to tax our coal for highway money, for instance. We need somebody there to fight that. We need people who can talk to those from the eastern part of the state and present our case effectively. That should be a major part of our campaign. Better representation in Richmond. Everybody we know laughs bitterly when they say Virginia stops at Roanoke. Our interests and the public interest must be seen to be one and the same."

The members present thought that B. G. made good sense, but there was no agreement about what person to put forward. They did agree that they should try to have candidates favorable to their association on both the Democrat and Republican tickets. That way they couldn't lose. B. G. took advantage of this agreement to suggest prospective candidates.

"I think we should try to place Hugh Beverley on the Republican ticket and Everett Lunamin for the Democrat ticket. I feel sure that Beverley will agree. I have already discussed the matter with him."

Everyone agreed that Hooper had made a good suggestion. "What about you, Moon? Would you be willing to be nominated for the Virginia Senate at the Democrat's convention?" Blalock Mullins asked.

Moon looked at his gray-haired, benevolent-looking questioner. He respected Blalock's common sense. He hesitated before making a tentative answer.

"I'm not a politician. I don't think I'd be a good choice. Why me?" "Because your family is heavily Democrat. Archibald MacCloud has been a red-hot Democrat for more years than I care to tell," Blalock argued.

"Besides, you can always lose to Hugh if you don't want to go to Richmond," B. G. Hooper added.

"You mean I should throw the election?"

"No. Just don't campaign hard and don't throw much money into your campaign."

"I don't like the idea of takin' a nomination under false pretenses." "Then campaign as hard as you want. We don't care whether you or Hugh gets the job—we just need one of you to get elected. If only one of you is nominated, we'll expect that person to try to win the general election."

After some more hesitation, Moon finally agreed to seek the nomination. He did not find the campaign very enjoyable even though he had a great deal more support than he had a right to expect. One reason that he had accepted the nomination was his desire to have a code of conduct for surface miners. He kept quiet about that, though. The main reason that he made an effort to win was his desire to put a crimp in the local drug trade. He hadn't forgot who had supplied Susan. He thought Rod still was slipping her dope. That had been his final thought before agreeing to run. Thinking like a politician, he didn't mention that when he accepted.

Archibald MacCloud worked long, hard hours to garner votes for Moon and encouraged the candidate to put more energy into the campaign than he had intended and to take greater enjoyment in the process than he had imagined he would muster.

"Democracy in action, boy, that's what we see here."

"I know, Papaw. I reckon I'm just not much of a politician. I don't care for baby kissin.' The main reason that I agreed to do this was an idea that I could cramp the style of Rod Mashburn and Sheriff Bo Mulberry. I'd like to end the easy access to pot that is a fact of life here, but I don't think that would make a good campaign issue."

Lunamin had to learn how to make a speech to a large audience. Despite his lackluster performance during the campaign speeches, Moon gathered a great deal of support. Archibald had considerable influence with the retired coal miners, and ODSUM members worked for him also. Moon himself relied on putting money into posters and other paraphernalia to show that he was a serious candidate. He made some speeches, and he improved with every speech, but it became obvious very quickly that Moon's oratorical skills needed improvement. The senatorial convention proved an exciting affair in spite of Moon's lackluster candida y. The delegates who gathered into the Clintwood High School gymnasium, thankful that the day was cool, displayed great enthusiasm for their respective candidates. Colorful banners proclaiming "Lunamin for the Laboring Man" and "Be Bold with Bolling" waved over the crowd to garner support for Moon and his opponent, Herbert Bolling.

Inspired by the crowd and their colorful banners, the introductory speakers managed to generate a great deal of enthusiasm for nominating a man to defeat whatever scurvy fellow the Republicans might nominate. Even Moon became caught up in the excitement of the event and made his best speech of the campaign.

"That's the best you've done," Archibald told him. "I reckon it just came upon me, Papaw."

To his great relief, Moon by two votes narrowly missed being chosen as the Democrats' candidate for the Virginia Senate. His defeat pleased Susan, who had not been at all supportive of his brief political career.

"It would be bad enough, Moon," she had nagged, "if you were running as a Republican, but you're trying to get the Democrats to nominate you. I think it's deplorable."

"Almost everybody in my family is a Democrat," he had answered, "You are just worried that I'd win and make a strong stand against the illegal drug trade."

Moon didn't admit to her that, for his own reasons, he agreed that it had been a mistake for him to seek the nomination, even though he might have done some good had he succeeded.

Hugh Beverley had succeeded in gaining the Republican nomination, so Moon felt an obligation to support him. Moon promised to throw all of his support to Beverley but insisted that his involvement in Hugh's candidacy be kept secret and that his aid be financial only. As far as the public knowledge went, he wanted to remain a Democrat. He didn't want Herbert Bolling's campaign or Archibald to know that he was supporting a Republican.

Politics in far southwestern Virginia, like that in much of the southern Appalachians, still showed the influence of the Civil War and its aftermath. Those who had supported the South during the war, the Hatfields, for example, tended to vote for Democrats. The McCoys had supported the North, and they tended to vote Republican. In the coalfields, this simple dichotomy of political issues was complicated somewhat because of the antagonism between those who supported labor unions and those who were adamantly non-union. Therefore, a McCoy who was a strong union man might become a Democrat voter. Archibald MacCloud was a Democrat by heritage and a confirmed union man—and therefore an ardent supporter of Democrat candidates. Moon saw no need to upset him over something that Moon did not care about deeply.

ODSUM managed to put part of its local plan into action. Only Blalock Mullins achieved a position on the Clintwood Town Council, but he managed to fend off the ordinance forbidding surface mining within the town by agreeing to an ordinance that strictly regulated blasting. That didn't mollify Dab Whacker altogether, but it satisfied the majority of the association's members, who thought but did not express openly their belief that Whacker was being unreasonable and giving them all bad publicity.

"I got the best deal I could, Dab," Blalock told him. "Now you just start using a little more common sense in setting off those charges. You'll be doing us all a favor."

Whacker grudgingly agreed. "I've just about finished that job anyway," he muttered.

Hugh Beverley became a strong voice for surface miners in the Virginia Senate. He could not prevent the passage of a coal-haul tax, but he did keep it to the minimum and wrote into the bill that the money raised would go to upgrading roads that were used for hauling coal.

To Moon's great relief, his monetary support of Hugh remained secret. He resolved not to become involved in politics further no matter how much encouragement he received. Allowing himself to be persuaded to seek the nomination because of a desire to deal with the drug trade was foolish he now believed. His brief experience with politics had shown him how much public scrutiny it entailed. He feared that he had too many secrets that might become public.

FALL COLOR

It was about two-thirty on a Friday afternoon in early October when George heard the call on his two-way radio.

"There's been an accident at Lunar Mining's Rubyrock job out at Fox Gap. Get out here in a hurry. Get the Coeburn and Black Mountain rescue squads on the way, too, if you can."

George turned his truck around and headed for Fox Gap. As he wound up the road from Guest River to Possum Gap, he couldn't help noticing the beauty of the leaves beginning to turn red and yellow at the higher elevations. The sourwood trees were already a deep maroon, the tulip poplars a bright yellow, and the maples were showing their more pastel yellows and pinks. The woods surrounding him battered his eyes with these brilliant colors. Nowhere else in the world but the southern Appalachians could a person find such glorious natural color.

Above, in the afternoon sun, a kettle of broad-winged hawks was circling ever higher above the Gap, catching the warm afternoon thermals to circle upward before gliding south down the long ridge to catch another thermal and rise again on uprising air. Marveling at their soaring ability as he watched them out of his rolled-down window, George heard the harsh scream of a protesting red-tailed hawk flushed from its hunting perch, a dead snag near the road. The sun shining on the bird's russet tail seemed to set it afire.

This doesn't seem like a day for an accident," George thought, "It's too beautiful."

Looking about him at the scars of surface mines that were just visible on the slopes around through the protective screen of oaks, hickories, maples, poplars, sourwood, and beeches, he feared the loss of that beauty when the leaves began to fall.

"There's just too much beauty being spoiled here, I reckon. Maybe the mountains are fighting back," he thought ruefully.

Wailing sirens interrupted his thoughts. George found a pull-off at the next curve and made room for the rescue vehicles that passed him at top speed, tipping a bit as they took the curve. In the cabs he could see the eager looks of the youths on their way to the mine site. This kind of excitement was what many of them thrived on, seemed to live for. No doubt about it, though, they did good work needed by the community.

Dust still lingered in the air when George reached the strip job. The rescue squad was at work collecting the body when George reached them. Moon and a couple of other men stood over the body of what seemed to have been a young man at one time, although it was difficult to tell much about him beyond that.

"Here's another toe!" yelled one of the rescue squad over his shoulder as George walked slowly up to Moon and the others standing with him. When Landsetter saw the body, he felt that he was going to throw up, but he managed to hold back the urge by focusing on Moon's face.

"Who had the bad luck, Moon?"

"Shorty Burk, Moon muttered, "I blame myself. I shouldn't have let him do it. He didn't know enough. Put in too much charge, got careless, and blew himself all to hell and back. I sure don't like to look at this. Reminds me too much of Nam."

"Why'd you let him set the charge, Moon?"

"Well, all the men were hell-bent to get to the Clintwood game tonight. Shorty practically got down on his knees and begged. We needed to have it done to be ready in the mornin.' So I let him. I reckon he was in a big hurry to get to that damn game too."

The thin, wiry man in a grimy shirt and blue jeans standing next to Moon shook his head. George recognized him as Moon's foreman on this job, Poss McNew.

"Don't go blamin' yourself, Moon. Shorty should have knowed better. We shown him a dozen times how to set a charge. Warned him not to get careless. Ain't nobody else to blame."

Moon shook his head. "Thanks, but that don't make it easier, Poss. I've got to tell his woman. She's three months gone. I reckon that comes with the territory, though."

While Moon talked with the rescue squad, George wandered around the mine site, as much from force of habit as a desire to inspect. The fiery foliage of a group of sourwoods and hickories left alone toward the back edge of the job caught his attention. There was movement in the treetops. A couple of squirrels were moving about in the glowing leaves waving in a light breeze. Wondering where those trees are that they had come out from the woods on, George surmisd.

"You'll have to come down off of your high horses to get back to the woods, fellows," he silently told them. "Those trees that were your avenue have bit the bulldozer dust. They've bought it, boys, just like Shorty. You'd better get back to the woods or you'll be the victims of friendly fire, too. Don't forget it's hunting season."

As Moon drove back to Abingdon to pick up Susan for the Clintwood-Winding Fork football game, he could think of little other than Shorty's death. It seemed to him that Shorty could have been his younger brother. In fact, he had been closer to Shorty than to his brother Tom, who had not even come back to Winding Fork with Verna on her last trip before Moon was drafted. Tom was a college boy now, doing graduate work, and he and Moon had not been close since Tom had become a teenager and had picked up his father's attitude toward Moon, or as James Jenkins still sometimes derisively termed him, "Tom's hillbilly bastard brother." Like their father, Tom and his sister Serena had done their best to fit in to the California culture and forget their mountain roots, but maybe they were having second thoughts now that their half brother was a millionaire many times over and could send Verna money for trips back to Winding Fork any time she wanted.

Besides bringing back vivid memories of mangled bodies in Vietnam, Shorty's death forced Moon to consider the brevity of human existence. A young life snuffed out suddenly can cause even the most unreflective human being to pause and ask, "Who am I? What is the meaning of my existence?" Lunamin accepted deaths in Vietnam as a matter of course, but his time with Gladys had had a profound effect on him. Though not totally exempt from self-examination, Moon had not wasted long periods of time in his life in reflection about life's meaning before Gladys Stayskill had become a part of his life. Now Moon had come to consider his life from many different perspectives.

Perhaps the aim of his existence should not be simply to become as wealthy as possible in as short a time as possible, Moon considered. In fact, he was coming to the conclusion that wealth was not even an end in itself but was valuable only to the extent that it could help its owner achieve a more fulfilling life. If true, it followed that he could not justify his pursuit of wealth to gain and maintain his marriage with Susan, as it was not helping him achieve a fulfilling life. He did not wish to accept this logic, however, for it seemed to negate almost everything he had done since returning from Vietnam. Andrew seemed a shining exception.

As he and George had watched the rescue squad haul off Shorty's body, Lunamin had looked about him and shaken his head.

"It's a shame to lose Shorty—all this beauty around us. Death's no respecter of persons or beauty. We all get cut down. But Shorty was so young. It go s harder when you lose somebody so young, I reckon."

"True, Moon. It's hard to accept. But you saw lots of death in Vietnam."

"I did, George. And I lost some good buddies. But it didn't hit me so hard then. We learned to live with it. I reckon I've changed some since then."

"There are some things more important than money, cousin?"

Moon surprised himself and George by remaining silent and merely nodding. He had been thinking about what was truly important to him. Just a few years earlier he had been certain of the answers. Now he knew none.

THE GAME

The night was clear and cool—perfect weather for playing football. The field was even better lighted than Moon remembered it. The school had added several sets of lights since the days that he and George had scored their triumphs there. Still, they were not the only people there who recollected their athletic exploits.

He and George were called forth with some other former players from the area and honored as part of the introductory ceremonies. When the master of ceremonies read Achilles Shorty Burk's name, he said that, because of Burk's untimely death that afternoon, Achilles could not take his place among the football greats that were standing on the field. He asked for a moment of silence in honor of Achilles.

As they returned to their seat, Moon bought chilidogs and drinks at the concession stand for Susan and him. It was amazing how much better these tasted at a game than they did elsewhere. Moon had never thought much about that before.

"I was hungry, Sue. These hot dogs are real tasty."

"That's just because you didn't have anything for supper. You didn't get home in time."

"From the mining job to Abingdon is a long drive."

"You could've started earlier. Acie and Fred can handle things well enough when you aren't there. They're partners. You don't have to be at the mine every time a machine starts up. It seems to me you'd want to spend more time with your family."

Moon didn't respond to what sounded like an accusation. Changing the subject, he reminded her of what a big event this game between Winding Fork and Clintwood had always been.

"Suzy, do you remember how big the pep rally before this game was when we were in high school. You really stirred us up with your pre-game cheers."

"Those were exciting times."

High school football is a big event in Southwest Virginia, Moon thought. Going to the games is the thing to do on Friday nights. Rivalries between towns have high priority in community life. Beating a nearby town's team brings glory to the student athletes beyond what would be gained in another region of the country. George and Moon were heroes. Though Moon remembered his excitement in the days when George played end and Moon played quarterback for Winding Fork, he could not find much enthusiasm for the game that night.

Susan showed enough enthusiasm for both of them. She relived her old cheerleading days. She was dressed fashionably for a sports event. Her outfit was cut low enough to reveal ample bosoms, but to her chagrin, Lunamin seemingly paid no attention to her outfit. Moon felt depressed over the death of Shorty, who had also played football— but for Clintwood High School—almost a decade after Moon and George had starred for Winding Fork. Shorty had been an All-State Division A halfback. He had set school records, too, just like George and Moon.

The cheerleaders were performing with great energy before the kickoff.

"Moon, pay attention, those girls are doing a great job!"

"You sound as though you'd like to get out on the field with them."

"I sure would. Of course, I may not have quite the figure for it now. Having a baby doesn't do any good for the figure."

"That's been over for almost four years. And you didn't lose your figure. If you had, all those men wouldn't be gawking at you and that revealin' outfit. There's Earl over there with his tongue hanging out watching you."

"Why, Moon, I think you're jealous." "Just statin' facts, that's all."

When the cheerleaders lapsed into inactivity, there was another moment of silence for Achilles Shorty Burk. The second announcement of his death did not escape Susan, as had the first. Surprised, she questioned Moon.

"Didn't he work for you?" Susan asked. "Yeah. Blew himself up this afternoon."

"Why didn't you tell me? You never tell me anything. That's why you were late."

Moon didn't answer. He realized the truth of the accusation. He and Suzy didn't have much to talk about any more. The playing of the national anthem gave him a temporary respite. Just as it ended, he was again saved—this time by Earl, who came up to say he lo—mainly to Suzy, Moon guessed, seeing how Earl looked at her and threw his arm around her. He was surprised that Susan tolerated Earl's familiarity, even though she didn't appear to care for his brashness.

"Hey Moon, hey Susan. Honey, you sure are a sight to look at. Moon better be careful, or some of us young fellows will sneak you away from him."

"You're a case, Earl. I heard you have lots of girls panting after you since you started driving the Lunar Flash. I'll bet they're just dying to run their hands through that red hair of yours."

"Not in your league, Suzy. They're all minor league compared to you. What'd you want to marry old Moon for any way—just 'cause he's tall, dark, and handsome—not to mention filthy rich? You should've offered some of us poor boys a chance."

"Why, Earl, if I'd only known you first, who can tell."

"I thought I saw you with some young girls just a few minutes ago, Earl," Moon observed. Moon didn't want to let Susan think that she was the only object of Earl's attention. He didn't feel any jealousy, he told himself, but he didn't want Susan to think she was anything special for Earl.

"I reckon second best might have to do. See y'all later." "Earl's a real case, Moon."

"The way he leered at you, you'd better watch out for old Earl."

"Oh, Moon, Earl may be obnoxious, but he wouldn't hurt a flea." "Not sober—but Earl can get mean when he's been drinkin.'" "You could say that about half the men I know, you even."

Moon's discomfort at the direction the conversation had taken made the noise of the Clintwood fight song welcome to him. Soon after the kickoff, he was lost in memories of the Clintwood-Winding Fork games in which he and George had played. This game was exciting even though much of the excitement stemmed from fumbles, blocked punts, and interceptions. At the end of the first half, the score was tied 6 to 6.

As usual, Susan enjoyed the halftime ceremonies more than the game, and with rapt attention she watched the cheerleaders and bands perform while Moon went to buy more hot dogs and drinks at the concession stand. She was so engrossed in the spectacle in front of her that she did not notice George Landsetter sit down beside her. George didn't interrupt her pleasure before the band marched off the field.

"Do you miss your high school cheerleading, Suzy?"

"I guess I do, George. Do you miss being the football hero?" "No, Moon always enjoyed the attention we got more than I did."

At this point Earl Campbell appeared with a blonde in tow and sat down beside Georg .

"George, I want you to meet Daisy Drumheller. Daisy, this here's George Landsetter, my educated cousin. And this sexy lady is Susan Lunamin, the wife of another cousin."

Susan was polite to Daisy and Earl, but she continued her conversation with George.

"Did you know about Shorty Burk?"

"Yep. I was out at the mine site after the accident. Shorty was in bad shape."

"He was all tore up," Earl added. "They looked for around an hour and still he was missin' a toe and a finger."

"That's gruesome. I don't want to know the details."

"Old Shorty was a real hot halfback when he played for Clintwood, but he's run for his last touchdown," Earl philosophized.

"A poet wrote that athletic fame is a garland briefer than a girl's beauty," George added. "Shorty died young, but his football heroics were already being forgotten. He may have gained some lasting fame as a victim of a mining accident."

"That's morbid, George. I don't want to think about losing my good looks, even to become famous."

"I don't think you have to worry any time soon, Suzy, but you know all men (and women too) are mortal. Therefore Suzy Lunamin and George Landsetter are mortal and generally we show the signs of age before we croak."

"You could find another subject if you tried, George. Who was that pretty redhead I saw you talking to earlier?"

"She's just a woman I know named Heidi Leaves. She's the head of LEAPS, an environmental group that's working for more effective reclamation laws. I'm sure you've heard Moon and other ODSUM members discuss her in unflattering terms."

"She's too pretty to be a do-gooder. You can't fool me that easily. You've got your eyes on her." "Hard not too look at Heidi."

"When are you getting married, George?"

"If and when the right girl shows up, not before." "You always were the cautious type."

"It saves a lot of trouble."

"But you miss a lot of fun. You just wait. You'll get caught one of these days."

VIEWING

There was a big crowd at Purgation Burford's funeral home, a large brick edifice on the main street of Clintwood. Purge's large parking lot was completely full. They were all there for Shorty's memorial service. Purge didn't have any other funerals at hand. He was devoting his entire attention to Burk's funeral. Attired in a dark blue suit and tie, Purge was tall and thin, but stooped forward unctuously, as if to offer condolences even when he was not greeting a mourner.

Purge's freckled face and puffy cheeks would have given him a satirical countenance had he not managed somehow to render it doleful.

Purge was busy greeting the family and friends when the Lunamins appeared in the doorway. He quickly glided toward them to offer his sympathy.

Saying hello and shaking hands with Purge as he and Susan entered the funeral home, Moon made his way to the guest book and signed it for Susan and him. As he turned round, he spied George Landsetter standing nearby.

"How're you doin,' George?"

"Glad to see you, Moon. How come you're not out at the strip mine? Cousin, you're losin' money."

"Now, George, don't try to rile me. That's out of line here, and I'm not takin' the bait. You know that nobody's workin' at Lunar today. Besides, there're other things than money."

"I know. But I'm surprised to hear you admit it again. Maybe you're not as hungry as you used to be.'

"People change. Give me credit for bein' able to change a little."

Moon turned and began making his way through the crowd into the viewing room to talk to Shorty's family. A little surprised, George attentively watched Moon move slowly from Shorty's father and mother to his sisters and brothers, shaking hands with the men and hugging the women sympathetically. There seemed to be genuine emotion in Moon's condolences. He wasn't just going through the motions expected of him. Then a voice beside Landsetter broke upon his observations.

"How are you, George?"

He turned to find Susan Lunamin smiling at him. She was wearing another revealing outfit like the one she'd had on at the football game but more in keeping with this sad occasion—expensive, in good taste, but certainly revealing her excellent figure.

"Fine, Susan, how about you?

"Pretty well, George. Of course, I'm just a neglected wife. Moon spends all of his time at his mines. I've got lots of spare time on my hands."

That sounded like a hint to George, but he pretended that he hadn't understood it.

"I thought you spent a lot of time doing the Book Circle and the Garden Club, Suzy. I see your name in the *Coalfield Endeavor* all the time even though you live in Abingdon. I don't see how you'd have much time to miss Moon."

"Mother puts all that stuff in the *Coalfield*, George. You're obviously still a bachelor. If you had a wife, you'd know better."

"Guilty as charged. I haven't met the right girl yet."

"A handsome fellow like you shouldn't have trouble finding a girl. I'll bet all the young girls are after you. And that Heidi Leaves. It wouldn't surprise me if some of the married women had their eyes on you, too, George Landsetter."

"That's dangerous talk, Suzy. I don't want to get shot." "Be careful then, but I don't need to tell you that."

Just then Earl Campbell approached and shook hands with George as he leered at Suzy. She pretended not to notice and, after a brief hello, made her way into the viewing room.

"That's a fine piece of ass," Earl said. "Suzy does have a great figure."

"Hit's a shame the way Moon neglects her."

"Yeah, and I don't think that Susan is suffering the neglect patiently."

"Moon better watch out. Might be others wantin' to mine on his claim."

"Do you have any ideas along those lines?"

"Not me, George, it's bad luck to two-time kin. Almost as bad as havin' a screech owl call to you at midnight."

George laughed a little to himself at Earl's superstitious nature as he eased into the viewing room and made his rounds with the family. He thought that there was more truth in what Earl had said than he himself cared to admit, but George certainly wasn't going to be the illegal miner jumping onto Moon's claim. Even if he were tempted, he and Moon went back too far.

The funeral service was held at Purgation Burford's the next morning at eleven. Purge and his helpers quietly and efficiently ushered the mourners into the mortuary's large chapel. The Wellford Gospel Singers were setting the tone of the service by playing and singing *The Old Rugged Cross, Over Jordan, O Beulah Land*, and other traditional hymns. Lamb o' God Flannary sat in front with head bowed preparing himself to give the funeral sermon.

Before the sermon, Fred MacCloud and Pudge Phillips, Shorty's high school football coach, offered testimonials to Shorty's brief life. An elderly, heavyset man dressed in a plain black suit, Pudge dwelled on Achilles high school athletic achievements and noted how well liked by his teammates he was. "I never heard a fellow player say anything negative about Achilles," Pudge testified.

Fred described Shorty as a young man who worked hard and was well thought of by his coworkers and employers. "He was always ready to help out his friends," Fred declared.

"Shorty was like a lily of the field cut off before it has had a chance to bloom," Lamb o' God Flannary proclaimed as he began his sermon. "Brethren and sistren, ours is a brief existence at the longest. Shorty's was even briefer than most. Ours is not to question the will of the Almighty. He wanted Shorty with him to run some heavenly touchdowns. We don't need to grieve 'cause Shorty was washed in the blood of the Lamb. We don't need to cry. We should shout with joy. Shorty's gone to a better place than this. Shorty's part of God's angelic choir now, singing songs for sweet Jesus."

Moon listened to Flannary's sermon as well as he could, but his mind strayed as the sermon grew in length. He wondered how much he was to blame for Shorty's premature joining with the heavenly choir. He would be more careful in the future about giving his men responsibility before they were ready.

Susan had to nudge Moon when the Wellfords led the group in singing a closing hymn. As they all joined in singing *What a Friend We Have in Jesus*, Moon resolved that he would provide extra compensation beyond the insurance for Shorty's widow.

Lunamin concluded that nobody could be certain of the future. Something unexpected could happen to him. He decided he should make a greater effort to spend time with Susan and Andy, but at the same time he longed to spend some time with Gladys.

FESTIVAL

The Mountain Heritage Festival took place at Clintwood on a weekend in mid-October. Moon had spent considerable time persuading Susan to attend. She really did not decide to go until she learned that Angie Setton and some of her other friends living at the Abingdon Riviera planned to attend.

The Saturday of the festival turned out to be sunny but crisp, not too warm, an Indian summer day. Moon was looking forward to a day listening to traditional music and seeing high school friends. George was to pick up Serafina and Archibald to bring them to the fair grounds. They were to meet at the festival gate at noon and then have a traditional mountain meal together.

The early cool weather had turned the leaves of the poplars yellow and the maples red even at the lower elevations. The various shades of green, red, and yellow offered a spectacle of gorgeous color lording it over equally colorful but less gaudy roadsides dressed with the blues of asters and chicory and the whites of wild carrot, yarrow, and old man's beard. Even Susan responded to the beauty of the rampant colors spreading wildly along their route. She pointed and told Andrew to look at the pretty flowers and leaves.

"The good Lord's been usin' his paint brush, Andy," Moon added. "It certainly is beautiful now. It won't last long, though. The leaves will fall off and winter will show all the ugly scars," Susan continued. "Those scars support the lifestyle you like so much."

"They're still ugly."

At the local fairgrounds, they bought tickets to the festival and entered the gates. Andy ran to Serena and Archibald as soon as he saw them. They hugged their curly-haired great grandson as Susan went to look for her friend Angie Setton. The rest of them made their way to the booths where food was being sold. All of them except Andrew ordered a meal of ham, turnip greens, soup beans, and cornbread. Andy held out for a hot dog with chili and a soft drink, but he was quite willing to join his elders in eating stack cake with apple butter and sorghum molasses on it.

"This here's good eatin', Andy," Archibald praised. "You should try some soup beans and cornbread anyways. I 'member many's a time that's all we had to eat when I was your age. No ham or turnip greens to go with 'em. We was mighty happy come spring and we could go out and pick us a mess of poke or wild salat greens."

"What's wild salat greens, Papaw?"

"Herbs growin' wild. Things like cressy greens, wild mustard, narrow-leaved dock, speckled dock (some calls it spotted primrose), and dandelion mixed all together. Course p ke's different—have to boil it in two waters, pour the first off, and put some wild garlic with the second batch."

"Your Papaw had rather eat from my garden patch now, Andrew," Mamaw pointed out.

"In the old days we had to eat what we had. Didn't have nothin' but salted meat and leather britches most of the winter. Wild greens in the spring tasted mighty goo —'specially when we cooked 'em with a little fatback. Times was hard. Why, people used to talk about Squirrel Annie livin' under a rock ledge on High Knob just like a wild Injun."

"Why'd they call her Squirrel Annie, Papaw?"

"I reckon 'cause that's what she mainly lived on." Andy listened intently as Archibald continued.

"She lived under an old rock ledge the Indians used in the old days. Some say Annie was half Injun herself. She sure lived off the land. Squirrel stew was her specialty, but she didn't turn up her nose at groundhog and 'possum. I'll bet she'd eat skunk in a pinch."

"You like the stack cake, Andy?"

George laughed, seeing smudges of cake and apple butter around Andy's mouth.

"Yep," Andy mumbled as he filled his mouth with another bite.

After eating, they went to the grandstand to hear the musicians and see the cloggers doing their traditional but noisy dancing style. They also planned to take part in the cakewalks and opportunities for audience participation in dancing. Saying he would join them later, Moon left the others to go to look for Susan. He found her at the art exhibit talking to Rod Mashburn. Rod greeted Moon as he walked up to them.

"Howdy cousin, enjoying the Festival?"

"Sure am, Rod. Came to find Susan to go listen to the music. Ralph Stanley's about to perform a set."

"Moon, don't worry over me. I'm enjoying looking at arts and crafts. I don't want to listen to music all afternoon. I'll come find you later."

"Don't be too long. You haven't spent any time with Mamaw and Papaw." Moon unhappily did as she asked, angry, but unwilling to show his anger in front of Mashburn.

Susan remained silent but grimaced at Rod when Moon turned away.

When Moon climb d into the grandstand and found his group, the Sorghum Cloggers were p rforming their dance routine with fancy high steps and clicking heels. Mamaw, Papaw, George, and Andy were all enjoying watching the flying feet moving to the rhythms of the Happy Hoedowners' music.

"Where's Susan?" George asked.

"She says she's enjoyin' the arts and crafts."

Before George could ask any more questions, the master of ceremonies Wild Bob Bolling announced a cakewalk. George told all of them to get in line and bought them all tickets for the cakewalk at twenty-five cents apiece. As they moved about in the circle to the music, Andy was having a great time.

"What happens next, George," Andy asked excitedly.

"When the music stops, we stop too. The person that's standing at the place designated by the master of ceremonies wins the cake."

The boy was almost at the right spot when the music stopped. Andy had a hard time containing his excitement after that, so Moon took him in his lap until time for the next cakewalk. Andy was even more excited when Mamaw won the second cake.

"I hope it's as good as yours, Mamaw," Andy said hopefully. "Probably better. We'll save you a sample for your next visit." "Could I go home with Mamaw and Papaw, Pa?"

"I reckon so. We'll have to ask your ma."

"I think I want to sample that cake too," George laughed.

Following Serafina's success at the cakewalks, they went back to their seats and listened to the many musical groups that offered a combination of music brought from the British Isles, music of similar form created in America by generations of traditional singers, and twentieth-century ballads. The singers for the most part were unconscious bearers of the old tradition.

They and the majority of their audience made little distinction between a ballad written yesterday and one hundreds of years old brought from the British Isles by their ancestors and passed down from one generation of singers to the next. George was an exception because some cours s he had had in college had dealt with the British ballad tradition. So he could distinguish between the provenance of the thirteenth-century ballad *My Goodman* and that of another Child ballad *O Death*. He knew the old songs from the newcomers like the American nineteenth-century ballad *In the Pine* and the twentieth-century Dock Moran Boggs' ballad *The Wise County Jail*, but most of the audience and singers made no distinction. They simply enjoyed the music and the musicians.

"Many of those songs are centuries old," George advised. "They're still as good as the new ones," Archibald judged.

There were also some Bluegrass tunes, but all of the music was played with acoustic instruments.

"Papaw, did you know the mountain dulcimer is the only original Appalachian musical instrument?"

"What about the hammered dulcimer and the dobro Isaiah Timmons plays?"

"No, the hammered dulcimer comes from the Chinese and the dobro developed in Central Europe. It comes from the Slavs."

"No matter. I like 'em. And guitars and fiddles too—all but those electric screechers."

When the groups performed instrumental numbers for the pleasure of those in the audience who might wish to show off their dancing skills, Papaw MacCloud offered onlookers a sample of his skill in flatfoot dancing. The first time Serafina danced with him, but after that she refused.

"If you want to kick up your heels like some young'un, Archibald, go on. But I've made spectacle enough of myself."

After several hours of music, George told Moon that he and the folks ought to be heading home soon, and Suzy had to be found if her permission was needed for Andrew to go along to Winding Fork with them.

"I reckon you're right, but I've already tried. See what you can do."

George hesitated, then agreed strange. even though he thought the request "Okay, I'll go find her."

George went to look for Susan with some misgivings. If Moon was ready to let him do his wife hunting, his cousin must not be as concerned about her whereabouts as he ought to be. He knew that Moon was dissatisfied with Susan's lack of interest in his outdoor pursuits, but he thought now that the problem must go deeper. Susan was beautiful, but she was extremely materialistic and rather superficial, George thought. Maybe Moon was beginning to think that he had made a bad bargain—that his marriage no longer seemed a good deal.

Perhaps it even went beyond that. George was still puzzling over the matter when he found Susan and Rod Mashburn sharing cotton candy. Landsetter could not avoid noticing a hint of intimacy in their passing the candy back and forth while eating it.

"Susan, Moon asked me to find you. I'm going to take Archibald and Serafina home soon, and Andrew wants to go with them. Moon says Andy has to have your permission."

"Well, tell Andy I said it's all right."

"Don't you think you should say goodbye to Mamaw and Papaw?" "Tell them goodbye for me, George."

"Should I tell Moon where to find you or should I tell him you're on your way to the grandstand?"

"Tell him what you want."

"I don't want to tell him what's not true."

"Oh, all right. I'll come with you. It's been fun, Rod." "Sure has Suzy. Are you certain you have to go?"

"I'd better. Goodbye."

Susan and George didn't engage in much small talk as they made their way to the grandstand. George tried, but Susan seemed angry and in no mood to observe social niceties. She responded as briefly as possible.

"Suzy, did you know that these performers are part of a living tradition, that they for the most part don't make a distinction between their modern songs and those that scholars have traced back six or seven hundred years. These sing rs are bearers of a tradition that probably pre-dates the Magna Carta."

"How interesting."

George could not avoid recognizing her sarcasm, but he was not about to broach a more dangerous topic indirectly. "Yeah, Susan. The Powell Valley Pickers sing a ribald ballad that comes down from medieval Scotland about a man who comes home and finds another man in his bed, and *The Cherry Tree Carol* is even older. A Harvard professor named Child declared the old ballad tradition dead in the 1890's, but it's still alive here in Southwest Virginia in the 1970's."

"I prefer the Beatles."

George thought back about the Powell Valley Pickers and their version of *My Goodman* that they presented under the title of *My Little Wifey*. They could hear the group playing it now.

"Suzy, that ballad that they're singing now, that's it, *My Goodman*. It's an old one. It goes back at least to thirteenth-century Scotland. That wife sure fooled her husband for a while."

"That's probably not so hard to do."

"Do you reckon that sort of thing happens nowadays?"

"I wouldn't have any idea. How about you, George? Do you plan to get found in bed with some other man's wife?"

"Not me, Susan. I don't jump mine claims."

George wondered whether Moon might come home and find somebody in his bed just as the husband in the ballad had. It wouldn't be so funny in real life, George thought. Susan would never convince Moon that some man's head was a cabbage as the wife in the ballad had hoodwinked her husband. He wondered if Moon would do something rash—kill Susan or her lover, or both. Probably not, he decided, unless Moon had been drinking. He had never s en Moon belligerent or acting foolishly except when he had had a little too much to drink. So far as George knew, Moon had never been falling-down drunk, but the incidents in Denver and Vegas indicated that Moon might act rashly if he drank a great deal.

When they reached the others, Susan greeted them coolly.

"Serafina, Andy can go with you for a visit if it's no trouble," she concluded.

"None at all, Susan. We always enjoy Andrew's visits."

"Maybe we could go by Winding Fork, too," Moon suggested. "Mamaw won a cake. We could sample it."

"No. I need to go home. I have some arrangements to make for a meeting tomorrow. Andy can spend the night, maybe a few days. Then you can pick him up."

Later, at Winding Fork, much of the prize stack cake disappeared quickly.

"Almost as good as yours, Serafina," Archibald judged. "That's high praise," George added.

"It's not nearly as good as yours, Mamaw," Andrew added. "Y'all just want me to bake a cake," Mamaw laughed.

George told Papaw what he had witnessed at the festival between Rod and Susan.

"I reckon that's why she was so frosty when she came to the grandstand. That girl's got above her raisin' I'm afeared."

"Papaw," Andrew asked, "what all is somebody getting above their raisin'?"

"Little pitchers have big ears," George noted.

"That means they think they're too good to live like they used to.

A story 'bout Jack comes to mind. Want to hear it, Andy?"

"Tell it me, Papaw."

Well, Jack's family was poor, but they was good people—farmers. Raised enough food for their own table but didn't have much left over to trade. Tried to live right, but Jack thought they was backward. Jack wanted to get ahead. Now Jack, he worked hard. He weren't no shirker. One day his pa told him to tear down the old shack that stood at one corner of their cornfield so's they could use the space to grow more corn. It was a big job, but Jack set right to it.

"He tore off the roof and the walls and then started on the floor boards. When he prized up the boards near one of the chimbleys, Jack spied an iron box. Nacherly he wondered what was in that box, so he took his crowbar and broke the lock and prized up the lid. 'By gonnies,' Jack thought, 'there's gold here.' He counted out 500 twenty-dollar gold pieces.

"That was a mighty big fortune back in those days, so Jack reckoned he was a rich man. He bought him a fine horse, a house in town, and a store where he set up business. No more farming for him, Jack decided.

Before long, he married the daughter of one of the richest men in town. She was mighty high-toned, caused Jack to forget where he come from. Jack was alivin' high off the hog. Trouble was, he wouldn't have nothin' to do with his family. Didn't visit his ma and pa. Pretended not to know 'em when they traded at his store. Jack had got above his raisin.'

"He was bad, Papaw."

"Yep, he was all right 'til he got above his raisin.' But Jack got his comeuppance. A big wind, a tornado it's called, come through town. Wiped out Jack's store and his house. Kilt him and his wife and children. No sir, it don't pay to get above your raisin.'"

"Is something bad like that going to happen to Momma?"

Archibald saw that he had gone a little too far in driving home his lesson.

"Don't you worry over that, Andy. Your ma's not nearly as far beyond her raisin' as that Jack I told you about. She'll be all right."

George wasn't so sure about that, but he kept this thought to himself and asked Andy if he wanted a story read before he went to bed. "It's about bedtime, Andy. Do you want me to read a story? How about Jack and the Beanstalk?"

"Yes, yes, George, please. I like that."

As he found the storybook, George thought that Moon might have found the goose that laid the golden egg, but he was missing a great deal of fun sharing time with Andrew.

HIGH ART

Not long after the festival, Susan had her revenge on Moon for dragging her to a folk festival in the wilderness. As part of her civic activities, she worked with the local arts council, and they had as part of their interests the support of ballet, theater, and the visual arts. Susan contributed both her time and money to the council's projects. Soon after the festival in Clintwood, the local children's ballet group sponsored by the council held its fall recital. On their way home from Clintwood after the festival, Susan told Moon to clear his schedule so that they could attend this recital together.

"You're supporting this group with your money, and I want you to support it with your presence at the recital. Those young people deserve an audience."

"My money should be enough. You sure give a lot of that."

"No. Those children need to have an audience. I want you to be there with Andy and me so that the boy doesn't see this as some female thing that real men don't do."

"Why don't we just tell him that it isn't sissy?"

"It's not the same. Besides, I've heard that some college football coaches require their players to take ballet. It improves their coordination or something."

Ironically, Moon was less hostile to accommodating Susan now than he would have been before Gladys had begun her program to transform him. He knew that Gladys would have some harsh words for him if he told her that he had refused to widen his intellectual horizons by attending the ballet. In fact, she had told him that they would see a ballet the next time he visited her in New York.

So Moon was a member of the audience who saw the aspiring local ballet dancers doing their best to emulate the greats of their art in a version of *Swan Lake*. What they lacked in skill they supplied with enthusiasm. Except when one of the performers made a really obvious mistake, Moon didn't know enough about ballet to understand whether they were performing well or ill. On the whole, he enjoyed watching them. He decided he might like to see some professional ballet dancers. He looked forward to seeing them on his next visit to New York.

"You're enjoying the performance, Everett. I can tell."

Moon decided that he had better not express too much enthusiasm, but he had to admit that it was more enjoyable than he had supposed, "It's not as borin' as I thought it might be."

Susan also demanded that Moon escort her to other arts performances. Again, he was not now averse to attending the theater, because Gladys had introduced him to some of the best theatrical productions on and off of Broadway. Moon discovered that Barter Theater productions and those of Theater Bristol were of a high enough caliber to compare well with those that he had seen in New York, and he had to admit to himself that he enjoyed theater-going. He admitted his pleasure about the theater to Susan.

"I like the theater building. It gives you the feelin' that you can escape from your everyday problems. And I liked that last show. What was the name?

"*Carousel*—it's very romantic. I'm surprised you liked it." "I reckon you don't think I'm romantic."

"That's not the first word that comes to mind when I think of you, Moon."

To Moon it appeared that he and Susan had more in common now than they had had before he was unfaithful, thanks to Gladys' tutoring. He wondered just how happy Susan would be to find out that his less grudging support of her civic activities was due in large part to another woman. He really was not able to fathom Susan's thoughts other than her obvious pleasure at spending money to attain social prominence. She was less jealous of his time now than she had been a year earlier. For the last few months she had not seemed very interested in what Moon did with his life as long as he did not interfere with her projects and accompanied her socially when she requested his presence.

Although Moon knew that Susan had found other men attractive and suspected she might be having an affair or two, he had no evidence of her infidelity firm enough to justify his seeking a divorce without her agreement. She certainly had not denied him conjugal rights. In fact, she was more adventuresome in bed now than ever, and she never complained of having a headache. To the contrary, she sometimes complained that he didn't fulfill his role as husband often enough. As Moon became more and more enamored of Gladys, he fell into a quandary about how to deal with his marriage.

Now, when Susan did make a rare complaint about his lack of attention to her or his lack of interest in the arts, he suggested the possibility of a divorce. To his bemusement, Susan told him that he was being silly and used all her admittedly considerable charms to excite him sexually. So what had begun as an ar ument usually ended up in sexual intercourse. If anything, Mo n's suggestion that they consider a divorce worked as an aphrodisia on Susan.

"There is no way," she told him, "that I will grant you a divorce."

"Even if you catch me in bed with another woman?"

"Even then, Everett. I might kick you out of my bed for a while, but I wouldn't divorce you. What would Momma and Daddy think? You've become the son-in-law they've always wanted now that your rough edges have worn off some. And you're the father of their adored grandson. No, Moon, if you want a divorce, you'll have to find a way to get it on your own."

Moon couldn't help cursing the irony that the more he changed to please Gladys, the happier Susan became with him. He felt trapped. He knew he couldn't stop seeing Gladys and trying to please her, but he saw that in the process he was creating an even greater dilemma.

He loved Gladys, he felt sure, but thus far he had not been able to convince her that she should marry him if he gained his freedom. He no longer believed that he loved Susan, as he once had thought, but she still excited him sexually. She had learned how to please a man in bed. When he inquired about the sources of her knowledge, she showed him the books that her friends had lent her and attributed her newly acquired expertise to them.

As Moon mused about his problem, the image of the New York street where Gladys' apartment building stood came into his mind as it often did now. He remembered her elegant but comfortable rooms and the sights and smells of that street where she lived. He remembered the hot dog stand on the corner. They had shared a foot-long hot dog with chili that he bought there one day. They walked over to the park across the street and sat on a bench to eat it. He longed for the touch of Gladys. Moon decided to send her flowers and to call from his Lunar Mining office as soon as he could.

In Moon's mind, Susan had become as much of a prostitute as Gladys. He felt Susan was much more interested in his money. She had apparently become completely satisfied with their situation and loathe to grant him his freedom. To her thinking, evidently, providing good sex was her part of what was now an obvious pay-for-play relationship, a relationship with which she seemed quite comfortable. For Lunamin, the marriage bargain was becoming less and less acceptable.

The dilemma seemed irresolvable.

STRIKE

Moon's encounters with the arts and his attempts to solve his marital problems were brought to a halt when the coal miners' union sought to unionize the many non-union mines in the region. Moon faced some more hard choices. For the most part, surface-mining companies were non-union. The union's strength lay in the work forces of the large companies with underground mining operations. Many of these companies leased lands to small non-union surface mining companies in order to avoid problems with union labor. When the strike came, therefore, a more complex situation existed in the coalfields than had been present during the strikes of the 1920's, 1930's, 1940's, and 1950's.

Many men who were working for non-union surface mining operations came from families with strong union backgrounds. Some of them were members of the union themselves. Just as the War Between the States had pitted family members against one another in Southwest Virginia and Eastern Kentucky, this coal strike sometimes tended to tear families apart.

The union's focus centered on non-union mines and the unionized companies who leased land to men with non-union backgrounds, but the men who worked non-union jobs were not necessarily hostile to the union. Still, many of them also could not escape the fact that they had families to feed. Lunar Mining was not exempt from these conflicting values. Moon knew that he had to keep his coal trucks running during the strike. He had made commitments that required him to deliver coal to the tipples, but he was not happy about his decision to keep mining.

"It goes against the grain," he told Fred and Acie.

They agreed. They all had family who were union men, and Fred had never given up his membership.

"Archie MacCloud ain't goin' to like it, Moon," Fred warned.

Acie nodded his head in agreement. Archibald MacCloud had never held with violence, but he was an unswerving union man.

"If we shut down, we'll throw a lot of men out of work and we'll have to dip into reserves to pay our bills. Besides, we have to honor our contracts. Haulin' don't seem like a good move, partners, but not haulin' could be just as bad or worse. ODSUM voted to keep haulin.' We'll be in trouble with Blackmun and the others if we don't."

"We better be prepared for trouble should we keep movin' the coal."

"Fred's right, Moon. Strikers ain't goin' to take kindly to our haulin.' They'll set up lines to stop it. There'll be trouble certain."

"There'll be trouble whatever we do. I don't want to cross picket lines, but long as we can find truckers, we can get the coal out. Boys, we have contracts to meet if we want to stay in business. I'll drive a truck if it comes to that. Hit'll be messy. It turns my stomach to do it, but we've got to get through this mess. We won't do more haulin' than we're obliged to," Moon said.

Lunamin kept pressing his p int of view. Acie and Fred finally agreed to continue operating during the strike despite their union sympathies and the dangers that would confront them. Moon wasn't happy about w at he was doing, but he didn't want to go back on his word given at the association meeting, and he didn't want to lose Lunar Mining's contracts. He had agreed to keep hauling during the strike, but he hadn't said how much he'd haul. He promised Fred and Acie that he would haul the bare minimum they needed to meet their contracts.

Papaw MacCloud wasn't going to praise him either, Moon knew. Papaw might even join the picket lines, old as he was. He still had lots of energy. For him, fighting the coal companies was almost as patriotic as fighting the Kaiser, or Hitler, or Tojo and Emperor

176

Hirohito had been. Though a peace-loving man, he hadn't shirked those fights when he thought his country was in danger.

Moon's attitude was also difficult to explain to Susan, whose family was more sympathetic to mine owners than to miners. She couldn't understand why Moon agonized so over his decision.

"Daddy says the miners should be glad to have a job at all. After all, they don't have any education. And it's not like the old days when they mined with pick and shovel."

"They still do dangerous work, and it takes skill to do it. They should get an honest day's pay for an honest day's work."

"But the mine owner takes all the financial risk, and he's the one that has to worry about the price of coal. You should know that. You're a mine owner yourself—and non-union at that."

"That doesn't mean I don't care about the men. My men get good wages. They don't want a union."

"That's right. And you're just one of the boys."

Moon grunted his displeasure with her sarcasm. Susan had never been able to convince him that becoming a mine owner brought with it a certain social status, social obligations, and social attitudes appropriate for these. She had convinced him to build the mansion in Abingdon and move there, but Moon was still a mountain boy from the hollows in his heart of hearts.

Moon looked upon his refusal to accept Susan's ideas about class as a refusal to betray important values. He was a firm believer in the political equality of mankind. He liked to hear George quote Robert Burns' lines about the dignity of man. Even George, a much more sophisticated man, still thought of himself as a mountaineer who would just as soon go squirrel hunting as go to a play at the Barter or a concert, even though he played the cello himself. So Moon was somewhat surprised when George told him of Susan's efforts to enlist him in her efforts to persuade Moon to become more of a gentleman. Moon heard of the resulting interaction from George. When Susan had appealed to George to try to encourage Moon to live a life more becoming to his newly acquired wealth, George had laughed at her.

"If Adam delved and Eve span, who then was the gentleman?" he queried. George then added a line from Robert Burns, "Old

Rabbie Burns said, 'A man's a man for a' that.'" Susan had snorted her disgust and walked off.

Labor unrest in the coalfields had been a fact of life for Moon and George as they were growing up. Their families had been union families because the men had been miners. Death by asphyxiation from "bad" air (pockets without oxygen), roof falls, and explosions had been a part of their daily existence, dangers accepted as part of the cost of gaining a livelihood. John L. Lewis was a revered figure, next only to Jesus Christ and Franklin Delano Roosevelt.

Lunamin understood where Susan's ideas originated. Susan's family was "town" Appalachian, having a long history of success as merchants in the region. Susan's uncle and grandfather had run stores in Isom and Norton, and her father owned half-interest in an automotive parts store in Clintwoo an active part in his business. even though he had never taken Susan's parents built their home so far removed from town that she had had to attend Winding Fork High School, but they were exceptions in their family. Her other relatives thought town the place to live. Many members of her family were involved in mine management, and the family owned a great deal of Pittston stock.

She approved of Moon's success as a mine owner and reveled in the money that his work brought in even though she grew angry at what she considered his neglect of her. She had found ways to compensate. She was a member of the Junior League, the Margaret Mitchell Book Club, and the Rhododendron Garden Club. She and her friends had luncheons in their homes and at the Martha Washington Inn, and then they engaged in somewhat cutthroat bridge playing. Moon didn't object to these activities. He thought Susan enjoyed them and they were appropriate for their new social status, but he felt in no way obliged to adopt attitudes that were at odds with the values he had learned from Archibald and Serafina.

Susan's other activities Moon only suspected. He believed that, in addition to busying herself with many civic meetings and social groups, Susan had an eye out for men who might be interested in her obvious physical assets, men with a little more sophistication than Earl Campbell possessed. He might be all right to deliver her supply of "hash" from Rod, Moon guessed, but surely he couldn't interest her as a romantic replacement for Moon. So Lunamin was unsure just how much Susan had strayed from her marriage vows. He knew that he himself had strayed, and he was reluctant to confront Susan with his suspicions or to hire a detective to confirm or deny them.

Lunamin was less reluctant to confront Susan about her attitude toward his work ethic and his egalitarianism. Despite her lack of sympathy for the miners on strike, Susan did not relish the idea of Moon's driving a truck to keep his coal moving. She felt that a man of his status should not lower himself to drive a truck, even in an effort to further his business interests. Moon considered this attitude ridiculous. "Everett, driving a coal truck any time is not something for the mine owner to do. And now it's going to be dangerous. What about me and little Andrew? What if you are killed?"

"I don't plan on getting killed. Anyway, you and Andrew don't have to worry. You're well taken care of financially, and Mamaw and Papaw MacCloud will see to Andy's raisin.'"

"You act as if your money is all I care about." "No, not all. You still seem to enjoy the sex."

"Not that you're around enough to provide much of that." Susan laughed at her witty sarcasm.

"Susan, you wanted to marry a successful man, a man who could give you money and social status. I gave you what I thought you wanted. I'm still the man who made the shift from dirt poor to filthy rich. But I'm not the kind that shirks a fight."

"Can't you hire somebody to drive the trucks?"

"Maybe. But it'll be hard. I'm not lame. I can drive anything on four wheels. Don't you remember one of my jobs that your family complained about? A year on a stock car team. I didn't drive in the races, but I sure did drive those cars enough to learn how to drive. And I'm a halfway decent mechanic, too. That's not something to be ashamed of. I'm willin' to humor your high-falutin' ways, but don't think you can make me into some stuffed shirt."

"No. It's obvious you're determined to be a redneck."

Explaining his decision to haul during the strike to Archibald MacCloud was even more difficult for Moon. He was more sympathetic to Papaw's reasons for wanting to keep his mine idle.

"Moon, you know how we feel about crossin' picket lines."
"Yeah, Papaw. I hate to do it. But I don't see any way out. I gave
my word at the ODSUM meetin.' I won't haul more than the bare
minimum we need to keep our contracts goin' and my loans paid up."

"But Fred says you plan on drivin' a truck." "Can't ask others to
do what I won't." "Boy, I may be one of them pickets."

"I figured as much, Papaw."

"There'll be nail boards to get your tires, brickbats through your
windows. If things get real hot, drivers might get pulled from cabs
and beat with bats and fists. I don't hold with violence, but crashin'
a picket line asks for it."

"Papaw, I'm between a rock an' a hard place. If the miners don't
beat up on me, some of my fellow strippers in the association will
tear me up. I figure to do just as little haulin' as I can get by with."

Serafina interrupted their conversation. "Archibald, you know
that Moon's honest. That's how we raised him. If he's given his
word, let him be. You don't care for such as go back on their word.
He's our young'un. We learned him. We stood with him when he
went into strippin' though we don't hold with it. He's agoin' to keep
his trucks runnin' and you're agoin' out on that picket line. You two
just be sure you don't hurt each other."

"I won't haul more than I have to, Papaw."

The strike was primarily against union and large non-union
mines. The small non-union mines were ignored at first. The first
week of the strike went by without much more than yelling and
cursing. The strikers concentrated on picketing the Pittston and
Paramount mines. These they closed down.

The union miners at the Pittsborough operations would not
cross picket lines, and the management at the Parapeak mines
declared a two-week holiday. By the end of the second week, however, the strikers recognized that coal from the smaller non-union
mines was moving at a rate great enough to keep the tipples busy
and the coal trains running. By Thursday the picket lines had formed
to prevent trucks from moving to the tipples.

Then the real trouble began for Lunar Mining. Many of the
truckers that ordinarily hauled for Lunar Mining and other small

operators decided to take their families to Myrtle Beach or to Atlanta to see Six Flags Over Georgia. An unusual number of others claimed to be sick, although Lunamin realized that they just didn't want to cross picket lines. Acie and Fred were willing to work at the mine and keep the equipment running, but they refused to drive trucks across the picket lines.

"If you want that coal hauled across them picket lines, Moon, you got to do it your own self," Fred told him, "Acie and me ain't truck drivers nor strike breakers."

"That's okay. I understand. It's my party. I got us into this. I'll drive. We've got a couple of other truck drivers willin' to haul as long as we take care of damages to their trucks and them. You fellows have any objection to that?"

"Nah, Moon. We'll go along if you don't ask us to cross them picket lines."

"Load me up, then. I'm goin' to haul."

He had bought protective equipment for driving, and he put on some of it. Driving toward Norton, Lunamin kept alert, not knowing where trouble might occur, but he didn't encounter any difficulty before he neared the tipple. He managed to avoid some nail boards in his path as he turned off the highway and onto the road to the tipple. The huge spikes jutting out from the boards could rip even a large coal truck tire. As he neared the picket line, he could hear the jeers of the pickets strung out across the road. When he got closer, he could hear some taunts hurled specifically at him.

"Lunar Mining should take a f... leap over the moon." "Scab, I'll bet your pa's turnin' in his grave."

Moon gunned his engine and picked up speed, scattering pickets to either side of the road yelling obscenities at him as he roared through. As he came abreast of the largest group, a brick cracked into his windshield and another into his side window.

Lunamin had prepared for this. He was wearing goggles to protect his eyes and a football helmet to protect his head. He managed to avoid the glass from the windshield and the first brick, but the glass from the side window inflicted a few minor cuts as the second brick hit him in the shoulder. With difficulty, he kept control of the truck and drove in to the tipple to unload.

At the tipple a small, roundish man with owl eyes behind his glasses came out of the manager's shack.

"You hurt bad, Moon?' asked Joe Pip, the tipple manager.

"Just a few cuts and a sore shoulder, Joe. Many trucks comin' through?"

"Only a few so far. Dave Blackmun's sending trucks in convoys with armed guards riding shotgun. He's just asking for trouble."

"Anybody shot yet?"

"No. But some strikers are talking about bringing guns tomorrow. Blackmun came with his trucks on the first run and told 'em he'd shoot any S.O.B. that stopped one of his trucks."

"Dave's got rock slag where his brains oughta be."

"He sure has brought the coal through. Made it a bit hotter for some of you other fellows, though. They'll take it out on you."

Moon ran the gauntlet back across the picket line and back to the mine. He found two drivers there waiting to see whether he made it back.

"From now on," Moon told the drivers, "we go as a group to increase our chances of getting' through."

They had heard about Blackmun. "You goin' to hire armed guards to ride our trucks?"

"No, my brains ain't made out of rock dust like Dave's. You carry a pistol if you want, but don't show it unless somebody points a gun directly at you. I'll give you goggles and a helmet and a padded jacket. So far those boys ain't usin' guns."

Moon and his drivers made three more trips to the tipple that morning. Then he told them to knock off for the day. "We've hauled all we need today. I'll pay you boys triple for what you've hauled. That'll make a full day's pay. We'll haul some more tomorrow."

They had hauled more than enough coal to meet the immediate obligations of Lunar Mining. Thus far they had escaped with minor scratches and bruises and a few shattered windows. Lunamin didn't want to jeopardize his men and machines any more than absolutely necessary. Maybe the strikers wouldn't confront Lunar Mining vehicles so harshly if they didn't see them much.

Moon knew ODSUM's members were determined to keep their mines working in spite of picket lines, rocks, bricks, nail boards, and threats. Executive Director B. G. Hooper and the board members alerted their allies in Richmond that they might need outside political help and police protection. Dave Blackmun's Red Dog Mining Company continued to invite maximum confrontation with the pickets, who answered the armed guards with rifles and shotguns of their own.

It was only a matter of time before someone used one of those guns. The next week the confrontation became more bitter. Moon heard about incidents from Joe Pip. On Wednesday somebody shot a tire on one of Re d Dog Mining's trucks, and some armed guards fired back, wounding several strikers. Return fire from the strikers wounded a truck driver. From the rear truck of the convoy, Blackmun saw what had happened and clambered out of his truck to assess the damage. Ignoring the taunts and curses, he strode up to the truck where his wounded driver bent over the wheel. There a large striker yelled at him as he looked at the driver's injury.

"Blackmun, you S. O. B., why don't you go to Hell where you belong?"

"'Cause I'd likely meet too many of your kin there, you bastard." This was not an insult the striker was willing to accept. He lunged at Blackmun with his placard that read "Union, Country, God!" Blackmun dodged the placard but not the fist that followed. He returned a blow of his own that knocked his attacker to the ground. Then he climbed aboard the truck, pushed aside the wounded driver, and drove the vehicle through.

When Moon heard about the incident, he laughed a little.

"I never said Dave was a coward. He's brave. He's a brave jackass." Fred didn't laugh when Moon told him about Dave's actions." "He'll get you all killed if he keeps pullin' stunts like that."

SHOOTING

Moon became more worried the next week. Blackmun's trucks continued to flaunt their Red Dog emblems at the strikers as often as Blackmun could get trucks loaded and moving to the tipple. The seemingly incessant stream of trucks he sent exacerbated the strikers' already raw nerves. Nail boards sprouting their steel points multiplied along the roadway to the tipple, and more and more bricks found their way through the windows of Red Dog trucks.

That week the strikers manned their posts along the road to the tipple under gray skies. The ominous skies cast a dark pall over a landscape that even on sunny days seemed a grim gray and black. Piles of coal and slag and rusty old mining equipment lent an air of desolation to the tipple area that contrasted starkly with the tree-covered mountainsides rising above it. Moon limited his trucks to one run, and the strikers reserved their harsher efforts for Red Dog trucks. "That Blackmun must not care what kind of bill he's runnin' up for blown tires and broken windows, not to mention doctor's bills," Archibald MacCloud, who had joined the strikers, said. He joked to young strikers standing around debating how to handle the next onslaught by the Red Dog pack.

"We've got to put the god-damn fire to them. We ain't got their f… attention yet," Jim Maggert cursed loudly. "Let's blow the bastards up." A small wiry, red-haired man, he had a reputation for possessing a fiery temper. The other miners had nicknamed him Rooster because his temper and his red hair reminded them of a bantam rooster and because he raised fighting cocks (and illegally put them into fights when the opportunity arose).

"Rooster, I think you have the right idea," Eben Ratliff, another young miner, nodded his approval and encouragement. Tall and heavy-set, Ratliff stood awhile debating with himself. His dark black cap matched his moustache and beard. His decision made, he went to his truck and pulled out a can of coal oil and a shotgun. Loading the gun, he stuffed extra shells in his pocket and carried the gas can over to Rooster.

"Be careful now. Those men ridin' shotgun might try gettin' your attention. Their trigger fingers may be gettin' itchy. If you try to blow them up, they may shoot to kill," Archibald cautioned.

"Don't lecture us, old man," Maggert snarled. "Just tryin' to calm troubled waters."

"I aim to make things hot for them. You old fellows have lost your nerve." Maggert's face had turned almost the color of his hair.

"Boy, I've been in two world wars and I've seen more killing and destruction than you ever dreamed. I hope you don't regret your hotheadedness," Archibald answered b fore walking off.

Rooster and several other young strikers began gathering up beer bottles and giving them to Ratliff to fill with the coal oil he had brought from his truck. After he filled them, he stuffed cloth into the bottles' necks. Maggert inspected the completed bombs.

"These might get them to mind us," Maggert bragged as he looked on these improvised weapons with a self-satisfied smirk.

Patting his shotgun, Ratliff announced his defiance. "I won't back down if those scabs start shootin.'"

Archibald MacCloud scowled at these young hotheads but held his peace. It was obvious these young hotheads wouldn't listen to him. Keeping his foreboding to himself, he walked over and sat down among a group of other retired miners sitting around a small fire.

"Well, boys, I tried to reason with those young squirts, but they ain't heedin' any advice from us old fogies. They're eager to start world war three."

"You done your best, Archie. Some of us tried, too. They's too full of piss and vinegar to listen." Tom Stoppard shook his graying head and shifted his tobacco to the other cheek before he spat a stream to indicate his disdain. "Them donkeys gonna bite off more than they can chew."

The old men did not have long to wait before seeing Tom's prophecy fulfilled. A line of Red Dog trucks appeared just as he made his pronouncement.

Maggert and Ratliff and other young strikers prepared to meet the trucks with their homemade bombs. As the Red Dog trucks rolled up to the strikers, they began to light the cloths in the necks of the bottles. Running forward, they threw the bottles at the trucks looming in front of them. The bombs began going off in rapid succession under the second, third, and fourth trucks.

From the lead truck and the next came shotgun blasts. The shooters' aim was hurried and poor, but the shots prompted Eben Ratliff to retaliate. Lifting his shotgun, he to k aim at the shooter in the lead truck. His blast shattered the truck's windshield but only grazed the shooter.

Scared at being cut by flying glass, Blackmun's man shot again, wildly. Other gun wielders in the trucks to the rear also fired some wild shots as lighted bottles sailed toward them.

Evidently one of the bottles thrown earlier had found its mark. The fourth truck apparently had a gas leak because one of the bombs had set it afire. The fire had spread quickly and the truck careened out of line as the two men in it jumped from the cab to avoid being burned alive.

Looking on, Archibald thought of the war scenes he had witnessed. Now he saw that his fear that real damage would be done had come to fruition. He didn't want the young men, foolhardy though they had shown themselves to be, to end up in jail or dead. He was relieved when they ran out of their firebombs and the shots subsided as a group gathered around the burning truck.

None of the other trucks received damage sufficient to stop them from delivering their loads to the tipple. None of those attacking the trucks received anything more than minor flesh wounds. Worried that the police had been called, the bombers disappeared from the scene while everyone was gazing at the burning truck.

When the trucks had passed, though, the men sitting near Archibald MacCloud watching the fire saw him holding his side where blood was staining his coat.

"Look here," Tom Stoppard yelled. "Archie's been shot. He's hurt bad. We got to get him to a hospital."

"I ain't too perky. I'd appreciate somebody drivin' me there." Archibald managed to stay conscious until they reached the emergency room.

HOSPITAL

oon heard about Archibald from George. A stray bullet from one of Blackmun's armed guards had hit the old man.

"Papaw will make it, Moon. The bullet went in his side but didn't hit anything vital."

"I'm worried, George. I love that old man."

"Me too, but the doctors say he'll be as go d as ever in a week or two. They're going' to keep him awhile to make sure he stays quiet. They think he might try to picket some more if they let him go now."

"They're plumb right. Hospital's things the best place for him until cool down."

After learning of the burned truck, Moon pressed B. G. Hooper to again contact Hugh Beverley and his friends in Richmond to influence a decision to send state troopers to Southwest Virginia. His message was urgent.

"B. G., we need help now. Before Dave and his dimwits cause more trouble."

"All right, Moon, I'll use strong language."

Moon drove to Winding Fork to pick up Mamaw and Andy to bring them to the hospital. He called home and left a message for Susan, who was away at some social function or other according to Elvira Popper. Elvira was vague. She really didn't know Susan's whereabouts.

Andrew had been at Winding Fork for several days, and Moon had been sleeping at Lunar Mining to keep guard on the equipment during the strike troubles even though Acie and Fred had hired an extra security guard.

"Poor Andy," Moon thought as he drove them to the hospital. "Neglected by his father and his mother. A lot like me. He's lucky to have Mamaw and Papaw."

The three of them found Archibald MacCloud a bit dazed from the pain-numbing drugs that he had received but still quite feisty.

"How're you doing, Papaw?"

"Not too pert right now, I reckon, but I'll be right smart in a day or two."

Serafina frowned, "Archibald, you behave. Don't give these people trouble. They be trying to help you. Hit would be shameful to hinder 'em right now. You're as stubborn as an old bull calf."

"Can't do much to bother 'em right now." "Papaw, you stay away from picketin,' you hear."

Archibald gave a non-committal grunt, "Go dig your coal, boy." George interrupted them. With him he had a young woman in blue jeans and an embroidered denim jacket She had a camera slung over one shoulder and a tape recorder in her hand. He introduced her to the group.

"This pretty young lady is Jennifer Coffey. You remember her, Moon. She's a reporter for the Roanoke paper. She's down here to cover the strike and she'd like a word or two with Papaw."

After the introductions were complete, George asked Archibald if he'd mind talking to Jennifer. "She thinks you'll be great copy, Papaw." Archibald grinned. "Shucks no, I don't mind. Besides, I couldn't refuse a woman with eyes as blue as hers. What do you want to know, young lady?"

"Don't pay attention to his flirtin,' Miss Coffey. He's still groggy from the pain killer they give him," Serafina apologized.

"Serafina, I didn't mean no harm—just tryin' to be friendly." Moon saw Jennifer grin as she took out her tape recorder. "Well, first of all, Mr. MacCloud, do you think you were shot on purpose?" "Nah, it was just a stray bullet. Them damned fools can't shoot straight."

"I hear there's been a lot of violence. Who started the violence, Mr. MacCloud?"

"Honey, when anybody crosses a picket line, there's bound to be some violence. But none of the miners carried guns until Dave Blackmun started havin' armed guards ridin' with his truck drivers. It was those armed guards that started the shootin.' So I hold Blackmun responsible for my bein' shot. He always was a damned jackass. Like his father before him. We worked in the deep mines together in the old days. Braddock Blackmun probably turned over in his grave when his son started sendin' his trucks across picket lines."

As the interview continued, Lunamin decided the time had come for him to drive to Abingdon. Things should quiet down a little now. He had been away from home a long time. Turning to Andrew, Moon hugged him and said goodbye.

"You take care of Mamaw, Andy. Get Papaw to tell you some stories when he's finished talkin' to the newspaper lady."

Leaving Mamaw and Andrew for George to take back to Winding Fork, Moon drove to his mine and checked the mine site. According to Fed and Acie, things were beginning to quieten, and Fred had agreed to spend the night at the mining operation. Moon called Gladys and chatted, then headed his truck toward Abingdon. She vied in his thoughts with Archibald as he drove east in the dusk.

When Moon arrived at the Abingdon Riviera, he found his home dark. Looking through the house, he could locate nobody and no note to indicate where Susan might be. He flipped through the list of telephone numbers in the book that Susan kept near the hall telephone. He called a few of the women he knew to be close acquaintances of Susan's and asked if they knew what Susan's plans might be. They told him that they had not talked to her for several days, so Moon called her mother.

"No, Everett. Susan hasn't been here today. Perhaps she went shopping in Roanoke and stayed a little longer than she intended. She's been shopping there a lot lately."

Moon drove down to the Tavern and had supper. When he returned to the house, Susan still had not appeared. The quietness of the large house caused Lunamin to feel a sense of loneliness. He went to the den and turned on the TV. He flipped the controls until he found a baseball game. By the time the seventh-inning stretch arrived, Moon was sound asleep on the sofa. He was still asleep in the den in front of the TV set when Susan's Mercedes pulled up to the house around one o'clock in the morning. She walked nonchalantly into the house, found Moon asleep, and went past the den to the master bedroom and took a shower. Then she went to the den and cut off the TV. Waking Moon, she told him to come to bed. Moon rubbed his eyes sleepily.

"Where've you been?" he grunted.

"I went shopping in Roanoke. It's late. I'm going to bed." Following her down the hall, Moon didn't ask any more questions.

He noted the time, but he wasn't certain when Susan had returned home because he knew he had dozed off around nine-thirty.

"You should have left a note.

Papaw?"

"Yes, is he all right?"

Did you get my message about "He was hit in the side, but it wasn't too bad—no vital organs hit.

Things seem to have quieted down now." "That's good. Come on to bed. It's late."

Kissing and fondling Moon, Susan encouraged his lovemaking. He detected no hint of displeasure with him in her actions. If anything, she seemed more active than usual after he thrust into her. He still found her beauty very alluring. He had no will to resist her even if he had felt less desire. They had not made love for some time, so Moon reached his climax quickly. To his chagrin, Susan expressed her dissatisfaction with this outcome and surprised when she took him in her mouth and kissed him until he was able to resume his thrusting. This time he had no trouble staying until she reached her climax.

"Welcome home, Everett. Maybe you won't stay away so long again."

Moon muttered what passed for agreement as he drifted back into sleep. He felt more like Susan's prize bull than her husband.

The next morning he wondered how Susan had become so proficient in oral sex. She had already left when Moon came down for breakfast. Elvira Popper cooked him eggs and bacon and grits. She was a good cook and housekeeper—that was certain.

"Elvira, tell Susan I'll have to be gone again for a few days. The strike's not over. I have to make sure we keep haulin.'"

"All right, Mr. Lunamin, but I don't think she'll like what all I tell her. She thinks you've neglected her."

Accused so many times, Moon had by now realized that he had neglected Susan, and Andy also. He felt guilty. He turned this feeling over in his mind, but the memory of the delights, b th physical and intellectual, he had experienced in Gladys' company proved stronger than his feelings of guilt.

As he drove to Lunar Mining, he ruminated on his life. "Mamaw and Papaw have given Andrew the attention and love he's needed," he thought, "but nobody else could supply Susan with the emotional life she needs. Susan hasn't given me the companionship I want either.

I've tried to please her.

She has what she said she wanted, all the material things including a mansion in town, not in what she terms the wilderness. If Lunar Mining doesn't weather this strike, she could lose some of this lifestyle that she holds in such high esteem. That lifestyle ought to be worth a few walks in the woods or a morning's fishing, but she doesn't appear concerned to meet any of my needs other than sex. And she does that more for her satisfaction than mine."

Lunamin couldn't fault Susan's leaving Andy with Archibald and Serafina so often, because they were giving the boy plenty of love. Still, he wondered how a mother could so easily leave the boy so long. Susan's idea of motherhood didn't square with Moon's. He myopically overlooked the fact that his mother had left him with her mother and father to raise entirely without her help.

Moon did recognize that Susan's materialism was at fault, but he had been as enamored with gaining material wealth as she, but unlike

Susan, he was beginning to find that these material things were less satisfying than he had supposed. "I reckon I have put too much stock in getting wealth and putting on a show," he judged.

Aware that Susan had unsatisfied needs, Moon still could not bring himself to believe that he was making the wrong choice in devoting his energies to the success of Lunar Mining. Without

Lunar's success, Susan would lack all of the material blessings she craved, might even be forced back into the wilderness she had sought so dearly to leave. "Susan would be even more unhappy with me if I didn't provide the life she's come to expect," he concluded.

A few days later Fred returned from Roanoke with news. "Smokies are comin.' I saw 'em up at Roanoke. They're headin' south in big numbers."

"Hope they stay calm. We have enough hometown hotheads. We don't need to import none," Acie replied.

The "bears" descended upon the coalfie ds in such numbers that there were soon no unoccupied motel rooms in the area. Despite the peace they brought, the police did little to win friends. They tended to view the strikers very negatively, as the reason they had been dragged from homes in the eastern part of the state to far southwestern Virginia. Their use of the terms "hillbilly," "local yokels," and even harsher, more vulgar epithets in describing the strikers not only alienated the strikers, but also many local people not directly involved in the strike.

Nevertheless their presence brought peace to the area.

Arrests of strikers quickly filled the Norton and Wise jails as full as the police had filled the local motels. Eventually these arrests produced the desired effect. With their leaders in jail, the striker's efforts were less organized. Whenever any striker threatened violence, he soon found himself in jail. As the local jails filled to capacity, the state police took arrested strikers to the jails as far away as Abingdon.

Now Moon had less trouble getting his coal trucks through. Still, he continued hauling only the coal he needed to pay the bills and contracts of Lunar Mining and to meet its payroll. He crossed the picket lines as little as possible, unlike Dave Blackmun and some other ODSUM members who pushed as much coal through the lines as they could.

Dave Blackmun and the others who followed his lead stirred up anger that would not easily go away, even long after the strike had ended. Moon was worn out from the strain of confrontation. He was relieved when the strike finally ended. He felt he had earned a rest. George's telephone call came at the right time.

DEER HUNT

George had proposed a hunting trip to Moon as soon as the strike troubles had died down. The leaves had begun to turn again. It was deer season. The trip from Southwest Virginia to Bath County had given Moon and George a chance to talk more than they had since before the strike had begun. Moon told George of his having asked Susan for a divorce and her refusal to give him one without a contest.

"I could hire a detective. She's havin' an affair." "You're sure about that, Moon?"

"Pretty sure, but that's not important to me except it gives me some leverage to get a divorce if Susan won't give me one some other way."

"That would be messy, and it wouldn't be good for Andy. Maybe you and Susan can patch things up."

"Susan is content to go on the way we are. She likes the money and the social status it buys. And the sex is still good."

"They say that's the last thing to go."

"I reckon they're right. Susan and me don't have much else in common but Andy and my money. Trouble is, I'm in love with somebody else."

Despite what he had witnessed at the festival, George was surprised to find Moon so definite about his and Susan's relationship. He knew that Moon and Susan had been attending plays and other cultural events together. Apparently Moon had attended these for some reason other than simply a desire to please Susan.

Arriving at their hunting ground early in the afternoon, they spent the rest of the day scouting for deer sign. It was dusky dark by the time they made camp at their campsite. After putting up a tent and cooking some steaks on the grill, they ate and drank some Irish coffee by the fire before dropping off to sleep. Moon sighed contentedly.

"It's good to be out in the woods after all that strike trouble."

"How did Lunar Mining come through the strike?"

"We came through all right, George. We hauled just enough coal to keep our contracts filled, but we didn't take on any new ones. We kept a low profile. Not like Blackmun and Whacker. Looked like they went out of their way to madden the strikers. After Papaw was shot, the strikers pretty much left my trucks alone."

Next morning they ate by lantern light, then drove as close as they could to where they were to hunt. The oaks still held almost all of their leaves, but there were enough fallen leaves to crunch under their feet as Moon and George moved as stealthily as they could through the woods. In the dark it wasn't easy to find a stand in the area they had scouted for deer sign the day before, but they had seen plenty of scat and other sign over a large area. They chose a draw below the area they had scouted and began their climb.

When they neared the top of the ridge, George took up his position on the left slope and Moon went up a few hundred yards higher on the opposite side of the draw. As they settled in, the dark began to shift to grays of lighter and lighter shades. The sun's movement across the sky could not be traced otherwise, b cause a complete overcast enveloped the sky above them and the surrounding ridges.

In the distance, they could hear the croaks of ravens—no doubt expressing their enjoyment of an anticipated feast on deer entrails provided by successful hunters. The air carried a hint of snow against George's face as he watched Moon disappear in the trees above him. He could not see Moon now, even with his binoculars. Behind him he heard a barred owl call "Who cooks for you?" and a ruffed grouse was drumming about a hundred yards up the ridge to his right. Underneath his feet, he could hear the shrill cries of shrews and the chirping of crickets.

George was still warm from the climb, but he settled himself down to wait while he listened to the sounds around him. He had been waiting about half an hour when he raised his binoculars again to Moon's position. A little higher up the draw from where Moon had disappeared, he spied a buck slowly moving down the mountain. About a quarter of an hour later, it passed by what be Moon's stand, but there was no shot or any other indication that Moon had seen it. The adrenalin rush that flowed through his body heightened George's perceptions as he prepared for the possibility that he would have a shot at the buck.

No sound broke the stillness other than the calls of raucous jays and the distant kek-kek-kek of a woodhen. George knew hunters disliked the woodhens or pileated woodpeckers because they alerted the deer to the hunter's presence, but this one was too far off to spook the buck. It was six or seven-pointer, a good rack. Slow y it moved away from where Moon must have been, but still no shot. It was Moon's shot, not his. Had Moon gone to sleep?

"He must have seen the buck," thought George, "and by now he's bound to have had a clear shot."

After what seemed like an hour but was actually only a few minutes, the buck disappeared into the woods on George's side of the draw. Landsetter continued to wonder whether Moon had gone to sleep after taking his position. A pair of ravens croaked derisively as they flew overhead, no doubt on their way to feast on the remains of a more successful hunter's kill. They did not fly in a straight, determined line but climbed high and then tumbled together in an intricate aerial ballet, all the while uttering what seemed guttural exclamations of joy. George recognized the antics of a mated pair, probably expressing their pleasure at the prospect of plentiful food. George thought that he understood their exhilaration. He wished that he could join them in their aerial acrobatics—"Casting off the surly bonds of earth," as that young Canadian pilot-poet had written. Landsetter remained below envying their acrobatic prowess until they passed over the ridge and out of sight, though he could still hear them for a long time.

The damp air carried sounds a long way that morning. Occasionally George heard a rifle shot in the distance, but he saw no other bucks that morning. An occasional doe or two passed by, but the only other animals that he saw that morning were a couple of chip-munks scurrying through the leaves near his station and birds moving through the trees above his head. He recognized chickadees, titmice, and an occasional nuthatch. He could tell the nuthatches easily by their strange habit of moving down the trees head first. They were traveling with the feeding flocks of woodpeckers, kinglets, and creepers.

Watching the animals gave George something to do other than count falling leaves. The leaves left on the trees retained some color and gave the forest a still-festive air, but each breeze that ruffled them brought a few leaves floating down. Already the ground had received a cover of new leaves that was growing deeper by the hour.

Back at camp, George asked Moon why he had not shot the buck. "It was your shot. Were you asleep?"

"No. He passed right by me. I was so busy enjoyin' the view that I forgot to raise my rifle. He certainly was a looker, eight points if you count the little ones."

"I recollect a time when you'd have poked fun at me for letting a buck like that go."

"Yeah. I reckon that wasn't so long ago. Maybe I'd rather look than shoot now. Anyhow, we can always get a doe on doe-day if we don't see another buck close enough for a shot. These woods are full of does. Bein' out in the woods, smellin' the bacon cook over the campfire, watchin' autumn leaves floatin' down from the trees. There're more reasons to be here than just killin' a deer."

"I couldn't agree with you more, old buddy. But when and where did you find this philosophical attitude you're displaying. I don't remember your being much of a philosopher."

"I reckon I think more about some things now than I used to. I've been a doer all my life. I haven't spent much time thinking about the meaning of things. Lately I've been thinking more about the pur-pose of all the gruntin' and sweatin' we do."

George mentally underscored Moon's assessment of himself, but he wondered what had prompted an active, unreflective man like Moon to become so conscious of his actions. Running the events of the past few years over in his mind, Landsetter wondered if Shorty's death might have contributed to Moon's thought processes, but it couldn't have been enough to explain Moon's transformation into a homespun philosopher. The only other thing that George could dredge up to explain the change in his cousin was Moon's dissatisfaction with his marriage, or perhaps the two things in combination.

"I can't say that I mind the change, Moon. But I can't help wondering what brought it on."

Moon became evasive. "I've been reading a lot lately. I even read the play you're always quoting—*Hamlet*. It makes you think about what we're here for."

The remainder of the week went by without their having another opportunity for shots at a buck. On the last morning, doe-day, George shot a doe, and they decided to take Moon's entire share of the meat to Archibald and Serafina. George planned to split his share between his parents and the food kitchen in Norton.

A cold front had moved in during the night, so they did not have to worry about the meat spoiling. Ravens circled overhead as they dressed the carcass. Were they birds of omen or just hangers-on waiting for their share of the feast, George wondered.

Snowflakes were b ginning to fall as they brought the deer to the checking station, and there was a trace of snow on the ground at Rural Retreat, but the ground was clear at Abingdon and Winding Fork. George put his share of the meat in his Datsun and drove out. Moon spent an hour or so with Archibald and Serafina before making the long drive back to Abingdon. Susan had left Andy at Winding Fork, so Moon had company on the drive.

"Did you shoot the deer, Pa?" "No, George did that."

"Did you see many deer?"

"We saw lots of doe. Just one buck came close enough for a shot. But I let him go." "Why, Pa?"

"He was just too fine to look at. I was too busy lookin' at him until it was too late to shoot."

When they reached home, Elvira Popper fixed them something to eat. Susan was shopping in Roanoke, she told Moon.

"Do you know when she'll be home?" "She said she'll be late."

Moon kept silent, but he wondered just how much shopping a person could do.

THE TAX MAN

Before Lunamin happened to discuss business matters with Tom Stanard, he had not realized that he might have trouble with the Internal Revenue Service. His conversation with his father-in-law caused Moon to realize that the IRS might consider Lunar Mining's methods of record keeping a little lax. Not that he had not tried to keep track of what he owed the government, but he and Fred and Acie had not always kept a neat office and could not put their hands on all the records they should have submitted to their a countant at tax time.

Lunamin had heard numerous horror stories about mine owners who had run afoul of the tax system. He was certain he wasn't in the position of some of the less law-abiding strippers who had tried to avoid paying any monetary homage whatsoever to Uncle Sam. Some of them had ended up broke and in jail. He did not have to worry about doing jail time, he thought, but he probably did need to tighten Lunar Mining's methods of financi l reporting.

During the first months of the company's operation, Moon and his partners had given little thought to taxes. They had been too preoccupied with the details of launching the enterprise, meeting bank payments, and (after they began hauling coal) adjusting to the handling of large sums of money. They had given little consideration to creating a paper trail to please the IRS.

After the first six months of Lunar Mining's successful operation, however, they began to consider the need for accurate reporting. As each man began coming to grips with his own personal tax reporting problems for the year, they began to understand that their newly acquired status as mine owners and the rewards that accompanied it had removed them from the simple tax bracket that they had previously occupied. Following some discussions about what to do, they decided to hire an accountant, who then, as far as they were concerned, would shoulder all of their tax problems.

Lunamin's worry deepened after he talked about taxes with Tom Stanard again on one of the rare family outings that he, Susan, and Andy had with her parents. Tom complained bitterly about the amount of record keeping he had to undertake to satisfy the IRS.

"I wonder if I might have trouble? We haven't paid careful attention at Lunar Mining, I reckon," Lunamin worried.

"If you don't provide your tax preparers with a record of everything you've done, you might be."

Moon began to fear that he and his partners might not be providing their accountant with as much and as a curate information as the Internal Revenue Service required. He and Fred soon agreed that they had a problem. What if they should face an audit? No matter how hard they tried, though, they could not convince Acie that a change was needed. He thought that the expense involved in hiring someone to keep their records in better shape was a needless waste of money.

"We've got to hire someb dy just to keep us right with taxes? I don't favor it." Acie saw no need to waste money on paperwork. "Maybe we could hire a person just part-time," Fred suggested. "That's the ticket, Fred, but we need some kind of system. We need somebody to organize the office and take care of filing the paperwork." "Don't see no need for it. Just wastin' money," Acie objected.

Acie remained unconvinced for months. By the time he had begun to see things their way, tax reporting time had come again. Though Moon was making an effort the keep better records, the tax payments of Lunar Mining proceeded as usual, and their accountant filed their report as he always had.

Lunamin gave little more thought to the matter until he received a letter from the IRS. It indicated that an audit of Lunar Mining's taxes from the previous year would be necessary and requested that Mr.

E. A. Lunamin, President of Lunar Mining, contact Agent Leonard Betterman to arrange for an interview and audit. Moon passed the letter on to Fred after he had read it.

"Sure looks like trouble, Moon. It's just what we were worried about."

"I reckon the horse has come back to the barn. But audits like this don't just happen. I'll bet the IRS got a tip. Did you talk to anybody about our problem?"

"No, nobody but Jauncie, and I told her not to mention it to anybody. Let's ask Acie."

They drove out to the Possum Gap job to find Acie, who was working on a bulldozer motor. Fred yelled at him from the truck, "They's something we got to ask you."

Wiping his greasy hands on a rag, Acie walked over to the truck. "Remember us talkin' about the tax man?" Fred asked.

"Sure. You and Moon still want to hire somebody?" "May be. Did you talk to somebody else 'bout it?"

"Let me recollect. Can't think of nobo y...maybe Rod Mashburn."

"That's where they got the tip I bet," handed Acie the letter.

"What tip?"

Moon guessed as Fred "Moon thinks the IRS was tipped off we're cheatin' on taxes."

"I knew Rod had it in for Moon, but shucks, I didn't think he'd do nothin' like that."

"No help now, but we've got to find all the records we can. What we didn't give to the accountant. And we'd better get our act cleaned up. Fred, you reckon your Jauncie would work part time?"

"Probably, just so's she could keep an eye on me."

"That'll keep it in the family. We need somebody we can trust. We've got to have better records. It's lockin' the barn door...but it might help a little now. And it'll sure help for next year."

As Moon and Betterman agreed in a telephone conversation, the auditor arrived at Lunar Mining's office two weeks later to do an on-the-spot audit. Moon had the papers that their accountants had worked from, and Jauncie had a box of papers she had collected in the office and from Acie, Fred, and Moon. Armed with these papers, they confronted Leonard Betterman. Middle-aged and balding, the IRS agent gazed at them with a steely blue stare that warned he was not to be trifled with even though he had reached only five feet two inches in height.

"We run an honest operation, Mr. Betterman."

"That may well be, Mr. Lunamin, but we have received information to the contrary."

"We may have been poor record keepers, but we haven't cheated the government."

"That remains to be determined." "Here is what all we could find."

Jauncie smiled at him as she handed him the box where she had put all the loose papers she had been able to find and the papers from the accountant. "You may wish to look through these, Mr. Betterman." Betterman spent the entire day sifting through the records and asking questions. His skepticism about Lunamin's honesty decreased as time passed, but he became more and more exasperated with Lunar Mining's record keeping. "Mr. Lunamin, I'm surprised that a company with a cash flow like Lunar Mining keeps such poor records," he complained the next time he talked to Moon.

"I know we have a problem. We've already improved our record keeping," Moon assured him. "Mrs. MacCloud's handling it for us now."

"I'm glad to hear it. I'd hate to go through this every year. As best I can determine, Lunar Mining owes the United State Treasury something in the neighborhood of $150,000 plus interest and whatever penalties the IRS assesses."

"That's a little steep."

"It could have been worse, I assure you. I tried to be lenient and give you the benefit of the doubt on close calls."

"I'd sure hate to see what all harsh is. But we'll have Jauncie to take care of us this year so that we won't find out."

"I'm relieved to hear that. I'd hate to have to do this audit every year. I'll send you a letter detailing my findings, Mr. Lunamin. You'll be entitled to an appeal, but my advice is to pay the bill and stop the bleeding. Penalties can grow fast."

"No doubt. Pay, then appeal. I'm turning the tax problem over to my partner, Fred MacCloud, Jauncie's husband. He's honest and he's patient."

Jauncie laughed. "He's also married to a woman whose first cousin's a first-rate tax lawyer."

"I suspect you'll need his help."

Leonard Betterman drove off in his 1950's Ford sedan without further comment. Lunamin, Fred, and Jauncie wondered just how ominous they should consider his last words.

"I think you should talk to our new tax lawyer right away, Fred," Jauncie suggested.

PROJECT AFRICA

It was some time after the strike before Lunamin could get back to New York to see Gladys. He called her often, and he was surprised but pleased when she told him that she missed him more than she cared to say. She told him that she had something to discuss. When he was finally able to fly to New York, Gladys met Moon's plane at the airport, but she didn't mention what was on her mind right away.

Though Moon could tell that Gladys had a new project in mind, he didn't ask what it was. She would bring it up when she was ready.

They went to dinner and a show, but Gladys still had not told him what she wanted to talk to him ab ut, even when they were in her apartment having drinks. The tasteful surroundings always compelled Moon's admiration. He looked around at a number of reproductions of landscapes by the French Impressionists that adorned the walls of her front room and told hims lf with some pride that he could now tell the style of Monet, Cezanne, Seurat or Van Gogh. He had spent a good deal of time in museums with Gladys.

"You could be an interior decorator, Gladys. Have you thought about that?"

"A little. I help friends decorate their apartments now and then. I've even taken on a couple of paid consulting jobs."

As they sat on the sofa, Moon fondled her and kissed her repeatedly. "It's been a long time, Babe. I've missed you."

"I've missed you too, Moonman. From the way you're acting. I think we ought to take our drinks with us to bed."

In the bedroom, a picture on the nightstand caught Moon's eye. It was a picture of him. "When did you take that?" he asked in a voice that he thought suggested hia surprise.

"The last time we were together. Don't you like it?"

"I do if you do. I think the photographer should receive compliments for being able to do so well with so poor a subject."

"I have a high opinion of the subject. I choose my subjects carefully," she laughed.

Moon undressed Gladys slowly as she undressed him. He had completely forgotten that they were supposed to discuss an important matter. Now he wanted her too fiercely to listen to or feel anything but their two bodies touching. Soon they were lying side by side on the bed. Moon had by now learned not to rush his pleasure, for Gladys had repeatedly impressed upon him that his enjoyment increased when he concerned himself with his partner's satisfaction as well as his own.

Kissing Gladys deeply, he fondled and kissed her breasts, her legs, and every other part of her. Gladys moaned her enjoyment. "You certainly respond to teaching well, Adamo."

"My teacher really knows how to make out a lesson plan," Moon responded.

Gladys laughed. "It's time for another lesson. Lie down on your back."

After Moon followed her instructions, Gladys kneeled above him. For the next half-hour she gyrated above him until they climaxed and collapsed upon the bed still twined together.

"Have you ever been abroad, Moon?" Gladys asked him later as she rubbed him down with oil using her delicate touch. As the lotion seeped gently into his relaxed skin, Moon could muster only a surprised grunt at first.

"Uh...well, no, Gladys, I never have unless you count my army tour in Nam. Why?"

"That's what I wanted to talk to you about. If you're ever going to become more cosmopolitan in your outlook, Moon, I think you ought to do some traveling. You need to see the world. You and I could go to Europe. We could see London and Paris and Florence. We could see Rome and Athens."

"I don't know that I'm ready for Europe."

"Where would you like to go, then? I want us to have some shared experiences beyond New York and the Gulf Coast. Isn't there some place you've always wanted to go?"

Moon, caught off guard, forgot his language a bit. "Yep. Sure would like a game hunt in Africa. I ain't done that. I've always wanted to go big-game huntin' in Africa, bring back a trophy or two for my den."

Moon sought to recover lost ground. "I have tried. Just to please you. But you asked me what I'd like to do. I'd like to go abroad if I could chase after some big game in Africa."

"I won't go on a hunt. You know how I fee ab ut killing animals. Have you ever thought about using a camera? You can take pictures of what you see. You don't have to have a head to hang on a wall. You can hang pictures. You don't hang me on your wall. I've given you pictures, but you can't even hang those on your wall. Do you have a camera?"

Moon had to admit that he didn't. He hadn't had time to fool around with photography. "Susan has a camera. I never saw much need to buy something I didn't have time to use."

"Soon we're going camera shopping," Gladys planned.

Moon felt his desire returning under her warm touch. He didn't want to argue. If she wanted him to buy a camera, he'd do it. He might even enjoy becoming a shutterbug, he thought.

"Okay, okay. I'll buy a camera."

Moon grabbed Gladys by the shoulders and pulled her down beside him. He took the lotion from her and poured it over her breasts with one hand and rubbed it in with the other. Moon found that he could not run his hands over Gladys enough to satisfy him or her. He did not think about what he was doing. It was simply that his movements led to more movement without thought—each movement bringing with it a warmer glow and the need for further movement. Nothing proceeded from the level of conscious thought.

Every passage of his hand came from some subconscious level where their bodies communed without conversation.

Gladys softly murmured poetry. "…We're knotted together in innocence and guile…" As she came more and more under the spell of his hands, other lines from Donne's *The Ecstasy* came to her lips from whatever part of her mind was still conscious. "'Love's mysteries in souls do grow…But yet the body is his book.' Let's read the book together, Adamo."

Gladys took some more lotion and began massaging Moon. The two of them kept their hands, covered with lotion, moving until the container was empty. They were the two lovers whose souls, interinanimated as Donne put it, formed the newer, greater soul that could converse the whole day through without a word being uttered.

A great prince had been lying in the prison of Moon's body. Gladys had liberated that prince. He wanted to touch every part of her body, to kiss her everywhere, to hold her tight, to tell her how much he loved her. He had known passion before, but he had never experienced anything like this. It was s x they were experiencing, but it did not seem like sex to him or her. Their bodies had been transported to another level.

The agony of impending separation weighed upon them. "Stay with me all night, Moon. Please."

"I will, Gladys, but I have to be back in Virginia tomorrow night." As their lovemaking seized complete control of them, their conscious minds succumbed completely to their senses. They gazed, touched, tasted, smelled, crooned, groaned, nibbled, and ate love in harmony.

"Oh, it's good. It's good, Sweetheart."

"I know. It's fireworks and sirens and…oh…an ocean wave…I love you, Moonman," Gladys moaned.

Later, exhausted, Moon collapsed beside her again, and she cradled him in her arms.

"Gladys, I've never experienced anything this wonderful before." "I know, Baby, I know."

Their talk became more and more disjointed as they kissed and nuzzled affectionately and gradually drifted off to sleep.

Next morning Moon woke as the sun streamed in through the window. It lighted the bedroom. Looking at Gladys beside him, he spent some time admiring her golden-brown hair above and below the waist. She wasn't an ad-man's dream, not a willowy clothes mannequin, but she was not plump. She was just fleshy enough to be termed gracefully buxom. Buxom, that was a word that Moon had newly acquired. Gazing at her, he couldn't resist touching her and passing his hand over her again and again. Gradually, Gladys came awake, felt his hands, and saw Moon above her gazing at her with an expression that she had never seen before.

"Oh, Moon, that feels so good. But I just hate to wake up."
"Don't. Let's just stay here awhile."

He leaned down and kissed her, and lay down close to her, drawing her to him.

"Adamo," she laughed, feeling him prodding her midriff, "I don't believe we finished last night. Let's see what we can do about that."

As he entered her, she sighed contentedly. They proceeded slowly, not wanting to rush their enjoyment, savoring their movements and then ceasing for kisses covering each other's bodies, then entwining again in different positions.

With Gladys' tutelage, Lunamin had developed a se f-control that he had never known existed, and when Gladys reached the peak of her enjoyment, he joined her and they collapsed onto the bed and off to sleep again.

Awake half an hour later, Gladys cooked Moon some scrambled eggs for breakfast.

"Things can't be the same anymore, Adamo. Last night was something new for me. I love you, that's certain now. That's a whole new ball game."

They laughed together at her joke, but Moon realized she was serious.

"I love you too, Gladys. Last night was something new for me, too, but I knew I loved you already. You know that. I can't stand the thought of you with other men. You ought to be able to live on what I've been giving you."

"Well, Moon, I may have to get another job. I haven't seen anybody else for a long, long time. I think I've been a kept woman. I think I may have to continue that. I don't think I can earn enough money with my college degrees in English to keep up the lifestyle to which I've become accustomed. Living in New York is expensive. Maybe I can become an interior decorator as you suggested. I'll see. If you want me to quit being an escort for good, you may just have to make me your favorite charity. I've grown used to luxuries. It will be difficult to give them up." "You know that's no problem, Gladys, but will you marry me if and when I'm free to marry?"

"That's a bigger step than I've prepared for now, Moonman. You have a ways to go with your education, you know. What about your reading list? What about our trip? That was what I wanted to discuss with you."

"I'm ready to go to Africa whenever you say we're fully equipped." "Okay, Mr. Lunamin, let's go shopping."

Before noon they had bought cameras, binoculars, scopes, tripods, and an assortment of clothing for an African tour as well as two air tickets to Nairobi, Kenya.

"Africa, here we come," Lunamin laughed.

"Moon, Honey, I'll do some studying about Africa. I wish we could go to South Africa, but the apartheid makes that out of the question. Lots of people go to Kenya, though. The Kenyans have parks full of strange people, big animals, and beautiful birds. You learn to use that camera."

AFRICA

Moon told Susan that he had business in Philadelphia, New York, and London and that he was going to do some sightseeing before and after meetings. He would be gone at least three weeks. She asked a few questions, but since Moon had legitimate business interests in all those cities he had mentioned, he supplied her with satisfactory answers. Besides, it seemed to Moon that Susan's questioning was a bit perfunctory.

In fact, he did have business with his stockbrokers and a coal buyer. He spent several hours in Philadelphia and more in New York speaking with financial advisors as he always did when he visited Gladys in New York. If they served no other purpose, these conversations rendered part of his trip tax deductible. After meeting with his stockbrokers in New York, Moon called Gladys and arranged to pick her up to go to J. F. Kennedy Airport The traffic was heavy, but they reached the airport in plenty of time for check-in.

It was a five-hour flight to London, but they slept a good portion of the trip. Their waking time they spent discussing what they were going to see.

"I'm looking forward to seeing elephants and giraffes outside a zoo, Moon."

"Lions are at the top of my list."

Their flight from New York to London on the first leg of the trip proved uneventful. During their layover in London, Moon spent some time dealing with coal brokers concerning some contracts for Lunar Mining, and then they took a taxi to see some of the city's highlights. They managed to see the British Museum, London Bridge, the Tower, and Kew Gardens. Then, tired but happy, they headed their taxi to Heathrow to board a plane for the flight to Nairobi, Kenya, where they would begin their African adventure.

"I'm glad we have to leave now. I've seen all I can stand. I don't think I could do any more sight-seeing today."

"I can tell you're ready for big game, Honey."

On the long flight from London to Nairobi their anticipation grew, whetted by promotional films provided by the Kenyan tourist bureau. Gladys was particularly fond of the wines provided by British Airways. They were free and plentiful and good.

In Kenya, they found that most people drank beer or wine rather than the water, unless it was bottled. Moon preferred the tasty and readily available African beer. He decided Tusker was the best. They had watched the tourist films closely. The animals and scenery were enthralling. They were going to see Amb s li, the Abedarres, the Masai Mara, the Rift Valley, and Samburu.

Lunamin understood that Gladys had planned the trip so that they could combine natural history with seeing the people of the remote areas. Besides Moon's new camera and camcorder, they both had a pair of binoculars. Gladys had also insisted that Moon buy a spotting scope with a tripod to use with the scope and the cameras. She had a plan for all this equipment, she told him—to use Moon's obvious love of the natural world to show him that there are other ways to approach nature than with a bulldozer, chainsaw, rifle, or shotgun.

Like all good Kenya tourists, they met their newly hired guide Terence Stavens waiting for them at the airport. A little below six feet, robust but not fat, he told them that he was a Yorkshireman who started out as a birding bum. His stay in Africa led to his meeting a young woman who took his fancy while he was birding at Lake Baringo. They married and he became part of the white establishment. Collecting their luggage, Stavens took them to their hotel.

"Rest a little and freshen up. I'll bring the lorry around in half an hour. Then it's off to the Nairobi National Park to begin your acquaintance with African wildlife. It's a short drive."

The drive to the game park gave them time to size up Stavens. They decided they liked his restrained but jovial manner. And he certainly knew the wildlife. He pointed out the ugly marabou storks, the small yellow weavers weaving their communal nests, and the awesome display of wild animals—elephants, gazelles, wildebeest, buffalo, and giraffes. They had seen large animals in zoos, and Moon had hunted big game, but the sheer size of the African landscape covered with so many large mammals was breathtaking.

"Everett, I hope you are catching some of this with your camera." "I'm trying. There's so much to shoot."

The Abedarres were their next Kenyan stop. They had chosen them instead of Mt. Kenya because Gladys wanted her Kenya trip to be crowned by another high peak, Mt. Kilimanjaro, which she had wished to see ever since reading Hemingway's short story set there. Terence Stavens told her that they should s e it well from Amboseli unless the mountaintop was completely covered by clouds.

"You should stay up late at the lodge in the Abedarres at least one night to see the nightly spectacular at the waterhole there. You can view the animals coming to the waterhole and saltlick at leisure from the observation room on the lower level of the lodge. You sit in comfort and look at elephants and rhinoceroses practically eye to eye, not to mention zebra, wildebeest, a lion or two, buffalo, wart hogs, and smaller animals."

Gladys hugged Moon. "It sounds delightful."

During the day when they were not out on a game drive, Gladys and Moon watched the visitors at the feeding stations around the lodge. The walkways to the jungle to the feeding stations offered flowers, birds, and animals as well. Gladys particularly enjoyed watching the mouse birds display the behavior that earned them their name. Clambering over vines to the trays of sliced fruits, the mouse birds looked like groups of large rodents with feathers, although closer inspection with binoculars revealed grayish-tan birds with crests and bright orange eyes staring from unfeathered blue skin surrounding them.

"They're cute. I can see why they call them mouse birds."

"They look more like squirrels to me," Moon said.

Often a colorful robin or thrush or bush shrike joined the mouse birds in the assault on the slices of papaya and other fruits. Ground squirrels competed with the birds for tasty morsels. The flowering shrubs and trees all around them attracted many species of iridescent sunbirds, gorgeous in their yellow, blue, red and orange plumages.

"These are the nectar eaters of the Old World," Stavens explained. "They fill the ecological niche that hummingbirds fill in the New World."

"Sunbird really is the right name, Moon. Their colors are so bright."

"I'm trying to catch their color on film."

After their morning excursion that included a rather close encounter with an old bull elephant, they had lunch at the Abedarre Country Club. As they drove in, a fellow in what passed for traditional native garb greeted them. The elegant meal offered them they agreed was an excellent way to "rough it." Gladys had wine and Moon ordered a Tusker to complement the food.

"I don't mind not drinkin' the water as long as they don't run out of this Tusker."

"You can always buy bottled water, Moon." "But the beer costs less."

"You could drink coffee or tea. They come with the meal." "I'll leave those to you. I'm definitely a Tusker man."

"I wonder whether our pictures will turn out all right. If they do, we'll have some wonderful scenic shots, not to mention that elephant and the sunbirds. The waterfall, the mountains, those flowering shrubs and trees—it's all so beautiful. I feel we're like Adam and Eve exploring Paradise."

"Don't look for an apple tree," Moon joked. "There may be a serpent behind it."

"I'm glad to see you've been reading Milton."

"Yeah. I really feel sympathy for Satan even though I side with Adam."

That evening, after eating dinner with others staying at the lodge, they gathered with the others on the balcony above the water hole to watch the animals come in to drink. Besides water, the waterhole provided the animals with a salt lick. The elephants in particular were sampling the salt in addition to bathing and drinking. There were big cows shooting water on themselves and their calves, then moving to the salt and snuffing the ground with their trunks to find it. Gladys and Moon busied their cameras photographing the elephants and the black rhinoceros that joined them before dark.

When it was too dark too use the cameras, they moved to the viewing room to continue watching the animals. As the night wore on, the room grew colder. Gladys went to their room and brought back a blanket. Underneath the blanket, the two snuggled as they watched the nightly spectacle. In the lights, they could see the night-jars flying back and forth across the water hole catching moths, and in the distance, just coming into the light, a herd of zebras were making their way out of the darkness to the water. Raising her binoculars, Gladys spied a young colt.

"Look, Moon, that little baby zebra's cute."

"Yeah, but he'd better watch out for that spotted hyena that's following him."

"He's ugly and mean looking."

"So's that wart hog over there. Only a blind mother could love him."

"Baby elephants are appealing."

The baby animals brought Andrew into Moon's thoughts. He wondered if he and Susan loved Andrew enough. Certainly they didn't pay the attention to him that these animals' mothers gave their young. Moon resolved that he would spend more time with his son.

They watched until two o'clock, then headed to their room and bed. Despite several blankets, they were glad to hold each other just for the body warmth. Terence had warned them, but they were not really prepared for the chilly equatorial night.

"Just like home," Moon observed, "high elevations bring cool nights."

From the Abedarres, they drove north to Samburu, a much lower, dryer region. The luxuriant forests and croplands of the Abedarres gave way to a much more arid environment where prickly acacia trees dominated the landscape. Whenever they stopped here and there to view the scenery or animals, people of all ages soon surrounded them, seemingly materializing out of thin air, eagerly accepting any sandwiches or other food left over from the tourists' box lunches.

"These box lunches are awful," Gladys judged. "I'm glad some-body will eat them."

"Somebody besides me," Moon added, "I'd prefer a mess of wild greens, even 'possum meat. I think some folks on we fare back home might turn down this food."

At the Samburu lodge, they had a pla e of their own, a round hut with a thatched roof. Terence Stavens explained that the smooth textures of the outer and inner walls were not attributable to concrete.

"Are workmen brought in to build these?"

"No. The women build these. They begin with two frames of wicker, one inside the other. Then they put together a mixture of water, mud, and goat dung. They fill the space between these wicker frames with this, and then add layers of the mixture to cover the frames. Finally they wet this down and work it to a finish almost as smooth as glass." These huts had a lavatory with a commode, a bidet, a washbasin, and a shower concealed behind a movable curtain. On the walls were painted scenes of zebras, impala, and giraffes.

Gladys tested the bed and found it quite comfortable, but they had to hurry to the main lodge for the mid-day meal. Cooked out-doors, the barbecued goat and antelope came hot from the grill. The food was delicious, and Moon was washing down large portions of it with Tusker. Gladys had to make certain they did not linger over the food. "Moon, don't forget we're planning to watch the Samburu dancers perform.

"All right. Let me finish this Tusker and we'll go."

As they made their way to the outdoor dance area, they spied a beautiful blue and tan kingfisher in the trees beside the stream that ran through the grounds. Moon was planning to photograph the dancers, but as they walked to the dancing theater, they came so close to the kingfisher that Lunamin raised his camera and took two quick shots with his 300mm lens before Gladys hurried him off.

"You've become an obsessive camera hound, Moon." "Your doing, Miss Stayskill."

The Samburu dancers were not visible when they took their places on the benches in the covered area beside the red dirt dance arena. Their wait was short. Soon they heard chanting to the left and turned to see a line of young Samburu warriors, tall and thin, dancing into the arena waving spears, jumping, and chanting. Their flowing red robes and red loincloths matched their reddened hair. In their dance, they leaped to heights that suggested they were all Olympic high jumpers.

"I sure hope these photos turn out."

"You're becoming an enthusiastic shutterbug." "It's a kind of trophy hunting, I reckon."

Gladys smiled. She was making real progress with her pupil.

The afternoon game drive produced many more photo opportunities. Moon was especially pleased with his shots of gerenuks standing on their hind legs to eat high foliage. These strange looking antelopes appeared to wish to be giraffes.

"Look, Moon, they rear up on their hind legs to get the tasty foliage too high for them on four legs."

"Gerenuks are like some people I know, always thinking what's beyond reach is better than what they have."

"Moon, that's not necessarily bad. Robert Browning said, 'A man's reach should exceed his grasp, or what's a heaven for.' We need to strive to be greater than we think we are."

"Honey, you're looking at one of the number one reachers of this world. I reckon I'm just a two-legged gerenuk."

"Me too, Adamo."

Late in the day as they were finishing their afternoon game drive, they passed a tree where a leopard had stored a kill. Their luck was running high. A large leopard came out of the bushes and moved across the track in front of their vehicle.

"If these pictures turn out, Gladys, you'll have something to scare your cat."

"No, he'll just think it's a big cousin."

From Samburu they moved on to the Rift Valley and the lodge at Lake Baringo. On the way, they encountered two Pokots, people who refused contact with the outside world. After some difficult negotiating by Terence Stavens and the proffering of money, the Pokot couple agreed to pose for photographs.

"I think we are like the Pokots, Moon." "Why's that?"

"Well, I guess you could say in a way we're defying society also."
"You may be right, but I'm not a Pokot. I don't charge for photographs."

"Maybe you would if you had less money."

"That's true. People do strang things for money."

At Lake Baringo, they found comfortable accommodations. They didn't envy the young Europeans camping out near the lake. The campers had to contend with hippopotamuses coming out of the lake after dark. Moon and Gladys congratulated themselves that they had a comfortable bungalow and didn't have to worry about hippo night visitors. They spent hours making love.

"We've been so busy, we've hardly had time to enjoy each other," Gladys said.

"We can try to make up for lost time,: Moon said as he began undressing her.

Walking to the lake edge, next morning, they watched the spear fishermen wade waist deep in the lake waters, seemingly oblivious to the crocodiles that also inhabited the lake. Stavens assured them that these crocodiles did not attack the fishermen, that they were strictly fish eaters. Remembering the giant crocs along the river at Samburu, Moon and Gladys found this explanation difficult to accept.

"I wish the fishermen luck. I'm happy to stay on croc-free land," Gladys said.

At other lakes in the Rift, salt lakes, they saw huge flocks of flamingos and watched the hot springs bubbling from the earth. "This part of Africa, the Horn, is sliding away from the continent," Stavens told them, the Rift Valley is famous for its geology, its scenery, and for the archaeological finds of the Leakeys."

"It's fascinating to think that we are standing where early man may have walked," Gladys mused.

"The live animals interest me more than the bones of those long dead," Moon said. "Bones don't make good trophies or good photographs."

"I like live animals, too, but it's so thrilling to know that we are standing here where the early ancestors of man roamed."

"What about those hippos?" Moon asked. "They're big. I've heard they're dangerous."

"They certainly are," Stavens said "You should know that hippos kill more people in Africa each year than do elephants, lions, or buffalo, though buffalo have a well-earned reputation for belligerency, and lions can cause problems for the unsuspecting. There was a Dutch couple that camp d by the river in the Masai Mara where they had been warned not to go. Lions came for supper and ate the campers."

Gladys shivered. "Masai Mara? Aren't we going there soon? "Yes, that's our next stop."

Leaving the Rift, they drove back to Nairobi and took a plane to the Masai Mara, in order to avoid the long, slow drive over the poorly maintained road to the Mara. At the airport, they looked out from the waiting lounge and saw their plane, an ancient DC-3. Terence assured them that it was a very airworthy craft. With bated breath, they awaited the weighing of their luggage.

"I reckon we should have packed a little lighter."

Stavens reassured. "Don't worry. You couldn't be much over the limit. A little cash will fix that." He was correct. They paid the few dollars extra and were soon on their way in a stripped down but reliable old carrier for an uneventful flight. At their camp in the Mara they were to be housed in tents—fairly luxurious tents, Stavens told them.

As they entered the Mara lodge to get their tent assignments, they encountered an American in shorts and a colorful floral shirt. Hearing them speak to one another and to Terence, he recognized them as fellow Americans and accosted them as if they were long-lost friends. "I'm a successful businessman from Cincinnati, Ohio. He loudly proclaimed how much Africa came short of what he had back home."

"Hello. You're Americans, too. I can tell. I'm Joe Goetz from

Cincinnati. I'm in auto parts, own six stores. Imagine being asked to sleep in tents at the prices we're paying. How scroungy can you be? These people here just don't do anything unless you flash a roll of money at them. Once I caught on, I did what was necessary, but it's not what I would call good service."

Gladys and Moon tried to hide their embarrassment and get away from their gaudily clad acquaintance as soon as possible.

"Moon, I believe we have seen the proverbial ugly American up close. And, unlike the one in the b ok, this one's really horrid."

"He's no credit to his country, that's certain. I reckon he's a walking ad for the people who say making money doesn't make a man better. I hope I've handled my good fortune better than that."

"I'm glad you see that having wealth brings with it a need to handle it well."

They found that their tent without much trouble. Erected on a concrete slab, it was spacious enough for four people. It also had very functional indoor plumbing. Moon's only complaint was that it lacked a double bed.

Gladys laughed. "I think we can figure out how to have sex on a cot. We could experiment. Let's take our showers together."

The next morning they clambered aboard a Land Rover just as the golden red ball of sun was breaking over the acacias on the horizon.

When they disembarked from that vehicle, they climbed aboard a basket attached to a large, colorful balloon for a ride in a many-colored chariot that carried them gently aloft. Rising from the ground in the first light, they could not help feeling a sense of awe at the huge golden expanse of grassland spread out before them dotted with grazing impala, buffalo, topi, zebra, and wildebeest.

"This ride is exhilarating, Moon."

Taking in all that he could, Moon only nodded his assent. The immensity of the landscape had stolen his words. He hugged Gladys and they laughed with pleasure. The more skittish animals stampeded at their approach, but the majority of them, used to the balloons, simply continued munching grass. Their ride took Gladys and Moon about ten miles before they landed and were served a leisurely English breakfast there in the field among the grazing animals and then taken back to the lodge in a four-wheel drive vehicle.

After lunch, they visited a nearby Masai village, where once inside the kraal or fence of sticks woven to keep out lions, hyenas, and other night visitors, they were greeted by the chief and a group of women singing a song of welcome. There were many trinkets available, and Moon bargained for several b ad necklaces for Gladys. Then they paid the small fee required to see the inside of a Masai lodge. They had to bend to move through the smoky interior. Moon told Gladys that he had seen coalmines whose ceilings were a great deal higher than these huts made of wicker and cow dung. He found it difficult to understand why such tall people (all of the men were over six feet tall) would have such low ceilings. Apparently the men and boys did little but sit around and swap stories a large part of the day while the women did the work.

"Don't the men do anything but loaf?" Moon asked.

"There are no lions to hunt legally now, and warfare is a thing of the past. It's difficult to be a traditional Masai warrior these days," Terence told them on their way back to the camp compound. 'Cattle tending is their main task."

Moon thought about the men's lack of occupation. "I reckon I would be at loose ends if I suddenly had no mines to direct."

Back at their tent, they chased off a marauding olive baboon. It had made its intrusion while they were gone. It appeared to have something white on its face. Evidently Moon had not closed the tent well enough. The baboon had found some bananas and other food in their tent, but it had also made a big mess with Moon's shaving cream.

"That explains the white face," Gladys chortled.

"Reminds me of that fellow at the lodge, butting in where he's not wanted."

The next morning on their game drive they encountered a pair of lions in the throes of courtship. They had left the pride and were "honeymooning." They may have had privacy from their pride, but tourists ogled the couple from several directions from five vehicles. For the most part, the male and female spent their time lying in the grass next to each other in sleepy repose. Every fifteen minutes or so, the male would mount the female. Then they engaged in a brief bout of intercourse before resuming their recumbent poses.

"Gladys, there's no savoring in the sex life of lions. That king of beasts reminds me of me before I met you."

"Lions seem to be rank gulpers. I don't see much savoring, that's certain."

"I wouldn't want to b a lion, even if he is the king of beasts."

Gladys smiled, obviously pleased at the manifest success of her teaching.

After what seemed to Moon to be far too long, they left the lion couple and continued their drive through the Mara. At a tree-lined waterhole, they spied a huge open-billed stork, and a little later they came upon a large collection of vultures tearing at the remains of an old lion kill. On their way back to the compound, they flushed a kori bustard.

"That's the largest flighted bird in the world," Terence told them. "I thought you told us at Samburu that the marabou stork has that title," Gladys objected.

"Yes, I did. It depends on whether you go by weight or by size. It's really a tie."

"The kori bustard certainly is better looking than the marabous. They're ugly. I give the title to kori on the basis of points for beauty," Gladys said.

Flying back to Nairobi aboard the old DC-3, Moon and Gladys talked about Amboseli. They were hoping to see Kilimanjaro, though Stavens had told them not to get their hopes too high, as the peak was often hidden in clouds. Gladys was worried that she might miss the mountain that had prompted Hemingway's famous short story.

They proceeded to Amboseli by Toyota van. Entering the park, they saw large areas of bare ground, some of it muddy.

"The heavy rains last year are just now evaporating. These areas will be bone dry before the next rains," Stavens explained.

On the road to their lodge, Gladys and Moon asked Stavens repeatedly when they could expect to see Kilimanjaro.

About two hours into the trip, his reply cheered them. "Any time now."

They were relieved finally to hear Stavens call out the name. "There it is."

They looked to their right and up where the cloud cover had dissipated.

"Oh, Moon, isn't it beautiful."

"Sure is. Reminds me of the Rockies."

For several minutes they stopped to see and photograph Mt. Kilimanjaro's snow-covered peak rising majestically above the surrounding plain. It was briefly unencumbered by clouds. Soon the clouds enveloped it again. They barely made the lodge at Amboseli by dark, but Gladys and Moon were jubilant about their good luck in seeing the famous mountain.

They were still glowing with enthusiasm when the time arrived for their morning game drive. The animals at Amboseli had less space to wander away from tourists, less area to roam than did the wildlife in the vast Masai Mara. Whenever an interesting animal was sighted, numerous vehicles congregated at the spot, seemingly out of nowhere. The most amazing sight to Gladys and Moon was the gathering of nine vehicles full of ogling tourists that occurred after Stavens found a cooperative black rhino that posed at length for photographs.

"This is more like a zoo than a wild place, Gladys, but the photos should be great."

"Our big game trophies," laughed Gladys.

"Yeah. But it's hard to get a picture without a vehicle in it."

The high spot of their Amboseli adventure did not occur until they were on their way out—a pair of cheetahs lounging under an acacia tree not far off the road, a chance to "burn" the last of the film they had brought.

"What a photo op," Gladys gloated.

"I reckon I'm getting to be a real shutterbug," Moon bragged. During the drive back to Nairobi and the flight back to New York,

Moon and Gladys spent their waking time re iving their adventure. The shared moments had brought them clos r to each other than ever, and Moon wondered how life would be if he and Gladys were living together permanently.

"Gladys, we need to be together all the time. It's harder and harder for me to live away from you."

"I know, but you're a married man." "I can't help that."

"Why not? Have you heard about divorce?" "She won't give me one. I've told you."

"You mean you haven't really tried to get free. Didn't you tell me she's having affairs? Why can't you find evidence and sue for divorce?" "I worry about how a messy divorce fight would affect Andrew."

"There you are. You have to decide what you want." "I want you to marry me."

"I haven't agreed to marry you, even if you weren't married. You are married, so there's no point in talking about our marrying."

Moon couldn't find any answer to that conclusion. Still, he truly worried about what a divorce might mean for Andrew. He didn't think he was using that just as an excuse as Gladys had hinted. Moon drank one beer after another as he assuaged his feeling of self-pity with drink.

When the beer failed to bring the needed relief, Moon switched to bourbon. Moon had been pushed back to contemplation of his life with Susan. Maybe he could persuade Susan to give him a divorce if he increased the amount of the settlement he had offered. After all, he was sure that she had ventured outside the marriage also. If necessary, as a last resort, he could hire some private investigators to accumulate plenty of evidence of her infidelity, he was certain.

THE LION'S DEN

 is flight from New York to Tri-cities was late in the evening. It was dark by the time that his plane reached the hub in North Carolina.

He attempted to telephone Susan, but there was no answer other than the machine's recording. His flight from Charlotte to Tri-cities was several hours late departing. After telephoning Susan once again from Tri-cities Airport without success, Moon got a call through to Lunar Mining and left a message. Next he called Fred at home. Then Moon got into his car, paid his parking fee and headed north toward the Abingdon Riviera. By then, it was nearing midnight.

It was past midnight when he turned off Interstate 81, headed toward Damascus, and prepared to turn into his driveway. Lost in his thoughts about how to resolve his dilemma with Susan and Gladys, he had just started to make the turn when a truck met him, lurched to the side, just missing him, skidded a little, turned back to the right, and then sped past on the highway toward Abingdon.

A little shaken, Moon pulled to his right and stopped, watching the pick-up in his rear-view mirror. It seemed familiar to him. After a few minutes, he started toward the house again. At the end of the long drive, he was surprised to see everything brilliantly lighted. The lights in the house and outside were all on.

At first Moon thought that Suzy was having a party, but he soon realized that there was nobody stirring. Using his garage door opener, Moon drove slowly into the garage and parked. Suzy's Mercedes was in its usual space. He got out and walked into the house, leaving his luggage behind.

"Susan!" he called as he walked toward the den. There was no answer. The house was still. Moon walked down the hall, past the kitchen, and into the den, calling as he went. There was no answer. When he entered the doorway of the den, Lunamim spied a body on the floor in front of the fireplace. Focusing his eyes on the body, he recognized Susan crumpled on the floor with his shotgun beside her. Quickly he strode to Susan and kneeled down beside her.

He felt her body. It was warm. Turning her over, Moon saw the wound in her lower chest and stomach and the pool of blood beneath her on the hardwood floor. She did not respond to his voice, and he could not detect her pulse. Suzy was dead. Moon fought off his urge to retch and examined the scene with all the calmness he could muster. He couldn't look at her body again for a long time. When he did look again, he found he couldn't help himself. He hurried to the bathroom in the utility room and threw up in the commode. After that, he went back and sat in the den near Susan.

For what seemed like an hour, he fought off the scenes from Vietnam that haunted him and the memories of Shorty's death that joined the present bloody scene in his mind. Susan's body still retained warmth and was not stiff. He guessed that she had been dead for a little while but that whatever had caused her death had not happened much earlier that night. It must have happened just before he reached home. At first Moon wondered whether Susan had taken her own life, but remembering the truck that had nearly hit him, he looked around. Whoever had been driving that truck probably had killed Suzy.

Before long, Lunamin found evidence that somebody else had been there that evening and had taken no pains to conceal the fact. There was a half-empty bottle of gin on the kitchen table and a number of empty tonic bottles beside it. An empty rum bottle in the trash caught his eyes next. Since Suzy had been a confirmed rum-and-coke drinker, Moon knew that another person had been there, probably Rod Mashburn. Rod liked to think that drinking gin and tonics was the height of sophistication. That didn't rule out suicide, but it certainly enlarged the possibilities.

When Moon had calmed down, he began a thorough search of the house. First, he searched everywhere for Andrew. He was afraid whoever had killed Susan might have taken the boy. Was it a kidnapping? Whatever had happened, Moon knew it meant trouble for him, but he didn't want the trouble to be compounded. His search revealed a rumpled bed in the master bedroom but no Andrew. The boy's bed had been made up; no one had slept in it recently. On the floor beside the bed in the master bedroom, he found a bracelet that confirmed his suspicion about Rod's having been there. The inscription on it read, "To Susan with love, Rod."

"I'll not give this to the police," he thought. In the heat of anger, Lunamin considered a more private revenge might suit him better. "Rod is a real bastard, but he is family," he told hims lf. Days later he would regret keeping the jewelry.

Abandoning his search for Andy, he went to the telephone and called Winding Fork. Andrew definitely wasn't in this house. Susan must have taken him to Archibald and Serafina if she expected Rod. She had enough sense to get the boy out of the way. Serafina answered the telephone.

"Mamaw, it's Moon. Is Andrew with you?"

"Sure is, Ev'rett. He's been listenin' to Archie's tales—gettin' ready for bedtime. He's in bed fast asleep now."

Lunamin was relieved that Susan's death had not been part of a kidnapping attempt. "Mamaw, Susan's been shot. She's dead. I just came home from the airport and found her with a hole blown in her by my shotgun that I keep over the mantel in the den. It's an ugly, bloody mess. It keeps runnin' through my mind even when I'm not looking at Susan's body. What'll I tell Andy?"

"Moon, keep calm, Honey. Whatever happens, Andrew will be all right. Archie and me will see to that. You take care. Archie and me will find a way to tell Andy the right way."

"Thanks, Mamaw. I have to call the police now. Goodbye."

As soon as he hung up from calling Winding Fork, Moon looked up the number of the Washington County sheriff's office and called them. He briefly told them what he had found and asked for somebody to be sent to his house to investigate. When he completed that call, he called Gladys in spite of the time. A sleepy voice answered.

"Gladys, I need to talk."

"Moon? Is that you? What's wrong? Do you realize what time it is? Where are you?" she asked in quick succession without giving him time to answer.

"Yeah, it's late. I'm back in Abingdon. Nearly two o'clock in the morning. Suzy's dead."

"What?"

"My wife is dead. It could've been suicide, but it sure looks like murder."

"Moon, you've picked a bad time to play a joke."

"No joke, Honey, my wife's chest has a blo dy shotgun hole in it and I've called the police. They'll be here soon, and they'll probably think I did it."

"Moonman, that's horrible. You call me later and let me know what happens."

"I will."

Moon went to the cabinet where he kept the liquor, took down some Wild Turkey, and p ured himself a double shot of bourbon and added a little ice. Then he sat down to sip the bourbon while he waited for the police. He didn't want to disturb anything else.

Lunamin considered that he would be a prime suspect, especially if the police learned about his wanting a divorce from Susan and her not willing to let him go. It would make for quite a sensational trial, and he was sure that District Attorney Hugh Macfee would love all the publicity that it would bring. Why, it might be enough to get Macfee that seat in the legislature that he craved. Bringing a rich strip miner to justice would be a feather in his cap with the environmentalists, Moon thought.

No, he couldn't expect Macfee to go easy with him. Moon was from over the mountain and Macfee wouldn't have to worry much about incurring the wrath of his family. Besides, Macfee and he had had words about surface mining. Macfee and he had also been at odds concerning Macfee's suspicion about drug use at Lunamin's house, and they had had some words about traffic tickets Susan had received. They had not met amicably. Knowing Macfee as Moon did, he thought the prosecutor wouldn't look very far for another suspect.

It wouldn't do for Moon to hire just any lawyer. The lawyers that handled Moon's business affairs were competent for civil matters, but he'd need a really good criminal lawyer if he faced a murder trial. Richard Graylock came to mind right away. The only problem, Moon thought, was that Graylock had been on the opposite side from Moon in a number of cases involving mining issues when Lunar Mining had been taken to court. Would Graylock be willing to defend him? Moon remembered that George and Graylock were close friends. Maybe it was time to ask a favor of George. Lunamin went back to the telephone and dialed George's number.

"George? Moon here. I need your help." "If it's something honest, I'm your man."

"I came home and found Susan with a hole in her chest and belly from a shotgun blast. From my shotgun. I shouldn't have left it hanging over the mantel loaded, but I did. I'm likely to be charged with killing her. Do you think that you could get Richard Graylock to defend me if I'm arrested?"

"Moon, have you been drinking?"

"No. Honest, I came home from the airport and found her dead." "Did you do it, Moon?"

"No, George, you know me better'n that. I reckon that bloody hole in her chest will stay with me a long time. It's runnin' in my mind along with scenes from Nam and Shorty's accident."

"All right, Moon, if you're arrested, I'll do my best to get Graylock for you. He won't come cheap for you, though."

"Thanks, old buddy. I'll pay what he asks. I'm not hagglin'."

A NEW GAME

The deputies from the Washington County sheriff's office spent the morning going over Moon's house and questioning Moon. He watched to make sure that they took note of the gin bottle, the tonic bottles, and the rum bottle as well as the empty glasses on the coffee table in the den where he had found Susan's body. As far as he could tell, they handled things carefully.

When the coroner had completed his work, the questioning of Moon began in earnest. They were eager to establish Moon's whereabouts during the day and evening. It was clear that Moon was already the chief suspect.

The deputy who questioned Moon was polite and businesslike. "Mr. Lunamin, we'd like to know your activities during the day and evening."

"I'd been on a business trip. I got in to Tri-Cities around eleven-forty-five and drove directly here."

"You didn't stop anywhere?"

"No. I called Fred MacCloud from the airport before I left there to check on things at Lunar Mining."

"What time did you get home?"

"Around quarter past twelve or a little before—I had told my wife that I would be home around 10:30, but my flight was late."

The police investigation revealed that Susan Lunamin's death had been a murder. Suicide was ruled out. There were signs that she had struggled with her killer. There were bruises on her face and arms, and she had the skin of someone under her fingernails. The time of death had been close to the time of Moon's arrival, anywhere from ten to one o'clock.

There were several sets of fingerprints on the shotgun: Susan's, Moon's, and those of two other people, but these unidentified finger-prints did not interest Washington County District Attorney Hugh Macfee. A rotund, balding man with great political ambitions, he habitually fingered his necktie during the press conference he called to announce his filing charges against Everett Lunamin.

Macfee was practically ecstatic to have a high- profile case dropped upon him just as he planned to run for the House of Delegates. His investigation revealed that Everett Lunamin had asked for a divorce from Susan Lunamin and that she had refused. It was common knowledge among all of Susan's friends and acquain-tances. Macfee didn't look further than Moon, who had opportunity and motive— and enough money to make this a sensational case. He hurried to announce his belief in Lunamin's guilt to the press.

"In a family matter," Macfee told anybody who questioned his bringing the case, 'it's usually the husband, not the butler. Besides, the person who finds the body is quite likely the murderer. In this case, Everett Lunamin wanted his wife out of the way because she wouldn't give him the divorce he'd asked for. He was frustrated and jealous of her affairs with other men. They argued and during the argument he killed her in a jealous rage. He'd probably worked himself up to a high pitch of anger on his way home from his business trip. He had motive and opportunity, and his prints are on the murder weapon."

Macfee wasn't about to let any qualms concerning the other fin-gerprints on the murder weapon thwart what appeared to be a ready-to-order homicide prosecution. He knew that there were other fin-gerprints on the shotgun, but he didn't worry about those. When a reporter for the Roanoke paper asked him if he were concerned about other prints on the gun, the prosecutor brushed the questions aside.

"Lunamin's prints are there—that's the important point."

He had his murderer, his case, and (he felt sure) his seat in the legislature.

Moon soon found that his quandary about his relationship with Susan had disappeared, only to be replaced by another, graver problem. Still, he found himself thinking of New York and Gladys. He longed to see and touch her. He remembered the times they had spent sightseeing on the noisy, bustling streets of the metropolis. He wished he could walk with her and have dinner at the Greek restaurant around the corner from her apartment. He remembered the joyful days they had just experienced in Africa—he wondered if she remembered their balloon ride. Then he had a thought that cheered him a little. If he could just escape from the trap Macfee was laying for him, he would be free to spend lots of time with Gladys.

ANDREW

For a while Andrew missed his mother enough to cry for her now and then, but gradually he became accustomed to being with Archibald and Serafina all of the time instead of just for a few days and nights at a time while Moon and Susan pursued their divergent interests. Serafina cooked all sorts of good things and hugged him a lot. One day when he missed Susan and teared up, Serafina cured his hurt with cookies. "You're my very own favorite curly-haired great grandson, Andrew," Serafina told him as she ran her hand through his brown hair.

Andrew looked up at her with his blue eyes and dried his tears. "Do you have any molasses cookies, Mamaw?"

"I think I may be able to find one or two Papaw hasn't found. You can eat them with some milk."

Sitting on the other end of the kitchen table reading the newspaper, Archibald overheard. He commented on Serafina's implied charge of cookie larceny with a loud snort.

"When you finish with those cookies, I'll tell you a story, Andrew." George laughed. He was sitting next to Archibald reading another section of the newspaper. "Don't rush through those cookies just to get to the story, Andrew. Be sure to give Mamaw's molasses cookies the attention they deserve."

Archibald MacCloud was a locally renowned storyteller who delighted in entertaining Andy with stories of the old man's exploits in youth and in the world wars as well as traditional mountain tales like the Big Toe, which Andy loved to have told at bedtime, when the gathering darkness made the story a little scary.

When Papaw-monster asked fearsomely, "Where's my big toe?" Andy would giggle, "I don't know. I ain't got it" and Papaw monster would pounce, saying, "Yes, you do, and here it is" as he grabbed Andy's diminutive big toe. The story had been really scary the first time that Archibald had told it, but now the telling of it had become a comforting bedtime ritual for Andrew.

While Moon had pursued his business and other interests and Susan had occupied herself with the local society and her private affairs, Andrew had received all the attention that a small boy could ask when he was with his great-grandparents. Uncles and aunts and cousins (especially George) often came by for visits with the old folks and gave Andy plenty of their time also. Everybody in the family felt sorry for Andrew because of the apparent neglect of his parents. More than the rest, George sympathized with Andy's situation. He kept hoping that Moon would eventually see that Andrew required more attention from his father.

Andrew particularly liked George's visits, because George always seemed to have candy or some little toy for Andy, and he would throw the boy up and ride him on his shoulders—something Papaw didn't do very much any more because Andy was almost five and getting heavy. And George could tell stories, too, about dinosaurs and other neat animals.

Often George and Papaw talked about boring things like mining: surface mining. Andy knew what that was. His pa (he didn't say Daddy unless Susan corrected him) had taken him to his mine and showed him the big hole in the ground, the piles of gray slate and black coal, and the big green and yellow machines that dug the coal and loaded it in the trucks.

"Are those machines all yours, Pa?"

"Sure are son. All but most of the trucks. Those belong to other folks. They just take the coal to the tipple for us."

"What's a tipple?"

"You've seen the one down at Norton. That's where they wash the coal and load it on the coal cars to haul it to people who use it. I'll take you to watch one work one of these days."

By the time Andrew had finished his treat, Archibald and George were once again immersed in a discussion of mining and politics. When Papaw and George had talked about mining so long that Andy got tired of hearing about it and tired of playing with the little front loader that George had brought him, he tried to get the promised story. He liked for them to tell stories, not talk about how better laws for reclamation (he wasn't quite sure what that was) were needed.

"Tell me a story now, Papaw. I've finished my cookies and milk."

Receiving no response, Andy waited patiently until the two men were silent to ask again.

"Please, Papaw, you promised a story. Georg , make Papaw tell us a story."

"I can't make Papaw do anything, Andy, but I'll bet he'll tell us about the time he got five turkeys with one shot."

"Papaw, did you?"

"Why, yes, I reckon I did that once. Or leastways some folks say I done it."

"Tell how, Papaw."

"All right. Now listen. One fall day your mamaw allowed that her larder was mighty nigh empty and we didn't have no turkey for Thanksgivin' dinner. 'Archibald,' she says (I know she's plumb set when she calls me Archibald), 'we need a turkey to give thanks over when all the young'uns come.'

"So I says, 'I'll get old Sureshot (that's my rifle) and go turkey huntin' up ferninst the next ridge where I heard turkeys awhile back.' So next mornin' I got me some shells and old Sureshot and headed up the ridge and over the top of it to where I knew them turkeys were rootin' after acorns.

"It was a fair morning to be in the woods for certain. The leaves were all red and yellow and the air had plenty of moisture from a heavy dew. Sound was acarryin'—'fore long I hear them turkeys scratchin' and talkin' low. I could just taste that turkey meat already. I crept up to them as quiet-like as a snake slidin' over plowed ground.

"When I could see three gobbles in front of me, I pointed old Sureshot in their direction. Then I gobbled. They all three raised their heads to look in my direction and I fired. Them turkeys was all in a line, you see, and my bullet went through one turkey head, and then another, and another. Three turkeys down.

"But my bullet kept goin.' It didn't stop there. Dang if that bullet didn't keep goin' 'til it hit a big dead branch. When that branch fell, it dropped on two turkeys scratchin' 'neath it and knocked 'em out cold. All I had to do was pick them birds up, tie up their legs, and tote 'em home with the three I'd shot dead. Them turkeys was sure tasty. Better'n tame or store bought."

"That was some shot, Papaw. Don't you think so Andy?"

George laughed as he asked the question, so Andy knew Papaw had stretched the truth a bit.

"What happened to the live turkeys?"

"One was a tom and the other a hen. We clipped their wings and kept them penned up to raise little turkeys."

Mamaw called Andy. "Andrew, it's bedtime."

"Do I have to Papaw? Could you tell me a story, too, George?"

"I'll tell you what, Andy, I'll read you a few nursery rhymes from that book I brought you if you'll go to bed now." George took Andy's hand. Andy went with him without more argument.

After Mamaw helped him put on his pajamas, the boy listened to George read some of his favorites—*Jack be nimble, Mary had a little lamb, Jack Sprat could eat no fat*...Andrew went to sleep as George read, "Hey diddle, diddle/The cat and the fiddle/The dish ran away with the spoon/The little dog laughed to see such sport/And the cow jumped over the moon." George slipped out of the bedroom and back to the porch with Archibald and Serafina.

"That trial will be tough for Andy, Papaw, but Moon's going to have a good attorney. Richard Graylock agreed to defend him. We know Moon didn't kill her. If anybody can get at the truth of what happened, Graylock can."

"I hope you're right, George," said Serafina. "I'd hate to lose another child. We lost Moon's pa in that mine, and our daughter left us. She wanted to shed her memories of this place, and James wanted to go west. Moon and that second husband of hers wouldn't have nothing to do with one another. So we raised Moon. He's like a son to us, and he's made of good stuff. Went a little crazy with all that money he's been rakin' in, but he's a good boy. Maybe all this trouble will bring him to see things different. Maybe when it's over he'll pay more mind to Andy."

George nodded agreement.

"He'd own up if he killed her. Moon ain't one to hide his faults," Archibald observed.

"You're right, Papaw. When I asked him, he said he didn't kill Susan. I believe him. We have to hope Graylock will get to the truth."

ON THE MOUNTAINTOP

usan's funeral hosted a less overtly emotional gathering than Shorty's had attracted. Except for her extramarital adventures, Susan had been determinedly middle class in religion and in her social life. So restraint and what Susan would have considered good taste determined the service. Moon left the arrangements to one of Susan's close friends, Angie Setton.

Angie was no beauty. Thin and mousey, she paid little attention to the latest fashions. In spite of her having little in common with Susan, she had been a good friend to his wife—perhaps because she had a son Andrew's age and they had been playmates.

"Angie," Moon had told her when he called for her help, "It's a lot to ask, but I know you could arrange a funeral that Susan would approve."

Angie appeared somewhat taken aback that Moon would be so careful of Susan's feelings. Moon misunderstood her hesitation.

"I'll be glad to repay you for your time and whatever expenses you have."

"Oh, no, Everett, I'll be glad to help you with the funeral arrangements. Don't worry about a thing."

Angie arranged for a viewing at the Maywood Funeral Home, a service at the First Methodist Church, and a short graveside service. She had questioned Moon about the viewing, whether there should be one and whether or not it should be open casket, and she had, despite recommending otherwise, acceded to Moon's desire to have an open casket viewing.

"It's not really the thing these days to have an open casket viewing, Moon."

On this point, Moon had been adamant. "Angie, folks from Winding Fork will expect it. It would be a shame to hide Susan's pretty face from her family and friends."

Though apparently again surprised at Moon's attitude, Angie agreed that Susan's beauty was undeniable. Moon gradually realized she was a little baffled that the neglectful husband described by Susan was this concerned with his dead wife's beauty.

"Everett, were you still in love with Susan when she died? I thought the two of you had nothing other than Andy in common anymore."

"Maybe it's guilt."

Seeing the quizzical look on her face, Moon hastened to set Angie straight.

"No, I didn't kill her. I loved her once. I didn't hate her. Let's just say that I have some good memories of our life together."

The viewing and the service at the Methodist church went by without incident. Most of the people in attendance were friends and acquaintances Lunamins had made since moving to Abingdon. Susan's mother and father and her aunts and uncles were the only family in attendance except for Archibald and Serafina, who brought Andrew.

For the graveside service, though, Moon brought Susan back to Winding Fork and the family's plot upon Pine Mountain. The ridge of the mountain rose up sharply above the valley floor, and here and there a clearing broke through the wooded mountainside. One of these clearings was the MacCloud family cemetery. It was well kept— Archibald MacCloud and other family members saw to that. The road into the cemetery was heavily graveled (Moon had seen to that) and the many family members that attended the funeral had no trouble getting up the drive and parking.

On the Saturday morning of the graveside service, the sun was shining in a partially clouded sky. Banks of fog were hanging low in the valleys below, waiting for the sunshine to break them apart. The mountain air was still cold on this November morning, although the temperature was rising as the sun ascended. Looking across the ridges, Moon saw plenty of evidence of ODSUM'S handiwork, but the remaining leaves of the trees still covered some of the violation of the mountainsides.

Old friends and family gathered around Moon. Fred, Acie, and all the others from Lunar Mining except Earl were there. Acie told Moon that Earl had called and asked him to tell Moon he was sorry, that he had to make a trip to Kentucky to appear in court on a DUI charge and couldn't be at the funeral. Moon accepted Earl's excuse without irritation. Earl always was getting into some scrape or other.

Moon stood and gazed out over the ridges a long time before joining Archibald, Serafina, and Andrew. Gazing at the natural beauty helped ease his mind. Not yet realizing the full impact of Susan's death, Andy stayed close to his paternal great grandparents and maternal grandparents.

"Andy, are you all right?" Moon asked after greeting the Stanards and his grandparents.

"Don't you fret about Andy, Ev'rett. We'll see to him. We're knowledgeable about raisin' our children's children." Serafina smiled and added, "We did a toler'ble job with you, Honey. We know you didn't kill her."

Just then, Moon spied Rod Mashburn standing at the edge of the crowd. Moon could not help being angry. Rod's face was full of remorse as he came up to Lunamin to try to make his peace.

"Moon, I sure am sorry about Suzy. You just don't know how sorry.'"

Moon glared at Rod. He was not very receptive because he had found the evidence of the gin and tonics in the den and had found further evidence of Rod's visit in the bedroom.

"I reckon I have some idea, Rod. You ought to be more careful of what you drop in other people's bedrooms."

Moon reached in his pocket and pulled out a bracelet inscribed "To Susan with love, Rod." Lashing Rod across the face with the bracelet, Moon prepared to send a fist to Rod's jaw, but Fred and Acie caught Lunamin's arms and held him.

"You better go, Rod. I don't believe you're wanted here," Fred said. "We can't hold Moon but so long."

"All right, Fred, I don't want to create a scene here," Rod said meekly before turning to leave. Watching Rod disappear down the gravel drive, Moon thanked Fred and Acie.

"I reckon a brawl would've messed things up."

Moon quieted down in time to greet the other mourners and thank them for coming. The gathering listened to the brief words of the Presbyterian minister that Angie had engaged, the Reverend Angus Maxwell. His high brow and heavy jowls set over a substantial body exuded a sense of solidity and stability that Lunamin found comforting. He was calmed by Maxwell's firm handshake and consoling words.

"I'm sorry for your loss, Mr. Lunamin. You can find comfort in knowing your wife will not suffer any more."

Without further conversation, Maxwell took a position at the head of the casket and lifted his hands to gather the mourners about him.

"Let us pray. 'The Lord is my shepherd....'"

After he had led them in the 23rd Psalm, Maxwell continued quietly. "We are gathered here to ay to witness the burial of Susan
Stanard Lunamin, a young mother taken from us in the flower of her motherhood. Her leave-taking of this world was violent, but she is now a recipient of the peace that passes all understanding. Her earthly cares are finished. We must give comfort to her family, to Everett Lunamin, her husband, and to Andrew, her son, and to her parents, Tom and Louella Stanard, who brought her into this world and cared for her youth.

"It is difficult to accept the death of those who die before they have run the full race of life, but we must accept the destiny that the Lord has appointed. The ways of the Lord are inscrutable to us. Here on earth we see as through a clouded glass, darkly. It is not for us to judge, oh Lord. Have mercy upon the soul of your servant, Susan Stanard Lunamin, and have mercy upon us who mourn for her. In the
name of the Father, the Son, and the Holy Ghost we commend her spirit to eternal rest. Blessed be the name of the Lord. Amen."

Moon joined the chorus of amens that echoed the Reverend Maxwell's, but his mind was not easy. He was immersed in guilt and bedeviled by a desire to know who had killed Susan, and why.

Thanking the Reverend Maxwell for his words, Moon told him that they were just right. "You said just what Susan would have wanted. Words of comfort. She didn't like a great show of emotion."

"I was glad to be of help." Maxwell gazed at the many ridges rising before them to the horizon. "This setting certainly is peaceful. I would wish for a final resting place as beautiful as this. If I can be of any further help, let me know."

After Moon had said his goodbyes, he walked over to where Acie and Fred were waiting for him.

"Take some time off, Moon. Acie and me can run things."

"I'll take you up on that, Fred. I'll probably end up in jail soon. That Macfee has his sights dead on me. He's not tryin' at all to do anything with those other prints on that shotgun."

WINDING FORK

The police were waiting to arrest Lunamin for the murder of Susan when he returned to his home in Abingdon. Using his telephone call to ask Serafina and Archibald to take care of Andrew and to tell George to call Richard Graylock, he repeated his declaration of his innocence.

"I didn't kill Susan, but it looks like I'll need some good lawyerin.'" "Don't you worry, Ev'rett. We know you'll be all right," Serafina comforted.

Moon had sized up Macfee accurately. He was determined to convict Lunamin. He even went out of his way to convince the judge that Moon was a risk for flight and therefore should not be allowed to make bail. If he had succeeded, Moon would have spent all the time waiting for his trial in jail.

Richard Graylock proposed that Moon be allowed bail and be released in the custody of Archibald MacCloud on the condition that he stay at the MacCloud residence in Winding Fork.

"The defendant is no flight risk, your honor," Graylock told Judge Grindquist. "He has no criminal record. His business and almost all of his assets and family are here in Southwest Virginia. His grandfather Archibald MacCloud is a veteran of two world wars and an upstanding member of his community in Winding Fork. He has agreed to take responsibility for Mr. Lunamin's appearance in court at the appointed time."

Judge Grindquist agreed to Graylock's proposal. Lunamin told Graylock that he was in no mood for a long delay. He didn't like to be thought of by everyone as a wife killer. For this reason, he urged

Graylock to have the trial date set forward as much as possible, even though the lawyer said that he needed time to prepare the case.

"Lawyer, I don't want my son thinking I killed his mother."

"I understand. I'll do my best to get the trial set forward. I hope I'll be ready."

The days at Winding Fork were peaceful and gave Moon a great deal of time with Andy, Archibald, Serafina, and his thoughts. On Moon's first day back with them, Serafina handed him the Bible they had given him when he was a boy.

"Read this. Start with the Book of James." "Mamaw, I don't much want to read right now." "You read it, Everett Lunamin. It'll help."

Like Archibald, Moon understood when Serafina gave an order that she did not expect to have ignored. He opened to James 1:12 and read. "Blessed is the man who endures trial, for when he has stood the test he will receive the crown of life which God has promised to those who love him."

Moon stopped and thought about this text. He was used to the habit of opening the Bible at random and taking the passage that came to a person's attention as a sign. Maybe it was meant for him to see this passage today. He certainly had endured trial, and he was certainly going to endure a trial for his wife's murder. He felt sure that he knew who was guilty of the murder, but Macfee had him, not Rod Mashburn, in his sights. Moon had to admit that he was a more tempting target. He was rich and a citizen within Macfee's jurisdiction—a prime example to show that the prosecutor played no favorites in doing the people's business. It wouldn't be half so helpful politically to convict a relatively unknown man from over the mountain.

As the days wore on, Moon spent much of his time walking in the woods or corresponding with Gladys and talking to her on the telephone. She promised to be at his trial, though somewhat disguised so that his ODSUM colleagues (if they attended) would not recognize her.

"You don't need our relationship to come out in court. That would be very damaging to your case."

"I reckon you're right about that, but I don't think anybody knows. George knows I'm in love with somebody, but he doesn't know it's you."

Moon couldn't help bragging about his progress on her reading list and his using the binoculars and camera that she had had him buy. He took them with him on his long walks in the fields and woods near his grandparents' place.

"You should have seen that pileated woodpecker, Gladys. I practically could touch his tail feathers I got so close. They're something to behold with that red crest. They're noisy. Hunters call them wood hens. Deer hunters don't like them 'cause they warn the deer. I just saw my first purple finch, too. A male. That deep red-purple male is something else. Now, tell me, am I using my time wis ly, or not?"

"I'm proud of you Adamo. You just keep reading and keep close to nature and you'll be all right."

"I will, Honey. Mamaw's got me back reading my Bible, too. I'm hanging in, but I've got another problem—a letter from the IRS."

"What did they want?"

"It's a follow up of an audit they did. I told you about that. Betterman says Lunar Mining does owe $140, 000 in back taxes plus interest and penalties. I've turned it over to Fred and his wife Jauncie. He's going to talk to our accountant and she's going to talk to her cousin who is a tax lawyer. I'm not supposed to leave Winding Fork."

"Can you afford it?"

"Yeah, if we have to pay that much, we can do it without tightening our belts much. We make that much on a good day when the coal prices peak. The IRS has a way of turning what you owe them into three or four times as much with penalties. We don't want the costs to mount. We'll pay and then appeal."

The leaves had turned their brilliant colors and had begun dropping from the trees even at the lower elevations when Moon's trial date was finally set. It would begin in late November or early December, so he did not have much longer to wait. He and Andy spent the days helping his grandparents with chores. Andy's help with the farm and garden work did not slow them down too much, and Moon for the first time was spending long hours with his son. When the day's work was finished, he would take Andy with him on his long walks in the woods. Whenever the boy grew tired, Moon tossed him up on his shoulders and carried him. They had great fun exploring Winding Fork together. It brought back to Moon's mind his boyhood adventures showing his sister Serena and brother Tom the wonders of Winding Fork.

On these walks, they saw chipmunks, does with almost fully-grown fawns, a raccoon family, and a number of box turtles and toads as well as birds. Moon showed Andy how to turn up rocks in the streams and logs in the woods to look for salamanders and to chew the bark of the cherry birches. Andy's favorite animal was the opossum, a strange animal, a marsupial with a pouch to carry its young, Moon explained to Andrew.

"It's like a kangaroo, Pa. I remember. George read me a story about a kangaroo carrying its baby in a pouch."

"That's right, Andy. The babies stay in the warm pouch until they're ready to deal with the world without their mother's help."

It occurred to Moon that he should have been the reader of that story. At least he was now making up for some lost time.

Moon couldn't help thinking of his grandparents' home in Winding Fork as his pouch that was keeping him insulated from an unpleasant reality. He knew that he could not escape the unpleasantness of the trial forever, and he really felt that he needed to get it over with as soon as possible, no matter how unpleasant. He couldn't believe that he would be convicted, but he knew of innocent men who had been convicted of murders they had not committed. He was lucky to be able to afford excellent legal representation.

Thinking back to his days with Serena and Tom, Moon decided that he needed to teach Andy all the things he had shared with those two in the days when his life was simple and close to the things that really matter. He did his best to teach Andy on their walks, and the two grew closer than before in a short time as the boy basked in the light of his father's attention.

The snow began to fall late in the evening on the Wednesday before Thanksgiving. By the next day, there were ten inches on the ground and the snow was still falling. It was a wet snow and the hemlocks in the yard were drooping under a white covering. Moon sat and watched the falling snow with Andy and Archibald. He couldn't help thinking how deceptive the white beauty could be. The whiteness covered all of the scars from the strip mines that adorned the ridges to the east and west. The high mountains looked pristine covered with their white mantles. It was restful sitting and watching the snow depth increase in the yard where they had set up a yardstick to measure the depth of the blizzard.

When the snow reached the two-foot mark, Andy began to worry about the birds and other animals. Archibald went out and cleared a spot near the house and scattered cracked corn and sunflower seed on the ground for the birds, because the traffic at the bird feeder had become so heavy.

"What will the bunny rabbits do, Papaw?"

"Don't you fret, Andy. They'll hole up until the snow stops.

They'll be snug under the snow houses they make, like them Eskimos in Alaska in snow houses."

Moon saw an opportunity for fun. "Soon's the snow stops, Andy, we'll build a snow man. Okay?"

"Okay, Pa."

The snow did not prevent their having a turkey dinner with

stuffing and gravy and lots of canned fruit and vegetables from Serafina's garden patch. George made it to Winding Fork with his parents in his four-wheel drive vehicle for the feast, so he was on hand to help Andy and Moon build a snowman when the snow stopped around four o'clock in the afternoon. While the building of the snowman was taking place, George and Moon threw a few snowballs—at the barn at first and then at each other.

Archibald had come out to watch, and with his help Andy managed to throw a few snowballs also. It was open warfare. They nevertheless managed to build a large snowman, almost large enough to satisfy Andrew, before dark closed in. Archibald and Andy found some pieces of coal to use for eyes and a nose.

Moon looked at the snowman critically. "He needs a hat," he judged.

"I'll get a hard hat from the Bronco," George offered. When George had placed the metal hat on the snowman, Andy laughed.

"He's funny-looking."

"He's a mining inspector like me," George claimed.

Moon had looked around and found a couple of branches to stick in the snowman's sides for arms. The builders then gave the snowman a final inspection and decided that he was now quite satisfactory.

Back inside in the warmth, Moon turned on the TV he had bought for Archibald and Serafina. She and Verna had been watching parades, but George, Sr., Moon, and George wanted to watch the Thanksgiving football game between the Miami Dolphins and the Pittsburgh Steelers. They drank a few beers and Archibald's Thanksgiving punch as they watched Bob Griese's replacement at quarterback, Earl Morrall, lead Don Shula's team to victory. Lunamin and George took the Dolphins' victory as a good omen. They were rooting for the Florida team because Moon had made a few bets with some other members of the surface mining association.

George told Moon of another good omen. "Moon, you'll be encouraged by the news I learned from B. G. Hooper just before I drove here. ODSUM has adopted that code of conduct that you pushed for. What do you think about that?"

"I'm glad to hear it, but it's hard to believe even though I kept tellin' you it would happen."

"B. G. said that the only hold-outs on the final vote were Dave Blackmun and Dab Whacker."

"That figures."

"Do you think Dab Whacker will stop raining rocks on people's houses now?" Verna asked.

"Not likely that he'll quit completely, Verna, but now he knows he'll have the association's members on his back if he does," Moon assured her.

George's news and the Dolphins' victory could not keep Moon from worrying about the ordeal he would soon face. Thinking of the rabbits and other animals hiding under the snow, Moon couldn't help wishing he had a blanket to hide under to avoid the trial ahead. Knowing he was innocent was not blanket enough. Innocent people were sometimes convicted, especially if the evidence weighed strongly against them and the prosecution was aggressive. He was lucky. He had enough money to hire top-flight legal counsel.

"I just hope my luck holds during that trial," he told George.

WITNESS

Moon was relieved when the trial finally began. The actual event was less daunting than the foreboding that he had felt. The courtroom had an air of solidity about it that had a calming effect even as Macfee called a number of witnesses to establish that Susan and Lunamin's marriage had not been an entirely happy relationship and that Susan had refused to give Lunamin the divorce he wanted. The prosecutor then established a time line that showed Moon had the opportunity as well as the motive to kill his wife. Next he called witnesses to establish that Susan had had affairs with other men, with Rod Mashburn in particular.

Finally, Macfee called Fred MacCloud to testify. Fred was obviously a reluctant but honest witness. Macfee was using his testimony to underline that Mashburn and Susan were having an affair and that Lunamin knew about this relationship. He also wanted to show that Lunamin and Mashburn had a history of antagonism. He wanted the jury to believe that Lunamin was a jealous husband who killed in a fit of rage because he could not get his wife to agree to a divorce.

The way it happened, according to Fred's testimony in court, was that Acie had been high on beer and Valium. Just before noon, Moon came by the maintenance shed and told Acie and Fred to go look at a bulldozer that had broken down early that morning.

"As we drove the old black pick up down the road toward the strip job, Rod Mashburn came by drivin' a red truck that matched his hair. The initials R.A.M. were spread on its doors. Rod waved to us to stop. When we got out and went over to him, he pulled out a half a gallon of moonshine."

"'Where're you headed, cousins?' Rod asked."

"'Down to Lunar's strip job over the ridge,' I told him."

"'Awh now, I've got all this liquor, here. I hate to drink alone.'"
"'Acie don't need, that,' I told him, 'He just done drunk a beer and taken four Valiums.'"

"Rod was fairly well liquored and a little belligerent. 'Another little drink won't hurt him,' Rod claimed."

"'Hell! Fred,' Acie said. 'We don't want the boy to drink alone. If he's gonna drink that liquor, then he's agoin' with us. We'll not let this stuck-up skirt chaser drink all that good stuff.'"

"I gave in. I knew I shouldn't but did anyway."

"When we got to the strip job, Acie and me started to work on the dozer while Rod sat by and talked and drank moonshine. After awhile, Acie took about six more Valium tablets and washed them down with the last of the moonshine in Rod's half gallon. By this time, Acie wasn't getting' much work done on the dozer, so I told him and Rod to go on and let me finish the job. They agreed to meet me at the Flamingo Lounge in Dornest. Then the two party-boys went off down the road talkin' big about the huntin' trip to Bath County they planned for the fall deer season."

Fred paused for a while until Macfee encouraged him to continue. "Please go on Mr. MacCloud. What happened next?"

"When I got to the Flamingo, I looked in Rod's empty Ford truck and saw another half a gallon of moonshine, one third empty. I found them inside. Rod was cuttin' up and carryin' on with the waitress, a good-lookin' blonde named Katy. She just happened to be the girl Acie was sweet on at the time. So Rod and Acie wasn't too friendly."

"'I'm gonna take that son-of-a-bitch up the road and beat the hell out of him, Fred,' Acie told me in a low voice."

"I tried to calm him. 'Nah, now, Acie, you don't want to do that, Honey. Let's get out of here. You two need some fresh air,' I told him." Fred testified that he got them out of the Flamingo and made them shake hands. They had another drink of moonshine to seal the handshake and then took off in Rod's red truck with Fred following in the old black pick up. Only they headed the wrong way and it took Fred some time to catch up with them and get them turned around. Later, on the way back to the maintenance shed, as they passed the Flamingo, they saw Acie's girlfriend Katy again and stopped.

"Katy was waiting for a ride. Acie pulled her into the truck with him and Rod. About a mile down the road near Katy's house, Rod's truck slowed up and a rifle was stuck out the window on the driver's side. Whoever was holdin' the gun (it had to be Rod) began to shoot at the Easter eggs hangin' in an egg tree alongside the road in front of Katy's. I drove up and told them to stop, and Katy got out of Rod's truck lookin' angry."

"'You should be more careful with that gun, Rod,' I told him." "'Why don't you shut up, you old fool,' Rod told me, 'Look how mad you've made Acie's piece of ass.'"

"'It wasn't Fred that shot my egg tree,' Katy yelled at Rod."

"'Well, bitch, why don't you just lay some more eggs,' Rod laughed."

"'Damn you, Rod, don't you talk to her like that.' Acie had struggled out of the truck and was shakin' his fist at Rod."

"'Oh yeah, what's to stop me?' Rod snarled." "'Get out and I'll show you,' Acie challenged."

Fred recounted that Rod got out holding the rifle. He aimed it and hit another egg on the tree dead center, smashing it. Fred said that he thought Acie was heading for trouble.

"'Take back what you said to her, damn you,' Acie glared." "'Make me,' Rod smiled, bringin' the gun around toward Acie." "Acie grabbed the gun and hit Rod in the face, staggering him.

Then he threw the gun aside and hit Rod again, as hard as he could, knockin' him up against the truck. Acie threw the truck door open, knockin' Rod to the ground. As Rod staggered up, he grabbed the rifle. That's when Moon came along."

"'Hey, what's all this about?' Moon asked." "'Moon, you just keep out of this,' Rod growled."

"Moon didn't seem to hear. He stepped between the two drunks and told them to quiet down. 'Acie,' he said, 'if you don't quit and get in that truck with Fred, you're gonna be out of a job, partner or no.' Moon grabbed the gun that Rod had picked up and was tryin' to get pointed at Acie, and that's when Rod got shot. Moon was just tryin' to keep Rod from shootin' Acie, that's all. It was just a flesh wound. Why, Moon drove him to the emergency room and then back to his truck." The jury listened attentively to Fred's testimony. When he paused again, the prosecutor asked him pointedly, "Mr. MacCloud, Mr.

Lunamin shot Mr. Mashburn, is that your testimony, yes or no?" "Yes."

Listening carefully, Moon wondered when Macfee was going to get to the main event. After all, he was being tried for the murder of his wife, not for accidentally grazing Rod.

"How long was this incident before Mrs. Lunamin's murder?" Macfee asked.

"About six months, I reckon."

"Did you see Mr. Mashburn again during those six months?" "Yes."

"How many times?"

"At least twice, as I recollect." "Tell us about those meetings."

"Well, the first time was over to Coeburn. He was at the gas station when I pulled up."

Fred paused, not wanting to go on.

"Go on, what happened," Macfee encouraged.

"He walked over and said howdy after he finished fillin' his truck. He started talkin' about how he was goin' to get even with Moon for what he done. I told him that Moon done him a favor, but he said he reckoned not, that Moon should've minded his own self."

Here Fred stopped again.

"What else did he say, Mr. MacCloud.?"

"He said he was goin' to even his score with Moon and that he knew just how to do it, that he'd been workin' on it for awhile."

"All right, Mr. MacCloud. When did you see Mr. Mashburn next?"

"Judge, do I have to answer that?" Fred looked at Judge Grindquist pleadingly.

"Go ahead, Mr. MacCloud, tell what you know," the judge ordered.

"When did you see Mr. Mashburn again?"

"I saw him up to Roanoke about a week later. I'd gone up for a Sportsman's Club Trophy Show."

"Where did you see Mr. Mashburn?" "In the Sundust Restaurant."

"Was there anybody with him?" "Yeah."

"Who?"

"Suzy Lunamin."

Moon listened to the hum go through the courtroom and wondered why he hadn't guessed sooner than he had that Suzy had taken up with Rod. He had suspected she was running around, but that it had been with Mashburn had surprised him a little at first when he found out. Then he decided that she saw Rod as a source to supply her with pot.

"Did they see you, Mr. Ma Cloud?"

"No, I don't think so. I sat on the other side of the room. They were too busy too notice me."

"Did you see them leave?"

"Yes." Fred's answer could barely be heard.

"Did you see anything else: Please speak up, Mr. MacCloud." "Yeah."

"Where did they go?"

"They walked across the street." "What was on the other side?" "A motel."

"What did they do then?"

"They went into one of the rooms."

"Did you tell anybody what you had seen?" "Yes."

"Who?"

"Moon."

"What was his reaction?" "Oh, he didn't say much." "What did he say?"

"He said he knew she was wild, that he suspected she was runnin' around on him, but he was surprised she'd stoop that low. She should've had better taste."

A ripple of laughter echoed in the courtroom. The prosecutor's reaction indicated to Moon that Macfee hadn't expected exactly that answer.

Fred was turned over for cross examination, and lawyer Graylock explored the answer at some length to emphasize that Moon had already believed that Suzy was unfaithful to him before he knew that Rod Mashburn had become involved with her and that Lunamin had evidenced little, if any, jealousy about her extramarital activities.

Listening to the evidence of Suzy's adultery, Moon wondered why he had put up with it so long without more complaint. He guessed that it was partly his own guilt and partly inertia. He wasn't the person now that he had been before he had met Gladys. He wondered whether she had made a new man of him, as she jokingly claimed, or whether she had simply stolen his manhood.

He knew some men who beat their wives for the mere suspicion that they had been unfaithful with another man. Some of them thought that just a phone call from another man was sufficient reason for a good beating. After all, that was what they had been taught—a good beating now and then was the way to keep a woman in line. But he knew that Archibald MacCloud didn't hold with that sort of wife handling. Why, sometimes Papaw laughed and called his family the kissing MacClouds.

After carefully considering the matter, Moon decided that whether or not he had got above his raising he did not care because his time with

Gladys had given him some of the best moments of his life. "I'd rather be with her than hit a four-foot seam of high-grade coal," concluded Moon. If he could survive this scrape, Moon promised himself that he would not rest until he had persuaded Gladys to marry him.

THE LAWYER

Prosecutor Macfee had established that Moon had motive and opportunity to commit murder. He had the murder weapon. It definitely was Moon's shotgun, and Moon's fingerprints were on it. Moon was worried even though he knew he was innocent of the murder, whatever his other sins against Susan might have been. He knew that he would have been better off with a jury of homefolks, real mountain people, but he would just have to accept the verdict of these townies.

He had a good lawyer, he was certain. Graylock was expensive, but Moon was aware that he had saved some people who had seemed as guilty as crows caught raiding a cornfield. When he first visited Lunamin, Graylock had told him not to worry. Moon was reassured by the confident manner of this small, thin, bespectacled man. His cherubic face and heavy shock of hair suggested that this man was mature but not extremely old. From past, not-too-happy experience, Moon knew him to have formidable courtroom presence.

"Lawyer Graylock," Moon had told him, "I hope you don't harbor any ill will toward me because of our past encounters."

"Certainly not, Mr. Lunamin. As I recall, your offenses weren't all that heinous," he had said in his most formal manner. Graylock's calm, confident demeanor reassured Lunamin.

"You are my client and therefore innocent. I have a theory. That truck you saw had to be driven by the real murderer. Now, it's important that we tie the murder to that truck driver. We need to come up with the identity of that truck driver. Who are the most likely candidates?"

"I suppose somebody that Suzy took up with. She had a lot of men friends, I'm told."

"Yes, that seems most likely. What we need to establish is which one of them was there that night."

"Well, Rod Mashburn and Suzy had been having an affair."

"That's right. We'll see what we can find out about his activities.

What can you tell me? He's a cousin of yours, isn't he?"

"Yeah, But so's half of Wise County. Rod's always been a skirt-chaser. He thinks he's hot stuff with the ladies. And maybe he is the kind of man they like. He's a little more sophisticated than most of the fellows around here. He and Suzy were definitely having an affair."

"I'll have my investigators find out about his activities that night.

Is there anything else you can tell me?"

Moon hesitated, then reached in his pocket and drew out a piece of jewelry. "I found this bracelet in the bedroom that night, and there were empty gin and tonic glasses in the den. Rod always drinks gin and tonics. Suzy didn't. Now that I think about it, there was something familiar about that truck that nearly rammed me that night. It could've been Rod's."

He handed the necklace to Graylock. "I should've left this for the police," he confessed.

Graylock examined the bracelet carefully and allowed himself a slight smile.

"We'll see what kind of alibi he has and if it'll hold up. It might be enough just to establish that he had opportunity if we can come up with a motive. All we have to do is establish reasonable doubt. So we just need to come up with somebody else other than you who had motive and opportunity. It would be helpful if Mashburn's finger-prints are on that shotgun."

"It's important to me to find the real killer, not just to establish reasonable doubt," Moon said. "I owe that to Susan and Andrew."

"I'll keep that in mind. Sometimes we have to settle for half a loaf."

"I'm in your hands, Mr. Graylock. I swear to you that I did not kill Susan. I certainly had a motive and the means, but I would never have killed her. I would never rest easy if my son Andrew thought I murdered his mother."

"I'll do my best to prove you didn't, Mr. Lunamin."

THE BRACELET

On Graylock's next visit to Moon he brought good news. He had witnesses that had seen Rod's truck or one like it on the road to Moon's house the night of the murder. He had a record of Rod's calls to Moon's house that day as well as witnesses who would testify they had seen Rod buying gas in Abingdon just before dark that evening.

Graylock had asked the police to check the unidentified fingerprints on Moon's shotgun with those of Rod, and they had come up with a match to Rod's, although there were still other unidentified prints on the gun.

"This gives me something to work with when I get Mashburn on the stand. Right now, we have enough evidence pointing to him that we should be able to establish reasonable doubt about your being the killer. We still need to find a motive."

Moon had had plenty of time to consider the situation. He knew that Rod was capable of violence, but he couldn't bring himself to believe Mashburn a woman killer unless the man was drunk and greatly provoked. Rod certainly never had to resort to rape to get what he wanted from women as far as Moon knew. If Rod was Suzy's killer, it must have been some sort of accident. The other set of unidentified prints kept coming back into Moon's thoughts. Who else had been there?

Moon turned these thoughts over and over in his mind, somewhat comforted by Graylock's assertion that, whether Rod was the killer or not, enough evidence against him had surfaced to make it probable that Moon would be acquitted. Mere acquittal wouldn't satisfy Lunamin, however. Moon knew that he would not rest easy unless the real killer's identity came to light. He still thought Rod was the murderer, but he wanted to see that proved in court.

After all, Suzy was his wife, the mother of his son, and he didn't want his son growing up believing his father had killed his mother. And he couldn't stop the image of Suzy's body with a hole blown in her from reappearing in his mind, somehow connected with the image of Shorty Burk's mangled body and corpses of buddies blown apart in Nam. When he told Gladys about this nightmare that impinged upon both his dreams and his waking thoughts, she immediately assessed them as figures prompted by his guilt.

"Moon, you use this time to continue that reading list. Take your mind off the trial and those feelings of guilt," Gladys said.

"I've been reading—a lot. You'd be surprised how much of your list I've covered. It does help."

He hoped Graylock was right. Moon didn't argue the point. He was willing to accept any plausible explanation. It was with relief that he went into court to hear Rod's testimony. Obviously Rod was a reluctant witness. He seemed surprised and a bit dazed when Graylock presented all of the evidence that he had assembled to point to Rod as the likely murderer.

"Tell me, Mr. Mashburn, didn't you have a motive as well as opportunity to kill Mrs. Lunamin?"

"No. I loved Suzy. I wanted to marry her."

"Yes, we have witnesses who will attest to that. But she wouldn't divorce Moon, would she? She wouldn't divorce Moon to marry you, and you killed her in a fit of rage."

"No. I loved her."

"You were there that night. You left this jewelry in the bedroom, didn't you?"

Graylock dangled the bracelet before Mashburn. Surprised, Rod took the bracelet Graylock handed him. Examining it with a bemused look, he answered faintly, "Yes."

"Would you please read the inscription for the court?"

After some hesitation, Mashburn complied, "It says, 'To Susan with love, Rod.'"

"Didn't you begin your affair with Mrs. Lunamin in order to gain revenge on Everett Lunamin?"

"That's true. But I fell in love with Susan. I told you, I wanted to marry her."

"But she refused you, and you killed her."

"No. That's not true. Suzy was alive when I left. I did take Moon's gun down off its rack over the fireplace, but I didn't kill her with it. I threatened to kill myself if she didn't marry me. She told me to stop being a fool and put the gun down. If I did, she said, she'd think about marrying me."

"So you claim that Mrs. Lunamin was alive when you left her. About what time was that?"

"It was about half past ten or a little earlier. She was expecting Moon to come home soon after that."

"Well, Mr. Mashburn, if you didn't kill Mrs. Lunamin, who did? It wasn't Mr. Lunamin. Was there anyone else in the house?" "Not that I know of."

"Do you think Mrs. Lunamin committed suicide, then?"

"No way, Suzy wouldn't have done that. She loved me too, and she was too good a Christian to take her own life."

There was a large ripple of laughter at Mashburn's introduction of religious scruples into this affair, and Judge Grindquist had to demand silence under pain of clearing his courtroom.

"Did you see anything that might lead you to believe that there was another person in the vicinity who might have committed this murder, Mr. Mashburn? In my eyes you are the most likely suspect, but we still have that other set of fingerprints on the gun that have yet to be explained. I repeat, did you see anyone else in the vicinity of the Lunamin's house?"

"I didn't see anybody else. There was a truck parked out on the road into Moon's when I left. I didn't think much about it until just now."

"Did the truck seem familiar to you?"

"Yeah, it was a red Ford four-wheel drive like mine, but there are a lot of trucks like that around."

Moon came alert at this disclosure. It had come back to him. The truck that he had seen was a red Ford. He had assumed it was Rod's after he found the bracelet.

"That's true," Graylock continued, "but do you know anybody else who owns one?"

"Yeah."

"Who? Name a few."

"Well, the first one that comes to mind is Earl."

"Do you mean Mr. Lunamin's cousin Earl James Campbell?" "Yeah."

Moon shook his head. "Earl? Was Earl Suzy's killer?" he asked himself. He stared at Mashburn as a hum of whispering ran through the courtroom."

After a few more questions, Graylock asked the judge for a continuance so that the police could compare the unidentified fingerprints on the murder weap n with those of Earl James Campbell. Graylock leaned over to Moon and congratulated him.

"Mr. Lunamin, you can rest easy. We may not have nailed Rod Mashburn, but we have shown that he had opportunity and motive.

Now we may have another p ssible murderer to give to the jury. It is an embarrassment of riches. Certainly the jury will have to concede reasonable doubt as to your guilt."

"I'm in your hands, lawyer."

"We'll do our best. My investigators will begin work on Earl today."

After court recessed, Moon drove slowly back to Winding Fork, his mind more on the events in the courtroom than on his driving. He might have misjudged Rod, he thought. Maybe he wasn't Susan's killer—just her lover. Maybe Rod's loss was greater than his. In spite of his worries and bemusement, Lunamin couldn't help laughing a little at the irony that the adulterous lover might have suffered a greater loss than the wronged husband.

Thinking back to the funeral, Moon wondered whether Earl's DUI charge in Kentucky had just been a creation of Earl's imagination. When Earl showed up at work again, according to Fred, he had scratches on his face. Maybe that was Earl's skin under Susan's fingernails.

Perhaps Earl had thought he couldn't carry off an act of innocence over Susan's dead body. He hadn't shown up at the viewing or the church. Earl was superstitious. Maybe he thought that Susan's wounds would open and bleed in the presence of the murderer. That was something often told as truth in the mountains.

At Winding Fork, Moon found George had arrived ahead of him and was visiting with Archibald and Serafina. He had already told them about the new events in the courtroom.

"Graylock says you've nothing to worry ab ut now, Moon."

"Yeah, that's what he told me. I hope he's right. I could believe Rod killed her, but Earl's hard to swallow."

"Either way, old buddy, you're in the clear." "Yeah, but Earl...."

Serafina patted Moon comfortingly on the shoulder. "Moon, Earl always was wild. somewhere's."

He's kin, but he's got some bad blood from

George remembered Vegas. "Earl's hot for practical jokes. Maybe this was one that went sour. We'll have to wait to hear what he has to say."

NO JOKES

hen Earl finally took the stand, he kept his eyes averted from Moon. He was not the confident, self-assured "ready-to-howl" Earl that Moon was accustomed to seeing. He didn't fare too well under the questioning of Graylock and became even less self-assured as the questioning went forward.

Graylock had had investigators hard at work since the day Rod Mashburn had told the court that the truck parked near Moon's house might have been Earl's. They had been able to trace Earl's movements the night of the murder in considerable detail. After work, late in the afternoon, he had found a so-called *adult* movie and had gone by Acie's to watch it with him.

According to Acie, they had had a few beers and a little moonshine, and Earl had taken the remainder of the liquor with him when he left a little before six. Earl appeared at a gas station at Abingdon a little after seven. That left him plenty of time to get to Moon's before Rod left. His time b tween then and one-fifteen, when he showed up at the Ruby Lounge in Abingdon and ordered a beer, was unaccounted for.

Graylock pressed him to account for his whereabouts.

"What did you do between seven and one o'clock that night, Mr. Campbell?"

"I just cruised around." "For what purpose?"

"Tryin' to find a little action." "What kind of action?"

"You know, women."

"Did your cruising bring you anywhere near the home of Mr. and Mrs. Lunamin in Abingdon?"

"It might have. I saw a lot of the town."

"Mr. Campbell, what would you say if I told you that the police have matched your prints with the last unknown set on Mr. Lunamin's shotgun? How do you account for your fingerprints being on the shotgun that killed Susan Lunamin?"

Whispers ran through the courtroom, but Judge Grindquist was so involved in the proceedings that he forgot to order quiet in the courtroom.

"I can't account for them."

"What if I told you that those prints are there because you fired the shot that killed her? Did you have anything to do with Susan Lunamin's death?"

Earl refused to answer. He invoked his constitutional right against self-incrimination.

"Did you wait outside until Rod Mashburn left and then go in and kill Mrs. Lunamin?" Again Earl refused to answer, using the Fifth Amendment as his shield.

"Did you watch Mr. Mashburn and Mrs. Lunamin making love? Did you kill Mrs. Lunamin in a fit of jealous rage?"

Earl still refused to answer. After a few more questions with no different respons , Graylock told the court that the defense rested, confident that sufficient doubt had been established to free Moon.

Macfee sat almost motionless and speechless as his assistants cleared their table of papers. An obviously disappointed man, the prosecutor jerked nervously at his tie. Moon was relieved but not completely satisfied. He leaned back and shook hands with George and Fred, who were sitting in the front row just behind him. He was pleased but deep in thought. Earl might have killed Susan, but why? The courtroom was for a time a noisy place as the audience compared notes about the latest surprises.

After Judge Grindquist demanded and obtained quiet in the courtroom, he heard final arguments. Graylock made short work of his.

He told his audience that his client was innocent beyond a reasonable doubt. Two men whose prints were on the gun but shouldn't have been had opportunity and motive to kill Susan Lunamin, who was dead when Everett Lunamin found her. An abashed Macfee left the chore to an assistant. Before Grindquist sent the jury to deliberate, Graylock assured Moon that he would soon be a free man. Moon gave the lawyer his thanks for a job well done, but he also voiced his skepticism about Earl's having had a motive to kill Susan.

"I can't believe Earl killed Susan intentionally."

"Leave that to Macfee, Mr. Lunamin. That man's eager to convict a murderer. He'll have to bring charges and make a case against Earl or Rod. All you need is a jury to determine that you are not guilty beyond reasonable doubt. With two other suspects having opportunity and at least one with a motive, I don't think you have anything to worry about."

"I hope you're right. I find it hard to believe Earl killed Susan. Rod I could accept easier."

They did not have long to wait. The jury deliberated a little less than an hour before bringing back a verdict of not guilty. Judge Gridquist dismissed them with his thanks and told the defendant he was free to go. Fred and Acie and many others rushed up to congratulate Moon, whose main emotion was relief. He still voiced amazement that Earl could have killed Susan.

Later, over celebratory beers at the Tavern, Acie gave Moon a plausible explanation.

"The way I see it, Earl was hot after watchin' that movie. He went alookin' for a woman. You know Earl. He was always alookin' for a woman and not often findin' one real cooperative unless he paid. I figure he came by your place and saw Rod's truck. So he parked out a ways and went on foot to the house. I'd say he looked around for lights and didn't see any inside except one comin' from the bedroom. Knowin' Earl, I'd bet he snuck around to the bedroom window and watched Suzy and Rod goin' after it. Together with that movie and all that liquor and watchin' them ballin' the jack big time, I'd bet old Earl just couldn't resist goin' in to the house when he saw Rod leave."

"So you think he tried to get Susan to screw him?"

"Sure looks that way," Fred agreed. "I'll bet he did. And I bet Susan laughed at him and turned him down."

"Sounds plausible," Moon admitted.

"Yeah, and then Earl most likely tried to force her," Fred added to the theory. "I'll bet she picked up the gun to get rid of him and he grabbed it."

"Then you think he killed her accidentally, that he grabbed the gun and it went off in the struggle?" Moon asked.

"Sure thing, Moon. I don't think he meant to kill her. Earl ain't that mean or horny."

That night Moon called Gladys to tell her the news. She had visited him for a few hours near Winding Fork and had been there in the courtroom to support him when he needed her, but she had flown back to New York after Rod's testimony.

"I knew you were all right after Rod testified, Moon. But I'm relieved to know that it's all over."

"There's a silver lining to these clouds that have been hovering over me, honey. I'm a free man now."

"That's right, you're single again."

"We have a lot to talk over, Gladys. I still want to marry you." "I'm ready to talk as long as you want, Adamo. Why don't we have our discussions on some neutral territory?" "Any time, any place. Suggest something."

"We like the Gulf Coast. I hear Galveston is very pleasant this time of year. Why don't we meet at Galveston? I'll fly out tomorrow and meet you in Houston. You can fly down and rent a car at the airport, and we can drive to Galveston."

"All right. Get your flight and let me know. I'll fly down to meet you."

ANOTHER COUPLE

fter the trial, George congratulated Moon and then found Jennifer Coffey and asked her to have dinner with him at the Starving Artist in Abingdon. Jennifer had been covering the trial for her Roanoke paper.

"I know you're relieved Moon is free. Let me write my story and send it in, George. I'll meet you later in front of the Starving Artist, say about eight."

"All right, great, I'll see you then."

At the restaurant as they ate, they discussed the trial.

"I guess you'd call it a happy ending," Jennifer said. "I'd love to know what is going to happen now to this mountain embodiment of the American Adam."

"I know Moon's been in love with another woman—that's a fact that didn't come out at the trial. Please don't print that. If it had come out at the trial, things would have looked even worse for Moon."

"Who is this secret love?"

"I don't know. Moon has never told me that."

"Do you think Moon will stay in Southwest Virginia?"

"I don't know that either. He hasn't said anything about leaving. I don't think he would ever want to live very far away from Winding Fork."

"So Moon remains in the mountains. George, are you ever going to leave these mountains?"

"I'll go, but I'll always come back. A poet I've read says, 'Being of these hills I cannot pass beyond.' I don't think Moon can pass very far beyond either."

"I know I keep coming back. It seems this place is a hotbed of news items."

"We ought to show you more hospitality. Then your visits wouldn't be all work."

"What did you have in mind, George?"

"For tonight, what about a drive up White Top to look at the stars? After that we'll have to improvise."

Jennifer agreed, and they were soon heading down the road to Damascus and up the winding highway to the foot of Mt. Rogers and Whitetop. The hour's drive gave them more time to talk. George explained to Jennifer that there had once been a resort hotel at the top of Whitetop Mountain. Eleanor Roosevelt and other famous folks had visited there.

"These mountains are different from thos in Wise County.

There aren't any coal seams here to entice people to strip away the mountainsides. Timber cutting has been the big problem here. It must have been quite a trek up this mountain b fore there were good roads and motorcars to travel them. Looking east from the summit gives a beautiful view on a clear day. A clear night with good moon-light ought to do the same. Many nights the top is shrouded in fog."

They were lucky. The top of the mountain was clear and the moon shone brightly as George pulled in to the parking lot near the summit. Jennifer looked out over the ridges drenched in moonlight.

"This is very romantic, George." "I think so, too, Jennifer."

George leaned over and kissed her.

"That was something I had begun to think you'd never get around to."

"I'm the cautious type, not like my cousin Moon."

"Do you think Moon's experience has changed him? He doesn't seem to me to be the same man I met when you took me out to the Lunar Mining operation>"

"He's a more thoughtful person now than I ever remember his being, and somebody has polished his rough edges. You wouldn't believe how many good books he's read in the past few years. Yes, I definitely think he's changed. Making money isn't as important to him as it used to be."

George kissed Jennifer again, thrusting his tongue deep as he reached under her bra. After that they engaged in very little conversation before the ride back to Abingdon an hour later to Jennifer's motel room.

"Do you have to go back to Roanoke tomorrow?"

"My editor says emphatically that I must. Otherwise I'd try to find another story here. He says that he has a pressing assignment for me in Lexington—something to do with hazing at VMI. Why don't you spend the night?"

George agreed, and Jennifer sent George to get some ice for drinks. "I have some gin and tonic."

When George returned, Jennifer had him fix them drinks while she pulled out a deck of cards. "Do you play poker?"

"Sometimes."

"Well let's play strip poker. How about seven card stud?"

* * *

As an exhausted George and Jennifer sat at breakfast the next morning, he wondered w ether he had brought her to see his mountains with a little sharper focus.

"On a clear day, Jennifer," George had told her, "a person can stand on the High Knob Tower and look way into North Carolina, Tennessee, and Kentucky. On a clear day in October when the leaves have turned but not fallen, a beauty covers all the scars of the strip mining. They are all still there, and they show up in full force when the leaves fall, unless the scars are covered again by a blanket of snow. That gives these hills another kind of beauty."

"I'd like to come down and look at the fall color with you."

"It's a date. The colors here are prettier than almost anywhere else in the world. Those up north can't compare with them."

"Better than we have in Roanoke?"

"A little, maybe, but beauty is relative. People who earn their livelihood from mining can find a beauty in a seam of coal dug and hauled to the tipple. Firebugs must think a fire's pretty. After all, everybody likes fireworks. It's not a simple matter to determine what's beautiful, either of the earth or its people.

Jennifer laughed. George paused. "I don't mean to preach."

"Yes, you do." She pulled him to her and kissed him. When he pulled away, she laughed.

"People and things are a combination of scars and beauty. It's as true of the mountains as of the city streets where men have covered the earth with concrete and asphalt in the name of progress. Improved land, they call it. And charge huge sums of money for a small piece of real estate with tall buildings all around. A strip mine is better than concrete spires raised up in the name of progress. At least we can reclaim a strip mine and grow grass and trees again."

George hoped he had changed Jennifer's outlook a little bit, but he wasn't sure. He thought he had at least convinced her to look beyond the stereotypes of Appalachia. Her last words, however, indicated an environmental conversion less complete than George had wished.

"Oh, George," she laughed "I know you love birds and bees and

flowers and trees. So do I. But 'progress is a comfortable disease' e. e. Cummings says. Maybe you can convince me eventually to love the natural world as much as you do. Why don't you come visit me in Roanoke and try? We'll play some more poker. I'll expect to see you this coming weekend. If my editor has me working, though, you'll just have to tag along."

George thought that a continuing attempt to educate Jennifer would be very pleasant.

"Okay, I'll see you Friday evening. Pick out a good restaurant where we can have a late dinner and listen to some music. There we will sit and eat and let the sounds of music creep into our ears, to paraphrase the bard. Then we can improvise. Maybe play some more poker. The next day I can to introduce you to more of the wonders of the natural world."

"And we'll talk about Moon and look at the moon again. I want to know what's going to happen to your cousin and see what effect a Roanoke moon can produce on you. Before you leave, let's have a few more hands of strip poker."

GALVESTON

By the time the trial had finished, November had slipped into December and December into January and cold weather had the mountains almost completely in its grip. As he looked at the snow falling while he waited for his flight, Moon was glad to have a reason for retreating to the warmth of the Gulf Coast. He flew into the newly built Houston airport on the north side of the city. It was surrounded on all sides by woods and agricultural land.

It was a huge airport, but he found Gladys without any difficulty. She was waiting for him at the car rental desk, just as she had promised. To Moon, she seemed more beautiful than he had remembered.

"Hello, Honey," Moon said as he pulled her to him and kissed her. "I sure have missed you all these months."

"Moon," Gladys laughed, "I missed you, too. But let's not make a public spectacle of ourselves."

Moon rented a car and, after a short wait, they put their luggage on the bus that took them to their rental automobile. Moon and Gladys hugged and kissed again after getting into the vehicle. Ten minutes later, Moon started the Ford Torino and turned it onto J. F. Kennedy Boulevard. The flat land on all sides presented them with a landscape quite unlike that of the mountains of Virginia.

Once out to Interstate 45, they headed southeast toward Galveston, where Moon had booked them into Gaido's. So that they would be close to the best seafood in town, he told Gladys. At

Galveston, he turned off onto 61st street and drove to the Seawall, the fortification built against ravages like those of the great hurricane of 1900 that had almost wiped Galveston from off the coast. Turning left, he drove east along the water's edge, keeping his eyes open for the sign with the fish that announced Gaido's.

Gladys gazed out into the surf beating against the seawall at high tide and beyond to the Gulf, where shrimp boats were sailing across the horizon with their nets down. "Look at all those birds hovering around the shrimp boats, Moon. I'll bet they're trying to get a shrimp dinner." "I think I'd rather get mine at Gaido's. The food is supposed to be excellent there."

The sun was beginning to set by the time they pulled into the parking lot behind the motel. After unpacking and showering, Lunamin and Gladys went to the dining room to find out whether the food was as good as they had been told. Moon asked for a table at the front window so that they could look out at the waters of the Gulf and watch the gulls hovering, looking for a meal. While they waited for their food, Gladys sipped coffee while Lunamin drank a glass of the local Shiner Bach as the darkness gradually descended over the water.

"This shrimp bisque is really goo ," Gladys observed as they ate their appetizer. "I could make a meal of this."

"I could make a meal of looking at you, Gladys. You've got to admit this is a romantic s tting. Look at that moon shining on the water. This should be romantic enough to tempt you to accept my proposal."

"We'll see, Moonman."

The dinner over, the two of them took a long walk down the Seawall to look at the ocean and listen to the cries of the seagulls still milling about in the glow of the street lights. Snuggling against Lunamin, Gladys pressed his hand hard in hers. "I've missed you terribly, Moonman. I don't want us to be apart that long again."

"No need. Just give the word and we'll get married."

Gladys laughed. "I think you've become stuck in a rut. Can't you think of another subject?"

"Now that you mention it, I can. Let's get back to the room. I think I can show you that I have at least one other thing on my mind."

In their room, Moon made good on his promise until the two of them finally fell asleep in each other's arms the next morning. It was late morning when they woke up. Sunlight was streaming into the room. Moon ordered brunch in the room, and they spent the remainder of the morning and early afternoon eating, making love, and getting dressed.

They decided to spend the afternoon driving south to see more of the coast. Gladys had a particular goal. She wanted to see a rare whooping crane. As they drove down the Seawall boulevard, they watched the Gulf's breakers throwing white foam spray skyward as they rushed to the beach. A soft southeast breeze was whipping the water in the brilliant sunshine. As they headed toward San Luis Pas and the bridge off the island, Gladys looked at the pastures searching for sandhill cranes.

"Look, Moon, there's a flock. With their heads and necks down they look like sheep, all but the one standing guard with his head up." At Freeport, they turned inland and headed south to Rockport, where they planned to spend the night. Above the large inland fields, Gladys and Moon saw immense flocks of birds, many white and some dark. These birds joined other birds already on the ground, causing the field to look like the snow-covered ground Moon had left in Southwest Virginia. Gladys had done her homework.

"Those must be the flocks of snow geese I've been reading about."
"That's the right name. The fields look like they're covered with snow."

They were excited when they saw the geese in one field rise like a swarm of huge white pillows and then saw the cause, a bald eagle soaring above, searching for a goose to feast upon. Moon had to agree with Gladys that they were witnessing a spectacular sight.

The next morning they were up early to board Captain Ted's catamaran for the trip along the Intracoastal Waterway through Aransas Refuge, the winter home of the last wild whooping cranes. A small, gray-haired man sporting a captain's jacket and hat greeted the passengers warmly as they came aboard. He gave them a safety lecture after everyone had arrived. Then they cast off.

The ride across Matagorda Bay was exhilarating for Moon and Gladys, who stayed topside on the upper deck behind the wheelhouse. They were warmly bundled, prepared for the wind chill. Having seen the sun rise in a clear sky, many passengers were not. They huddled below in the cabin, drinking coffee and hot chocolate. Gladys had prepared Moon. She had been on enough boat rides to know what to expect.

"Dress warmly," she had told him.

"But Gladys, it's warm and the sun's shining." "Here, yes, but it's different out on the water."

Bundled against the wind, they had the upper deck almost to themselves as they watched for the fins of harbor dolphins breaking the surface of the bluer water in the bay. Occasionally one of the dolphins rose from the water enough so that they could see blue sky between the animal and the water.

From time to time, Captain Ted's raspy voice came over the loud speaker and pointed out landmarks or identified birds and other animals. Flocks of sea ducks rose from the water ahead of the boat and flew across the bow and away; Captain Ted steered close to oyster bars that rose out of the shallow blue-green waters of the bay.

"Folks," Captain Ted warned, "those oyster bars provide some tasty food, but they can tear a boat or a person apart if you're not careful. They lurk under the water to catch the unwary."

Gladys pressed Moon's hand. "We know about hidden dangers, don't we?"

As they approached the oyster bars, Captain Ted alerted his passengers to look at the birds on them. Huge white pelicans adorned some of them, dwarfing the nearby oystercatchers, whose black-and-white suits and huge blood-red bills caused Gladys to exclaim with appreciation.

"Moon, those oystercatchers are sexy birds." "I think they're funny looking."

"The two things aren't mutually exclusive."

As they neared the marshes of Aransas, redheads and pintail ducks took flight. Once alongside the marshes, they began to see herons of many different varieties and, to the greater delight of Gladys, roseate spoonbills.

"Look at those funny beaks, Moon. They're weird but beautiful birds. They glow in the sunlight. They're like huge pink roses."

"You're my rose. You're glowing too."

Captain Ted encouraged everyone to enjoy the spoonbills. Then he identified the great and snowy egrets, the great blue and little blue herons, the gorgeous tri-colored herons, and the comical reddish egret, whose fishing tactics consisted of running madly about with wings outstretched. He also pointed out the deer feeding on the higher ground back from the marsh.

"White-tails, Gladys, not as big as those western mule deer, but prettier. It's hard to imagine that those pretty creatures can eat themselves to death by ruining their habitat. If it weren't for hunters, they would die of disease and starvation."

"A very rational defense of hunting—I'd rather let wolves or mountain lions do the job. keeping habitat, do they?"

Strip miners don't help them much in

"Why, no, I reckon we don't. But you should take into account that most people aren't willing to live next to wolves and mountain lions, so hunting is a necessary evil."

A few minutes later, Captain Ted warned everyone that they were approaching the first territory of a pair of whooping cranes. "Whooping cranes mate for life," he lectured. "They defend winter feeding territories as well as their breeding territories on the northern prairie. These have a young bird with them. It's the one with the tan feathers. It will stay with them until they return to their nesting grounds. Then they'll kick junior out."

The cranes continued feeding in the marsh close to the waterway as Captain Ted maneuvered his cat close to the shore and kept it there for his passengers to take pictures and look their fill.

"Aren't they beautiful, Moon?"

"They're something to look at, all right. They're alert for danger. One of them always has a head up looking around. I reckon they're used to boats with gawking humans coming around. Maybe they're people watching. Anyhow, I'm getting some great pictures."

"If they're watching us, they must have a sense of humor then."

"Maybe. Animals have more sense than people think, Gladys." "And did you hear Captain Ted say they mate for life?"

As the boat headed north, they saw many more whooping cranes. Captain Ted explained that they were seeing a large percentage of the world's remaining wild whoopers. He told them that the flock at one time had been down to fifteen birds.

"They've come a long way back," he continued. "Now some cranes are being bred in captivity, but this is the only wild flock. Scientists found the breeding grounds up in Canada and discovered that these birds lay two eggs but usually raise only one chick. The scientists have been taking one egg from whooping crane nests and hatching them at Patuxent in Maryland. So now there is a captive flock."

"I'm glad the cranes didn't disappear, Moon. It would be a shame to lose forever something so b autiful."

"Yeah. That's just the way I feel about you."

Gladys smiled and grabbed Moon's hand. "I don't want to lose my Moonman either."

On the trip back, Captain Ted pointed out some loons. "Have you ever heard a loon call?" Gladys asked. "Can't say's I have. What's it sound like?"

"It's eerie, like a wild woman wailing for a lost love. You can hear them on the lakes in New England in the summer."

"Maybe we can go there and listen to 'em this summer." "Maybe."

They spent the afternoon driving around Rockport harbor, visiting the Marine Museum, and watching the gulls and shorebirds on the beach and the waterfowl on the freshwater lake on the inland side of the city park. The museum took a bit of time. It was full of photographs and other mementos of sailing days gone by. By the time they were finished looking through the exhibits, it was four o'clock.

"I can appreciate the photography here, Gladys." "You're a photography buff, now."

On the drive back to Galveston, they watched the sun setting across the fields plowed for spring planting. Strange formations of clouds in the evening sky shone red, pink, and yellow. In the glow, Gladys told Moon, she saw herons and cranes and deer.

"You have a vivid imagination."

"I know. I've imagined you as a handsome prince and me as the princess you've awakened from a long sleep."

"You're my princess, that's no lie."

"And you're handsome. I'm beginning to think you're prince material."

Moon thought about that while Gladys considered the accuracy of her statement.

"Moon, I'm going to tell you about a Greek story. Pygmalion fell in love with the ivory statue of a beautiful woman he had created. He prayed to Aphrodite to make his beautiful statue a flesh-and-blood woman. I understand how Pygmalion felt. I think I'm your Pygmalion and you're my creation even though you were already flesh and blood. I'm definitely in love with my Moonman, but I can't live with you in Southwest Virginia. You have too many bad memories for us to be happy there. Maybe you couldn't be happy living outside the mountains. But there are other mountains—perhaps the Rockies or another part of the Appalachians. Probably the southern mountains would work better, because you wouldn't be far from your family."

"I'm willing to go where you think we can be happy. I do like the mountains, and I wouldn't want to be too far from my grandparents. Andy needs them."

"Everett, I know you have enough money to give up mining despite your legal fees and your difficulties with the IRS. And you and I could even adjust to a much simpler lifestyle if it were necessary. But you aren't a man who would be happy with an inactive life. I think that a college education would open possibilities for you. The more I've run the idea through my mind, the more convinced I am that soe college for you is the answer for us."

"I think I could stand some college if you are with me."

"If I marry you Adamo, I want us to be a pair of whooping cranes, mated for life. If you would go to college, we would have much more in common and you'd have the basis for another career. Maybe you could get a degree in landscape architecture while I could take some courses in interior decoration. Think about it. We could set up a business, Lunar Solutions for exterior and interior decorations. You'll handle the outside and I'll handle the inside. Think about it."

"That's quite a bit to take in."

"I know you could be successful in college. You are one of the quickest studies I have ever known. Why not education and a new career to put the finishing touches on my Moonman? You think about a little college."

"If you say I should, I'll think ab ut going to college and taking up a new career." Moon was pleasantly surprised when Gladys gave him a quick kiss.

That night, after a meal of shrimp gumbo and red snapper, Moon again asked Gladys to marry him. She told him not to rush things.

"I'll give you an answer of some kind before we leave Galveston. For a few days, let's just enjoy ourselves without worrying about the future. It'll be fun knowing that we are just an ordinary couple. I will let you give me an engagement ring, Moon. How's that. It's not a final answer, but it will do for now."

"I reckon I'll live on hope."

After dinner, they strolled down the sidewalk along the Seawall, listening to the surf and enjoying the sea breeze. Gladys pointed out the moon to Lunamin.

"Look, Moonman. The moon's almost full. Tell me, are you any kin to the man in the moon?"

Lunamin laughed. "I don't think so. Are you any kin to the cow that jumped over the moon?"

"No, but I've leaped over you often enough. Does that count?" In their room, they watched the news. Propelled by a northeaster, a snowstorm was hitting Southwest Virginia and moving up the coast toward New York.

"We're down here in the sunshine while the snow is flying up north. You have to admit that coming here was a good idea," Gladys laughed.

"I've always said that you have looks and brains, too."

That night their lovemaking was extraordinarily extended and yet rather subdued. They had not ceased when daylight had begun to break. Exhausted, they fell asleep in one another's arms and did not wake until well after eleven o'clock. They decided that it was too late for breakfast when they woke, so they showered and walked to Gaido's restaurant section for brunch. They had seafo d again. Gladys had crab and Moon opted for the special on grouper. They decided that the tip they had heard about Gaido's was true. The food demanded superlatives.

That afternoon they explored again. Following signs to the ferry, they took the free ferry across Galveston Bay to the Bolivar Peninsula and drove up the isthmus, stopping to see Fort Travis, Bolivar Flats, and High Island on their way to Winnie, where they planned to eat at a Cajun restaurant known as Al-Tee's.

In former times Fort Travis had been used to guard Galveston Bay, but now it was a tourist attraction. Touring the old fort didn't require much time, but they found a strange little bird standing on one of the concrete drainage features. As they approached, it ducked into the drainage pipe below where the bird had been standing, but it peered out at them.

"That bird is cute, Moon."

Consulting the Peterson birding guide she had brought with her, Gladys told Moon that it must be a burrowing owl. She handed Moon her binoculars to get a closer view of the bird.

"Strange looking, I'd say. He's found himself a concrete burrow."

They spent more time walking along the seashore at Bolivar Flats. The ships in the Gulf waiting to go up the ship channel to Houston attracted Moon's attention, but Gladys paid more heed to the hermit crabs scurrying about with their adopted seashell homes.

"Moon, this shell guidebook says that these crabs find an empty shell and take it over. When they quickly outgrow that shell, they crawl out and find a bigger one. They don't seem to worry much about housing."

"Good for them. I think some people spend too much time thinking about houses."

"I guess we change our clothes a lot more than these hermit crabs change their shells, but I'm glad we don't have to find new skins."

"Me too, I like your skin, whatever you put around it."

The numbers of birds overwhelmed them. Gladys tried to flip through her guide to identify them, but she was only partially successful. What she could identify she pointed out to Moon. Flocks of hundreds of avocets and other shorebirds flushed ahead of them and waders eyed them warily.

"Look at the white pelicans, Moon. They're huge. It says here that they spend the winter here and fly up to the Great Plains to nest. There aren't many brown pelicans now. The DDT killed them off. But they're trying to bring them back."

"There sure are plenty of the white ones."

Moon saw a strange grayish bird with a reddish neck running about crazily, lifting its wings and running back and forth as if possessed by some demon.

"Gladys, what is that? That bird is funny. Do you have that in your guide?"

She looked in her Peterson and showed him a picture. "That's a reddish egret according to Peterson. It's a kind of heron. We saw one from Captain Ted's boat."

The bag that they had brought with them for seashells filled, they headed back to their car. On their way along the coast road they passed through a number of small settlements. Moon marveled at the way people built their houses on stilts next to the Gulf.

"You'd think people would have better sense. They don't read the Bible, I reckon. It says not to build your house upon sand."

"You can see why they like it, though, and you'd have a hard time finding a place around here where you could build without building on sand."

When they crossed over a bridge where there was a crowd of fishermen, Moon drove off the highway to look at the Bay, and Gladys consulted her tourist guidebook. "This place is called Rollover Pass, Moon. The pirate Jean Lafitte brought his loot here, put it on wagons, and rolled it over to boats on the bay."

At High Island they saw land rising up above the surrounding area. And there were trees all over this high spot. Away from the high places where the houses sat, many oil rigs were pumping oil.

"That's the Texas version of black gold, Gladys."

"Moon, did you know that this field is one of the oldest in Texas? The travel book says that High Island is a salt dome and that there is a large oil field underneath."

"Looks easier than coal mining—they just dig the well and then sit back and let the pumps do all the work."

That evening at Al-Tee's, Gladys and Moon ate their first alligator. "It tastes a lot like rattlesnake to me," Moon judged.

"Maybe so, I wouldn't know about rattlesnake. I think it tastes like chicken."

Moon preferred the red beans, rice, cornbread and sausage. He had asked the waitress to suggest a real Cajun meal, and this was what she had told him to order. "I sure do like your Cajun cooking," he told her when he was finished.

They made the drive back to the ferry in the dark. The days were still short. While they were riding across to Galveston Island, they got out of the car and stood to the front of the ferry, letting the breeze blow spray in their faces and listening to the gulls calling their eerie laughter.

"I think they're laughing at us, Everett."

"With us, Gladys, with us. They can see we're happy."

That night they stood on the boardwalk and watched the surf for a few hours. Then thy went inside and cuddled in one another's arms for several hours before Moon pulled Gladys to him and kissed her repeatedly, on the mouth at first, running his tongue deep into her mouth, and then kissing every part of her. Gladys moaned her pleasure. "Adamo, in the middle ages lovers talked of hearing the nightingale sing when they were making love. I want to hear the nightingale sing all night long. I hear it singing now. Don't let it stop singing tonight, Adamo."

They woke about eleven the next day. The sun was shining into the room. The nightingale had sung the night through.

"Gladys, I know you love me, too. I want you to marry me now."

Gladys decided that the right moment had arrived for her to clearly repeat her requirements for marriage to Moon, to state what he would have to do to get her consent.

"Moon, we've discussed what I want. All right, Moon, I will marry you, but only when you meet my conditions. We've talked about them. I'm not trying to be difficult It's just that, if I marry you, I want it to last. I want us to be paired like the whooping cranes, for life. You seem to be everything I've dreamed of, but you still have some rough edges I want polished.

"I know I can do that."

"We'll have to live where nobody knows us. I know you'll never leave the mountains, but we can go to some mountains other than those in Southwest Virginia after we finish preparing for our new careers, perhaps somewhere in North Carolina near Asheville. I hear it's beautiful there."

"All right. I'm willing to become a Tarheel, if that's what it takes." "And you have to adopt some line of work more friendly to the environment than surface mining. I don't want you commuting back and forth from Asheville to Lunar Mining." "That's a big step, Gladys."

"I know, Moon, but I don't think you'll miss tearing the earth to pieces. Our happiness is worth some sacrifice. Both of us have changed a lot. I think we can change some more. I like the idea of being an interior decorator. You put that idea in my head. I think a business like the Lunar Solutions we discussed would be a perfect solution for us. Whether we do that or not, I wouldn't want you to continue mining. You'd spend too much time away from me."

"Gladys, Lunar Mining came into being because I thought I had to prove my value to Susan and her family and all of the other people who looked down on me. I was a rank materialist, I admit, even though I hadn't been brought up that way. But I reckon you are right in thinking we need to make a clean break with the past I'll think about it and see what arrangements I can make."

ABINGDON

lmost two months after the trial, George telephoned Moon several times but received no answer. He tried for days without success. He hadn't run into Moon at Winding Fork. Archibald and Serafina told him that Moon seemed busy making plans. Finally, George decided to drive over to Abingdon to see how Moon was reacting to having escaped almost unscathed (though a little poorer) from the judicial system.

George had heard from Fred MacCloud that Moon was selling his share of Lunar Mining to Fred and Acie on an installment plan. Fred didn't seem to know much else. If he did, he wasn't telling. George wondered why Moon would quit his company. He thought that, unless Moon had changed greatly, he would want to recoup his losses. He couldn't imagine his cousin sitting around counting his money. Moon had plenty of money left, even after the lawyers' bills and the IRS. His sale of his part of Lunar Mining should give him a steady stream of income for a long time. He just couldn't imagine Moon's quitting. Getting money had been his driving force for so long.

As he drove east, Landsetter drank in the beauty of the mountains surrounding him. "No sign of strip mines here," he thought. "No coal seams. It's too bad that such great scenery has to be destroyed to dig at the coal. Moon's black gold comes at a high cost."

Pulling in to the Abingdon Riviera, George drove to the entrance of Moon's long drive without coming to any conclusions about Moon. The sarvis or serviceberry trees were in full bloom, and some of the dogwoods and cherries were showing signs of bloom. It was a beautiful day, but George worried. He didn't see any signs of activity as he drove up the long, tree-lined drive, but as soon as he stepped from his vehicle he heard the sound of a twenty-two rifle coming from behind the house.

Fearing the worst, George rushed across the lawn beside the house to see what was going on. He found Moon sitting on the deck behind his recreation room with a twenty-two rifle cradled across his knees. Moon was tenderly caressing the rifle with one hand while he drank from a bottle of beer with the other. From the wide-open French doors of the recreation room drifted the sounds of *Wild Bill Jones* playing on Moon's hi-fi system.

"Hey, Moon, old buddy, what's going on."

Moon turned and gave George a slow, happy smile and pointed to the cans on a board about fifty yards from the deck. He lifted the gun and shot another can.

"I'm celebrating,' George. I'm celebrating' my freedom that I'm soon to lose."

"I hear you sold Lunar Mining. Is that a fact?"

"True, George, that's as true as the fact that bears live in the woods. I'm selling this mansion, too, as soon as somebody ponies up the cash."

"Moon, are you drunk?"

"I have had a few beers, but I don't even have a buzz on."

"Well, I understand the freedom part, but how come you're about to lose it again?"

"You remember that woman you saw me with on the airplane?" "Sure, I thought I might have seen her again at your trial, but I wasn't certain."

"Well, George, Gladys Stayskill has made me an offer I cannot refuse."

"What kind of offer?"

"She has agreed to marry me if I make a few more changes. I've agreed to them all. George, the troubles besetting me have led me to a new perspective on life. I've been taking from the land. I plan to spend the rest of my life putting back. I'm going to college to become a landscape architect."

"That woman must be persuasive."

"Life should be more than a cash transaction or a barter agreement. The land's like a pretty woman. She needs to be handled gently, with respect. I wanted to make money, plenty of it, but I don't hold with rape of women or the land. I reckon I ought to have known it all along. Papaw and Mamaw taught us better than to worship Mammon. It just took me a long time and the tutoring of Gladys Stayskill to learn the lesson."

"You certainly have changed. That woman is a magician—or a witch."

"She's the best thing that's happened to me, no fooling. George, I want you to be my best man again."

"Moon, I'm proud to call you cousin. I'd be honored to be your best man at this wedding."

"You're on. But this one will be quiet, just a minister and witnesses. We want to start a new life without creating a spectacle. Then I'm off to college and a new career."

"Good for you, Moon. What about Andy?"

"Mamaw and Papaw will keep him for awhile. Gladys has met him and thinks he's a bright, adorable young man, and Andy thinks she's beautiful. When he's comfortable with her being his new mother, he'll come to live with us. We'll come back as often as we can while I'm studying landscape architecture. Gladys is going to take some courses in interior decoration while I'm working on my studies. We're going to start a company called Lunar Solutions."

"So Mamaw and Papaw get to raise another Lunamin?" "Andrew needs me, I know, but Papaw's a good substitute—might be better for Andy right now. Papaw sure tells better stories." "It's definitely temporary?"

"Yes. It's best for Andy to stay with them until he's ready. This way he'll be close to his maternal grandparents too."

"I'll look in on him as much as I can. Andy and I are buddies." "Thanks, George. One of these days I'll be Andy's buddy too, instead of just his pa. We got close while I was waiting for the trial."

CPSIA information can be obtained
at www.ICGtesting.com
Printed in the USA
FSHW020111070721
82849FS